WARRIOR BROOD

IT IS THE 41st millennium and the world of Heró-
dian IV is as good as lost. The nightmarish tyranid
hive fleets have descended from the depths of
space and are swiftly devouring every living thing
on the planet. When Inquisitor Kalypsia and the
Deathwatch Space Marines are sent to investigate
a vital outpost on this doomed planet, they find a
terrible secret, one that could spell a fate worse
than death for Kalypsia and her warriors – maybe
even for the whole of humanity!

More Warhammer 40,000 from the Black Library

DAWN OF WAR
by CS Goto

The Gaunt's Ghosts series
by Dan Abnett

The Founding
FIRST AND ONLY
GHOSTMAKER
NECROPOLIS

The Saint
HONOUR GUARD
THE GUNS OF TANITH
STRAIGHT SILVER
SABBAT MARTYR

The Lost
TRAITOR GENERAL

The Ultramarines series
by Graham McNeill

NIGHTBRINGER
WARRIORS OF ULTRAMAR
DEAD SKY, BLACK SUN

The Soul Drinkers series
by Ben Counter

SOUL DRINKERS
THE BLEEDING CHALICE
CRIMSON TEARS

A WARHAMMER 40,000 NOVEL

WARRIOR BROOD

C S Goto

A BLACK LIBRARY PUBLICATION

First published in Great Britain in 2005 by
BL Publishing,
Games Workshop Ltd.,
Willow Road, Nottingham,
NG7 2WS, UK.

10 9 8 7 6 5 4 3 2 1

Cover illustration by Phillip Sibbering.

A CIP record for this book is available from the British Library.

ISBN 13: 978 1 84416 234 5
ISBN 10: 1 84416 234 6

Distributed in the US by Simon & Schuster
1230 Avenue of the Americas, New York, NY 10020, US.

Printed and bound in Great Britain by
Bookmarque, Surrey, UK.

See the Black Library on the Internet at
www.blacklibrary.com

Find out more about Games Workshop
and the world of Warhammer 40,000 at
www.games-workshop.com

IT IS THE 41st millennium. For more than a hundred centuries the Emperor has sat immobile on the Golden Throne of Earth. He is the master of mankind by the will of the gods, and master of a million worlds by the might of his inexhaustible armies. He is a rotting carcass writhing invisibly with power from the Dark Age of Technology. He is the Carrion Lord of the Imperium for whom a thousand souls are sacrificed every day, so that he may never truly die.

YET EVEN IN his deathless state, the Emperor continues his eternal vigilance. Mighty battlefleets cross the daemon-infested miasma of the warp, the only route between distant stars, their way lit by the Astronomican, the psychic manifestation of the Emperor's will. Vast armies give battle in his name on uncounted worlds. Greatest amongst his soldiers are the Adeptus Astartes, the Space Marines, bio-engineered super-warriors. Their comrades in arms are legion: the Imperial Guard and countless planetary defence forces, the ever-vigilant Inquisition and the tech-priests of the Adeptus Mechanicus to name only a few. But for all their multitudes, they are barely enough to hold off the ever-present threat from aliens, heretics, mutants – and worse.

TO BE A man in such times is to be one amongst untold billions. It is to live in the cruellest and most bloody regime imaginable. These are the tales of those times. Forget the power of technology and science, for so much has been forgotten, never to be re-learned. Forget the promise of progress and understanding, for in the grim dark future there is only war. There is no peace amongst the stars, only an eternity of carnage and slaughter, and the laughter of thirsting gods.

CHAPTER ONE:
MANTIS WARRIORS

[Three Days Remaining]

THE GROUND CONVULSED and shuddered, as though retching at some violation. In the haze of his peripheral vision, Shaidan glimpsed a sudden flash of orange light and snapped his head round to face it. On the horizon, across a sea of seething arachnid bodies, a shaft of flame lanced into the dark sky, incinerating a brood of flapping gargoyles that screeched helplessly into its path. A fraction of a second passed before the engine core detonated and the barely visible Mantis Vindicator exploded into a burst of destruction, sending concentric shockwaves of flame rippling through the dark ocean of insectile tyranids. A moment later, a sleet of molten, alien flesh rained down on the command squad, sizzling with heat and toxins. But already the distant ring of death had been overrun by a wave of talons and claws, each intent on reaching the Mantis Warriors' command post.

'The Vindicator?'

Shaidan pulled his eyes away from the ruin of the tank and turned to face his captain. 'It's gone.'

Audin nodded a brief acknowledgment to his librarian. 'How long till the Thunderhawks arrive?'

'Minutes,' answered Shaidan calmly, as his spun his crackling force staff and drove it through the bony neck of a diving gargoyle, its barbed wings clattering in shock. 'Just minutes, but perhaps too many.'

The Mantis Warriors, captain ducked under the claws of a swooping beast, firing off a volley of bolts into the advancing ground swarm as he did so. As the gargoyle overshot, Audin slashed blindly behind him with his power sword and rent the creature cleanly in two.

'We must hold this vantage point until the hawks arrive – it is our only hope of extraction.'

'Understood,' whispered Shaidan, exhaling through gritted teeth as he fought to free one of the bayonet blades of his force staff from the skull of the snarling beast at his feet. With an imperceptible nod of his head, Shaidan sent a jet of blue light dancing along his staff, bursting the hormagaunt's head into shards of alien bone and freeing his blade. Not for the first time, Shaidan offered silent thanks to the Emperor for this unusual weapon – a double-bladed force staff forged in the long forgotten fires of Badab Prime. As he pulled it clear of the carcass, his weapon jerked backwards and sliced the barbed wing off a gargoyle diving towards Lodur, the standard bearer, sending it sprawling across the roof of the bunker. Without even breaking the rhythm of his bolter fire, Audin swept his power blade across the skittering creature's throat, silencing its screeches.

Lodur showed no signs of noticing. All of his attention was focussed on the brood of hormagaunts struggling to breach the line of Mantis Warrior Devastator Marines to the west of the bunker. His melta-gun hissed with superheated death as the giant banner of the Mantis Warriors rippled in brilliant greens against the night sky.

Spinning the force staff to clean the blades, sending threads of ichor and sparks of power flicking off into the ever darkening sky, Shaidan turned again to survey the scene developing below them. The Second Company was in full retreat. Some squads had already been extracted, hoisted out of the mire of talons and teeth by the shimmering green Mantis Thunderhawks. This bunker was their last stand. Theirs were the last human feet on Herodian IV, and theirs were barely human.

Looking south, in the near distance Shaidan could see Sergeant Magnir and his Devastator squad blazing away from an island of rock in the jagged sea of xenos organisms. They had been surrounded and cut off by the tide of tyranids that flowed over the desert towards the command bunker. Magnir had made a stand, buying a few vital moments for the command squad to reach its vantage point. But now, peppered from the sky by balls of bio-plasma, vomited from the screaming guts of circling gargoyles and besieged on all sides by broods of braying termagants, Magnir's squad was a fury of death and glory. Shaidan watched the flashes of lascannons and great plumes of fire from the heavy flamers. He saw an arc of flash points, defined by the continuous discharge of heavy bolters, arranged in a disciplined, defensive line. Atop the highest rock, Shaidan could see Magnir himself defiantly battling the swooping gargoyles with his chainsword.

Away from Magnir, over to the east, immediately in front of the bunker, were Sergeant Hoenir's Terminators. They were holding a line against impossible numbers, their storm bolters unleashing a continuous torrent against wave after wave of barbed claws and taloned feet. A huge bank of dead, arachnid aliens was growing in front of them, like an organic sea defence. But the swarm just kept flowing over the barrier of its dead, uncaring and utterly unsentimental.

A cloud of gargoyles pestered Hoenir's Terminators from the sky, but they were little threat to the ancient armour of Mantis Terminators. When they came too close, Hoenir would swat them away with his power sword, or the Terminators would shred them with their chainfists. And from the top of the command bunker behind them, covering fire strafed over the heads of the Terminators, riddling the gargoyles with bolter shells; Veteran Marine Balder was encamped on the roof of the bunker with his trusted heavy bolter, relentlessly loosing hellfire shells into the cloud of flying creatures. On impact, the shells exploded into tiny stars in the night sky, sending fragments of deadly shrapnel splintering into the brood. Balder's fellow veterans were in formation around him, discharging volleys of lasfire from their multilasers, providing support for Hoenir's squad.

Silently praising the might of the Mantis Terminators, Shaidan turned away to the west, where Sergeant Ruinus's Devastator squad was falling slowly back into the bunker's precinct. Their heavy bolters were cutting swathes from the advancing horde, but it was a losing battle. The numbers were simply too great. Brother Nerthus was behind the line of his battle-brothers, firing salvoes from the squad's lascannon, attempting to knock out the largest of the tyranid foes: giant warrior creatures on whom the bolter shells appeared to have little effect. Ruinus himself was in the centre of the retreating line. His boltgun had been spent long ago and he was in the thick of the hormagaunts with his power fist, smashing the giant scything talons and cracking tyranid bones with lightning speed and ferocity.

Circling over the heads of Ruinus's squad like glorious green and gold avenging angels were the Assault Marines of Sergeant Soron, their jump packs blazing with fire against the encroaching darkness. The Assault squad rained frag grenades into the organic sea, creating miniature ripples of flaming death, buying precious moments for Ruinus's Devastator squad below. With flamers, bolt guns and chainswords, Soron's Assault Marines fought to keep the gargoyles off their retreating battle-bothers, struggling to part the clouds of flying aliens, desperately trying to keep them away from the command squad ensconced on the roof of the bunker.

Bringing his attention sharply back to the command bunker, Shaidan cracked his force staff into the rockcrete at his feet, sending a javelin of power forking through the humid air and smashing into a six-legged, viciously taloned creature leaping towards Chaplain Aegir. The hormagaunt seemed to disintegrate as it flew and the chaplain turned just in time to have his ornate death-mask splattered with charred fragments of the alien.

For as far as Shaidan could see in every direction, there was nothing but arachnid forms, barbed scales, dripping claws and the glint of sharp teeth. The sky itself was crying with toxins and the air was thick with microscopic parasites eating into the Mantis Warriors' lungs: the planet was beginning to be consumed by the tyranid hive. The swarm was without end and it pushed forward relentlessly, fixated on annihilating this last point of resistance on Herodian IV. The last stand of the Mantis Warriors' Second Company was all but over.

BEHIND THE GURGLING cries of the gargoyles and the ceramic clashing of claws, Magnir could hear a faint whistle. Distracted for a fraction of a second from the frenetic action around him on the rocky summit, the Mantis sergeant was thrown from his feet by the impact of six clawed legs, pinning him against the rock face. The creature stood over him, trapping his limbs under its own, dripping with blood and fizzing with streams of

toxic ooze. The hormagaunt threw its head back and
screeched, raising the giant scythes that protruded from
its massively muscled forelimbs. Magnir stared straight
into the red eyes of the alien beast, watching its unthink-
ing hate pour back at him through the streams of saliva
that puddled into the eye sockets of his helmet, glinting
with bestial passion. He struggled against the xeno's
hold, thrashing with his own inhuman strength, but his
limbs were trapped beneath the weight of the beast and
pierced with its vicious claws.

A splintering crack cut off the hormagaunt's victorious
keening and Magnir watched one of its fore-scythes shat-
ter under the impact of a hellfire shell. The beast reared
in shock, screaming into the darkness below, its red eyes
searching for the source of the shot. The shell ruptured
on impact, sending a rain of lethal fragments riddling
into the beast's chest and peppering against the power
armour of Magnir beneath it. As the creature shifted its
weight, Magnir ripped his right arm free, dragging his
flesh across the claw that pinned him down. A flash of
searing pain shot up his arm before his enhanced nervous system shut down the pain receptors.

More bolter shells hissed over his head, impacting on
the rock all around him. Gargoyles fell from the sky like
insects, shot through with gaping holes where lascannon
fire had ruined them, or deformed into molten lumps
were the squad's multi-meltas had cooked them.

The tyranid beast was ignoring the frenzy around it, its
attention having been tugged back to Magnir as he freed
his arm. It drove down with its remaining scythe, straight
towards Magnir's primary heart. But the injured sergeant
was ready, parrying the thrust with his chainsword, pushing it off target. The talon slid along the serrated blade of
the sword, sending sparks of bone cascading into Magnir's face. The creature screeched in frustration and then
pain, as a volley of fire from Magnir's squad at the base

of the rock found its mark, strafing the hormagaunt's hardened thorax. It twisted away from the fire, stabbing down with its talon with desperate ferocity. Magnir pushed upwards with his chainsword, letting it slide along the creature's talon, transforming his parry into a thrusting attack. In a sudden moment of agony, the giant scythe pierced Magnir's shoulder, running straight through into the rock below. At the same time, the sergeant's chainsword punctured the tyranid's abdomen, where it whirred, churned and spat alien flesh. For an instant there was peace, with each silenced in shock and pain. Then the hormagaunt simply stopped moving and fell sideways onto the rock beside Magnir, the gaping wound in its abdomen already filled with tiny maggots greedily consuming their host.

Magnir took a breath, waiting momentarily for his Larraman's organ to kick in and stop the rush of blood from his wounds. Then, in the background, he heard the whistling again. Climbing back onto his feet, the Mantis Marine scanned the scene below him. Off to the north he could see Audin and the command squad holding the extraction point, supported on each side by squads of Devastators and Terminators. On the crest of the command bunker was Lodur, the Company's standard bearer, his melta-gun glowing fiercely in one hand with the Chapter's banner held high in the other. The brilliant green and gold of the standard stirred Magnir's heart; the flaming Mantis claw at its centre seemed to shine like a beacon of hope.

He strained his augmented hearing, filtering out the frenzy of battle around him: the whistle was getting gradually louder – something was whistling through the air above his head.

'Ordnance!'

The spore mine flew straight over Magnir's position, clearing the sea of creatures between him and the command bunker in a couple of seconds, arcing through the air on a gentle parabola. It came down just short of the command squad, busting against the side of the bunker with an organic splash, sending jets of toxic bio-plasma squirting across the rockcrete. Even from this distance, Magnir could see the rock-crete melting away where the viscous ooze splattered against it.

In his mind he calculated the trajectory of the mine, following its path back down to the south, deeper into the ocean of claws behind him. Sure enough, there, in a tiny circular clearing in the midst of the advancing horde, was a bulky, giant quadruped with a hideous deformity protruding from its back. Every minute or so the massive beast convulsed, lurching backwards as the immense muscle spasm fired a spore out of the growth on its back.

Magnir surveyed the distance between his squad and the biovore-cannon to the south. It was about two hundred metres, thick with a seething mass of tyranids. But, turning to the north, he knew that there was no way that his squad would make it to the command bunker either. Moreover, watching the impacts of the spore mines against the walls of the bunker, he knew that the exposed command squad would not last much longer against such an onslaught.

'Devastators!' he cried from his elevated position on the rock promontory – reaching his decision without hesitation. He knew that his squad could hear him, despite the frenzy of battle below. He raised his chainsword into the air, pointing across the swarm to the south, to the organic cannon that was spitting spores of death into the air, and called again. 'Devastators! For Redemption! For the Mantis Warriors! For the Emperor!' In immediate acknowledgement, his squad turned their guns to the south and released a united salvo.

Magnir leapt from the summit of the rock down into the wave of gaunts that broke against the fire of his squad, his spluttering chainsword alive with the promise of death.

THE IMPACT OF the spore-mine shook the bunker, and Audin planted his feet against the shockwave as it rippled through the rockcrete, never once breaking the rhythm of his fire. The smell of toxins and vaporised rock meandered through the clouds of smoke, easing between the lashing talons and swooping claws of the incessant gaunts. In the background, filtered through his Lyman's ear implant, Audin could hear the thud and whistle of another spore mine on its way.

'Incoming!' he yelled.

The fleshy spore bounced into a slide as it hit the roof of the bunker, skidding across the ichor-slicked surface as though it were on ice. Its tail thrashed viciously, trying to find a crack or protrusion on which to anchor itself. Audin launched himself into a roll, taking his weight on his shoulder before spinning back onto his feet, boltgun coughing. The rest of his squad parted to let the mine slide between them, never taking their eyes from the swarm of incoming tyranids that threatened to overrun their bunker, never relenting in their barrage of bolter shells, flames and bursts of melta.

Shaidan saw the danger first, but it was already too late. The spore slid desperately past the front line of veteran Marines, who hardly seemed to notice it or its flicking and snaking tail. In the heart of the squad, banner held proudly and defiantly to the heavens, Lodur stood immovably, his melta-gun hissing with power.

'Audin – Lodur!' yelled Shaidan over the tumult, directing his captain to the threat.

The Mantis Warriors' captain spun on his heel, seeing the danger just as the call reached his ears. Lodur himself glanced down at his feet just in time to see the impact of Audin's bolter shells punch the spore off course as it slid towards him, pushing it off to the side. The head of the spore seemed to buck in indignation as it slipped off the far side of the bunker, its tail lashing and twisting in a desperate attempt to find a hold. Suddenly, a tendril darted out of its tip, flicking itself around Lodur's ankle and constricting until his armoured boots started to buckle. With an anchor point at last, the spore caught its fall and started to pull itself back onto the roof of the bunker.

Lodur felt the pressure around his leg but his reactions were not swift enough. As the spore was dragging itself back up onto the bunker, its weight was pulling Lodur towards the edge. Sensing the danger, the standard-bearer drove the armoured stem of the standard down into alien tentacle and rattled off a volley of fire from his bolter, shredding the liana with a line of small explosions. At the same time, a forest of rope-like tendrils flashed out of the spore and caught hold of Lodur's arms, jamming his bolter and binding the Mantis Warriors' standard into his hand. The Marine thrashed against the constrictions that enveloped him, battling to save the Chapter's standard from being drawn into the braying mass below. But it was no use; the vines held him fast and the weight of the spore mine dragged across the ichor-slicked roof, finally tugging him off the edge with the Mantis standard still fluttering in his hand.

As soon as Lodur cleared the roofline, the spore exploded, and the rain of bio-plasma followed his fall into the swarm of gaunts below. Before he hit the ground, his armour had already dissolved, and as he thudded into the earth he was instantly consumed by a wave of alien teeth.

'Lodur!' cried Shaidan as he bore witness to the standard-bearer's heroism, his yell lost in the cacophony of battle.

He clenched his jaw to harness the hate that rushed into his nervous system as he watched his battle-brother's life smothered and the Chapter's standard torn to pieces. With a curdling cry he vaulted off the bunker and launched himself down into the swarm, his power staff spinning into a storm of blue lightning. He landed with a crunch, just a couple of metres from the desecrated body of Lodur. The Mantis Staff burned in his hands, spinning rapidly and defining an impenetrable orb of power around him. Its blades sliced through limbs, claws and talons, sending tyranid blood and specks of blue power showering out into the xenos sea around him. He could feel the power of his forefathers coursing through his body, giving him strength, feeding the staff that seemed alive in his hands.

From the roof of the bunker behind him, a volley of hellfire shells punched into the swarm before him. Balder had seen Shaidan's purpose and had abandoned his firing point on the east side to provide cover. As Shaidan scythed his way into the breach cut by the veteran Marine, the gaunts swarmed all over him, hiding him from Balder's view. The librarian was rapidly submerged and yet his staff flared and power ran through his veins: the sphere of lightning etched into the deadly sea by his weapon could not be breached and he left a wave of ruined tyranids in his wake as he fought his way forwards, deeper into the swarm.

With a sudden explosion of power, his staff spasmed in his hands as it spun. The flare cleared a radius around him in all directions, incinerating gaunts and sending their charred remains scattering into a wide fountain. In the fraction of a second of clarity that this provided him, Shaidan stooped to the ground and snatched up the remains of the Mantis Warriors' standard, thrusting it into the air with a flourish. The tattered remnants of brilliant green flapped in the heavy air. As he did so, volleys of supporting fire raked out from behind him – Balder's veteran Marines had formed a firing line along the bunker's edge. In their midst stood Chaplain Aegir, his Crozius Arcanum held high, glowing with power. Behind the tumult and the screeches of the gaunts around him, Shaidan could hear the cheer raised by the Mantis Warriors all around: the Mantis Claw would fly until the last Marine left Herodian IV.

A sudden blast of purple ripped through the air above Shaidan's head, arresting the moment of glory and smashing straight into the magnificent figure of Aegir, knocking him off his feet. Shaidan turned on his heels, snapping his attention round to the source of the blast. Over to the east, he could see Hoenir's Terminators tracking their fire across the ever growing ridge of corpses before them. At the summit of the mound, surrounded by a faintly glowing purple aura that seemed to deflect even the most focussed volleys from the storm bolters, slivered three ungodly serpents. Their heads were monstrously disproportionate to their snaking bodies, and they were pulsing with energy. The other tyranids squirmed around them, keeping a perimeter of clarity that throbbed and oozed with warp taint. The light spilt down the bank of dead gaunts, lapping against the awesome armour of the Terminators. Shaidan recognised the new creatures at once: zoanthropes – tyranid sorcerers.

The three monstrous worms were oscillating slowly, gradually synchronising with each other, bringing their energy fields into resonance. Then, with a blinding flash, another javelin of warp energy speared out across the night sky.

Shaidan knew their target with absolute certainty.

'Aegir!' he yelled up to the heavens as he swung his staff, circling it above his head and decapitating a ring of snarling gaunts. He stole a glance at the roof of the command bunker just in time to see Aegir, back in position in the middle of the firing line, bathed in a terrible light.

The purple taint flickered around his armour and hissed as it came into contact with the Crozius, sending plumes of warp-steam wafting into the air. With a thunderous crack, Aegir's armour suddenly exploded outwards, sending shards of adamantium darting into the line of veteran Marines around him. The Crozius fell to the ground as the chaplain's body simply blinked out of existence, sucked through the breach in reality into the unspeakable realm, where daemons salivated in anticipation of his soul.

With a cry of anger, his blood boiling with hatred, Shaidan lanced his staff into the thorax of a hormagaunt that leapt toward him, shattering the creature's carapace in an explosion of brilliant light. He screamed into the swarm that vengeance would be his and then set off in the direction of the Terminators.

THE SERGEANT'S CHAINSWORD bit through the carapace, chewing the shell into splinters and then thrusting into the soft flesh inside, where it whirred freely, churning the termagant's organs into mush. Magnir pulled his blade free as he punched out with his left hand, fending off the elongated talon of a leaping hormagaunt, before turning his spluttering sword in a tight arc to sever the creature's forelimb completely. His shoulder winced in pain, but he forced the injury into the back of his mind – no time for that now.

As always, Magnir was leading his squad from the front, spearheading the thrust towards the giant biovore that had planted itself just out of their reach, releasing salvo after salvo of spore mines towards the besieged command squad on the bunker. Magnir glanced to the north just in time to see a tremendous blast of purple fire consume Chaplain Aegir as he stood defiantly amongst his battle-brothers on the bunker.

'Aegir!' he yelled in horror.

Magnir had known the chaplain for nearly forty years.
Innumerable battles had been fought in that time, as the
Chapter quested around the perimeter of the Imperium,
searching for evils to slay, desperate for its own redemption. The two Marines had been recruited together from
the forgotten wastes of Nanthrax III, as the Mantis Warriors had swept through the system clearing out the
remnants of an ork invasion force.

Magnir's Devastator Marines advanced in a ring, loosing lances of lasfire, volleys of bolter shells and waves of
melta in all directions as they moved. Magnir drew his
squad deeper and deeper into the quagmire, hacking a
path with his sword and his fists. The enemy was relentless: lightning-fast hormagaunts leapt from all sides,
their six legs kicking wildly and their giant front talons
thrusting for impact against the isolated Marines; wave
after wave of smaller termagants formed banks of resistance, firing off a constant sleet of fleshborers – tiny
beetles that gnawed into and cracked the adamantium of
the Mantis Warriors' armour; winged gargoyles circled
overhead, vomiting balls of toxic bio-plasma into the
tiny circle of Marines and shooting off fleshborer rounds
from their symbiote weaponary.

Dropping his head in determination, Magnir lowered
his giant armoured shoulder and barged forwards into
the mass of gaunts before him. He could hear the crunch
of bone and the serrated grind of barbed claws dragging
across his armour. Then there was a sudden drop in resistance and he burst through into a clearing, stumbling
and slidding to a halt before the massive figure of the
biovore. Behind him, Magnir could hear his squad penetrate the defensive line around the organic cannon.

'Covering fire! I need twenty seconds!' he called, knowing that his squad would not fail him.

The squad spun on their heels, facing back into the
seething tyranid sea through which they had just waded.

They formed a perimeter around their sergeant as the sea pressed in against them, threatening to overrun them with sheer weight of numbers.

The biovore just ignored them. The eyes of its huge head were closed and the terrible muscles along its back convulsed. With a sudden, ear-splitting screech, the creature threw back its head and bucked. The deformed bulk on its back contracted in a ripple and then coughed out a spore, which was catapulted into the air towards the command bunker. Then its head turned, as though the massive creature was irritated by an insect on its skin.

Sergeant Magnir was already on the creature's back, hacking into the spore cannon with his chainsword, grinding his way through the awesome lattice of bone and muscle. The creature reared up onto his hind legs, letting out a thunderous cry. But Magnir drove his blade deeper into the beast's back and gripped the hilt with both hands, using it as an anchor against the violent motion of the creature. With a terrible crack, the biovore smashed its front feet back down to the ground. Without looking, Magnir realised what the crack must have been and he yelled out in fury. The sounds of bolter fire from his squad below had stopped suddenly and the remaining flashes of lasfire looked pathetically small against the vast sea of blackness that swarmed around them.

Unclipping a chain of frag grenades from his belt, Magnir made a final call to the remnants of his squad. 'For the Mantis Warriors! For Redemption! For the Emperor!' He could faintly hear the return call of a single voice buried beneath the wave of tyranid screeches and the lashing of teeth and then he plunged the grenades into the churning cavity in the biovore's back. The creature bucked in pain, but, with a whip of his long-trusted chainsword, Magnir detonated the grenades.

* * *

'INCOMING!' CALLED AUDIN as the telltale whistle grew louder. He turned his power sword in a crescent around his head as he surveyed the remains of the command squad. Fragments of Aegir's armour were scattered over the roof of the bunker, but his body had simply blinked out of existence. There was a deep cavity at the edge of the roof where Lodur had been incinerated by the spore mine, and talons were beginning to reach through the breach from below. Over to the east, Audin could see Librarian Shaidan scything a path towards the Terminators, the remnants of the Chapter's standard held aloft in defiance. Balder and the veteran Marines were still fighting, apparently undaunted by the epic scale of the siege. Heavy bolters and multi-lasers spat fragments of death into the surrounding swarm with precise discipline and astounding effectiveness. Audin himself, planted in the middle of the roof, was fending off the swooping gargoyles with his power sword whilst rattling bolter shells into anything barbed that showed itself over the roofline.

For once the spore mine overshot, as though its aim had been interrupted. Audin strained his eyes against the darkness and the increasing humidity, scanning the sea of tyranids off to the south. He could see nothing but the apparently never ending ocean of glinting claws and flashing teeth – the evil sheen of ichor-coated arachnids in the faint light. Then suddenly there was a burst of muffled light in the near distance. Flames erupted into the sky in rainbows of oranges and greens, as though chemicals were being burnt. A series of smaller explosions followed as flaming projectiles were ejected into the air, dragging tails of green fire, before exploding into fireworks that rained burning toxins down into the swarm around them.

Scanning his eyes to the left, Audin searched for signs of Magnir's Devastators on the rocky promontory where they had been stranded during the retreat. Nothing. Then it suddenly made sense and Audin whispered a silent prayer for his heroic sergeant.

As RUINUS STARED out into the swarm, new beasts were starting to appear menacingly amidst the teeming tyranid mass, cackling over the heads of the smaller creatures. The giant shapes punctuated the swarm like skyscrapers in a sprawling skyline. They bristled with claws and talons that projected several metres from their forelimbs and with ugly organic protrusions that could only be weapons of some kind. As they advanced, the smaller creatures seemed to part before them like an impossible ocean, as though commanded. A flicker of memory licked at Sergeant Ruinus's mind. He could vaguely recall moments of Audin's briefing before the Mantis Warriors made planet-fall only a day earlier. Something about giant warriors and psychic nodes. Ruinus had not paid a great deal of attention – he had just been eager to get down onto the surface and start devastating some aliens.

A rattle of bolter shells punched through the space between Ruinus's line of Marines and one of the new creatures. Ruinus himself fired off a spray of hellfire shells a moment later, approving of his squad's strategic choice: focus on the new giants. But the shells just ricocheted off the massive beast, or burst into shrapnel that flicked pin-points of death into the sea of gaunts at the monster's feet. In response, the giant warrior planted its rear feet and leant forward, balancing the immense recoil of its weapon as it spasmed, releasing a jet of tiny specks racing towards the line of Devastator Marines. A fraction of a second later, the specks splattered against the armour of Marine Haldrus, standing firmly with his multi-melta fizzling from his shoulder; he was instantly speckled with smudges of deep green and red.

It took a second, but then he started to scream. He threw his weapon to the ground and started clawing at his armour, scratching at the adamantium plates and yanking desperately at the seal of his helmet. His battle-brothers drew into a defensive ring around him, buying him some time to deal with the invisible attack. But then it was over. Haldrus slumped to the ground motionless, and thin trickles of bloody tissue oozed out of the little holes in his armour, which hissed and bubbled with toxicity. From out of one of the holes in his helmet squirmed a shiny, black-headed worm, grimacing with daggered teeth and blood.

In the seconds that it took Haldrus to die, the giant xenos warrior had broken into a charge. The smaller gaunts were scattering out of its path or simply being trampled under its feet. As it ran, it sprayed more devourer worms towards Ruinus's squad from one of its bizarre organic protrusions and the other monstrous warriors nearby were closing in on their position. Meanwhile, the tide of talons and claws continued relentlessly, and the Devastators were battling for their lives.

'Nerthus! Use the lascannon! Bring that thing down!' cried Ruinus over the clattering din, hoping that the heavy gunner could hear him.

Nerthus steadied the cannon on his shoulder and took aim at the charging beast, citing a point between its augmented rib-cage and its colossal jaw. The creature kept coming, leaping and bounding like a monstrous insect. Nerthus fired, but the lance of light seared through empty space where the beast had been mere moments before. Fifty metres. Thirty. It was getting too close, but Nerthus couldn't get his line of sight.

Javelins of lasfire jousted out from the Devastators' position, flashing over the heads of the swarm but dashing by the side of the charging warrior beast. The smaller gaunts lashed at him with their own huge talons and peppered the air around him with fleshborer shells. Ruinus was there to defend him, sticking the muzzel of his heavy bolter into the mouth of a leaping hormagaunt and crushing the head of another with a weighty stamp. Fifteen metres.

'Nerthus, now!'

The lascannon erupted, sending a blast smashing into the abdomen of the tyranid warrior as it leapt through the final distance between them. The force held the beast immobile in the air for a fraction of a second, arresting its momentum, before it crashed to the ground a couple of metres in front of the line of Marines. As one, the Devastators raked their fire across the fallen beast, spraying it with hellfire shells, lasfire and chemical flame. The swarm of smaller creatures seemed to sense the pain of this great beast and a piercing scream spewed out of the tide – its talons and claws lashing with renewed ferocity.

But the tyranid warrior wasn't finished yet. Despite the close range barrage from the Mantis Warriors, which had shattered and splintered the creature's talons, the warrior beast sprang back onto its feet, ichor gushing from its tortured form and it screeched with defiance. Its weapon coughed once more, splattering Nerthus with a spurt of tiny devourer worms. As it threw its head back to bray, Ruinus was on it, launching himself full length at the beast's thorax with his combat knife clenched in his left hand. The Mantis Warrior sergeant punched the blade through the petrified bone that protected the creature's vital organs, and then he smashed the knife straight through with the weight of the boltgun in his other hand. With the barrel jammed into the cavity, Ruinus clicked the weapon onto automatic and pulled the trigger, kicking himself away from the thrashing warrior beast as he did so.

The gun spent dozens of hellfire rounds into the interior of the creature, each shattering and exploding into myriad splinters, lacerating the beast's internal organs and liquefying it from within. For a second the giant warrior remained on its feet, shuddering with the staccato of explosions in its body. Then it crashed to the ground, crushing a clutch of smaller gaunts as it fell. A piercing cry erupted from the ocean.

The Devastators were already back in their firing line, loosing disciplined volleys into the relentless swarm. However, at the moment that the giant fell, the tyranid mass seemed to hesitate. It stopped pressing and some of the creatures even appeared to turn on each other – impaling themselves on talons and claws. The raking fire of the Marines started to make inroads into the seething mass.

'Devastators, pull back into the compound! Pull back behind the walls!' Ruinus could see their moment of advantage – but it was not the promise of victory, only the faint hope of survival. The other tyranid warriors were charging in their direction. Their lascannon was gone, together with Nerthus. He himself was reduced to a combat knife. This was not the time for stupid heroics. 'Pull back!'

WHEN SHAIDAN BURST out of the swarm into the Terminators' pocket of resistance, the giant armoured Marines were a blaze of fire. Their storm bolters spat a merciless hail of shells into the horde, felling the creatures in broken waves, building a massive wall of tyranid corpses in front of their position – a decaying tsunami. Any beast that managed to slip through the spray found itself impaled by a power fist or shredded by the sputtering whir of a chainfist. The broken and ruined remains of such creatures were scattered on the ground by the Terminators' feet. Not a single Terminator had fallen in the onslaught, but Shaidan could see the danger of the new serpentine enemies that seemed to float and slither into view on the crest of the ridge of corpses, flaring with warp-taint.

The storm of bolter shells just bounced off the purpling haze of power that emanated from the pulsing creatures. They seemed to be oscillating in a complicated, syncopated rhythm, occasionally phasing into resonance with each other and sending warp-flares spewing out into the night. The bursts of energy were growing more and more frequent until the heads of the beasts snapped round in unison, focussing their gazes on one of the Terminators and releasing an awesome beam of crackling purple. It punched into the chest of the ancient armour, lifting the Marine off his feet and throwing him clear of the defensive pocket. He landed with a thump, crushing dozens of gaunts under his huge weight. Shaidan watched the flight of the Marine, and then horror crept over him as he saw the head of a termagant burst out of the huge cavity blown from the Terminator's chest by the warp-beam. The creature leapt clear of the dead Marine and launched itself towards the clutch of Terminators – but it was shredded in midair by a sleet of bolter shells. Meanwhile, the fallen Marine was swamped beneath a frantic pile of gaunts and a flood of tiny, slithering creatures poured into the hole in the Terminator's armour, consuming the Marine inside with a forest of tiny teeth.

'Terminators, retreat!' cried Shaidan. 'There is nothing that you can do here.'

As he spoke, the librarian thrust the tip of his force staff into the ground, sending jabs of lightning coruscating through the sand, frying a brood of gaunts in front of him. From the top of the staff, a pulse of energy lanced over the heads of the enemy creatures, smashing against the psychic shield of the zoanthropes. On impact, there was a huge explosion of uncontrolled warp energy, instantly incinerating a radius of tyranid creatures and pluming into a dome in the sky.

In support, the Terminators turned their guns onto the zoanthropes, letting loose with everything into the midst of the energy field. The fecund darkness was riddled with bursts of light, concussive explosions and clouds of smoke. But, when the cacophony calmed, floating effortlessly above the massive crater that had been blown into the bank of tyranid corpses, the zoanthropes appeared unharmed. And through the new breach in the improvised tidal defences below them poured brood after brood of gaunts.

'Hoenir, retreat,' said Shaidan calmly, turning to face the Terminator sergeant and imagining the anger simmering behind that ageless helmet. The Mantis Terminators had never turned their backs on any enemy. 'There is nothing to be gained here. Nothing.'

The Terminators continued to blaze away into the relentless onslaught. For a moment Shaidan thought that Hoenir had not heard him or, even worse, was ignoring the order. Then, crackling into the open vox channel in their helmets, the Terminators heard the voice of their sergeant: 'Ordered retreat. Fall back into the compound. Defensive ring – constant fire.'

Before the hiss of static that followed the order had even faded from their ears, the sergeant's voice barked with renewed urgency. 'Cancel that order. We have a new target.'

Lumbering into the breach in the line before them, crushing the smaller creatures under the weight of each of its ponderous steps, came a huge beast. It towered over its brethren, and ignored them utterly. It stood on its hind legs, twice as tall as a Terminator, and, in place of forelimbs, there were two giant scythe-like talons, easily longer than a man. Its head protruded forward, with an immense jaw shimmering with jagged teeth. From a bizarre growth sticking out of its abdomen protruded an ornate, bony barrel.

Shaidan stared at the monster and realised immediately that this must have been what had taken out the Vindicator earlier. He looked up to where the zoanthropes had been, and just saw their tails slip from view down the other side of the bank of xenos corpses – as though leaving the monstrous carnifex to deal with the Marines. For a moment, Shaidan wondered whether the sorcerous serpents were searching for a weaker point in the Mantis Warriors' defences. They were after the command squad.

'Hoenir. I must get back to the captain.'

'Understood. May the Emperor guide you, brother Shaidan.'

Shaidan turned to face the sergeant and nodded his acknowledgement to the veteran warrior. 'For Repentance and the Emperor,' he whispered, pausing before scything his way into the sea of creatures between him and the command bunker.

THE TERMINATORS HELD their firing line, concentrating all of their ranged fire on the carnifex whilst battering the slashing hormagaunts and biting termagants with their power fists. Hoenir swept tight arcs with his power sword, slicing through alien flesh with each sweep, as his storm bolter coughed a continuous flurry into the face of the immense advancing beast.

The carnifex lumbered towards them, hardly slowed by the terrible impacts of the Terminators' fire. The strange bony barrel in the creature's chest started to shake and then, with a scream from the beast itself, a clutch of tiny fragments fired out, like shotgun pellets. The beast kept wailing as thousands of the tiny pods were scattered into the air in front of the blazing Terminators. For an instant, Hoenir thought that everything was going to be alright after all – these tiny pods would be no match for his squad's ancient armour. But then, as though triggered by some silent signal, the pods exploded into life, sending barbed vines and hooked tendrils spreading and growing in all directions at once.

The rapidly expanding web sent feelers running over the armour of the Terminator squad, where tiny hooks penetrated the joins in their armoured plates, anchoring the strangler-vines and dragging the web towards the Marines. Hoenir shifted his attention from the carnifex itself to the thrashing vines that were attempting to lash around his powerful limbs. His power sword flashed with life, hacking through bunches of tendrils and severing creeping shoots. But the vines kept coming, growing thicker and thicker and Hoenir could feel his movements slowing as though constrained by tremendous weights.

Looking across to his squad, he could see them all struggling under the onslaught of liana and alien foliage. Most of them had stopped firing at the carnifex as they thrashed around to free themselves from this close range threat. Those with chainfists were making an attempt at a defence, but they were fighting a losing battle. Those without bladed weapons were now almost immobile.

Hoenir slashed violently with his power sword, freeing his storm bolter once more. He recommenced firing at the carnifex and watched in awe as the hellfire shells just bounced off the creature's hide, lacerating clumps of nearby gaunts like paper. It was as though the swarm had known how to neutralise the advantages offered by the Terminators' awesome firepower.

Two shuddering thuds shook the ground, and Hoenir turned his head to see two of his Terminators collapsed onto the floor, completely cocooned in the barbed stanglers. There was an incredible tension in those vines, which grew thicker with alien muscles as he watched. Then, in a sudden release of tension, the tendrils ripped apart, scattering the limbs of the Terminators in all directions. The abdomens and heads of the Marines were left

on the ground where they fell and Hoenir caught a last
glimpse of his battle-brothers before they were hope-
lessly buried beneath a frenzy of talons and claws, as the
smaller gaunts overran their position.

The rest of the squad were not faring much better.
Hoenir could see that a number of their chainfists had
been bound into ineffectiveness, and the Marines were
grappling with the alien plants with their other hands,
having discarded their boltguns in the interests of self-
preservation. The carnifex, now at close range, was
simply dousing them with more and more of the seed
pods, as the web of vines grew thicker and more impenetrable.

The increasingly vulnerable and immobile Terminators
were now also under constant attack from the hormagaunts, which seized the opportunity to leap into battle,
kicking out with six clawed-limbs and skewering the
Marines with their elongated talons. Hoenir was now the
only Terminator with a functioning storm bolter and he
had his work cut out to keep the vines from binding his
arms. Even so, his feet were immovably planted into the
ground, and completely overgrown with liana. He was
slowly being assimilated into the organic structure of the
plant-life.

As Hoenir despatched the pouncing hormagaunts with
hellfire shells and slashed at the barbed stanglers with his
power sword, he focussed an immense effort of will into
his legs. There was one last trick in his box and he would
play it on that cursed carnifex if it was the last thing he
did. The servos in his armour whined and screeched in
resistance as he struggled to turn his body. Just a few
degrees. Just a few would be enough at this range; the
carnifex was almost on top of him.

With a sudden jolt, Hoenir's body spun round, pivot-
ing on his right leg, his left having been severed,
wrenched from his waist and dragged down into the mire

of tendrils and thorns. In the fraction of a second before he lost his balance and fell into the thrashing sea of barbs, spikes and spines, Hoenir ducked his head towards the monster and activated the cyclone missile launcher on his back.

In a flurry of power, the missiles seared over his head, punching deeply into the flesh of the carnifex. They burrowed their way deep inside, like giant maggots, before detonating. With an immense convulsion, the massive creature exploded outwards, sending chunks of sizzling flesh raining into the swarm. A huge fire ball erupted from the heart of the beast, blasting outwards in a wide radius, incinerating dozens of broods of tyranids and reducing the barbed tendrils to ashes, cleansing the dead bodies of the Terminators.

'THERE!' CALLED SORON, pointing into the heavily clouded sky with his chainsword, raising a cheer from the surviving Marines with his apparent salute. The Assault Marines had come down out of the sky and regrouped on the roof of the command bunker, reinforcing the depleted command squad. Around the base of the bunker, inside the walls of the compound, were Ruinus's Devastators, their strategic retreat having brought them right to the very feet of the command squad.

'I see it,' answered Captain Audin, straining his eyes to catch a glimpse of the Thunderhawk as he thrust his power sword into the abdomen of yet another gargoyle, which tumbled out of the sky and slid across the slick roof of the bunker. 'Ruinus, get your squad up here for extraction. Soron, give that drop ship some support.'

Soron brandished his chainsword, rallying his squad for one last flight and then kicked his jump pack into life. Energy poured out of the bottom of the pack, propelling the Marine into the air, with his chainsword roaring into the swirl of gargoyles above him. From below, a javelin of lasfire seared through the air next to him, clearing a path for his squad to break through the cloud of creatures. As the Assault Marines burst out of the whirl of talons and wings, the night sky seemed to leap into life, punctuating their vision with pinpoints of light as the stars welcomed their angels home.

The Thunderhawk was already descending, its weapons batteries alight with lasfire, ploughing great troughs into the tyranid swarm that surrounded the command bunker on all sides. Off to the east, a great explosion of fire sent ripples out through the sea, only to be quashed by the sheer weight of numbers in the horde. Soron could see the gargoyles pestering the Thunderhawk, peppering it with pathetic splatterings of fleshborer symbiotes. But the aliens were also getting in too close for the gunship's weapons to be effective, latching onto the wings, trying to destabilise the descent of the craft. Some were even throwing themselves into the exhaust vents, presumably to clog the atmospheric cooling system and overheat the engine. For a moment, Soron wondered how these mindless animals seemed to know what to do.

Pushing all such thoughts from his mind, Sergeant Soron organised the Assault Marines into a defensive formation, escorting the Thunderhawk down into the roiling mass of alien life below. Their jump packs roared with fire as the Assault Marines stood guard around the Thunderhawk, matching their altitude to its, defining a ring of death around their only hope of extraction with bolter shells and the constant whir of chainswords. From below came salvos of fire from the remnants of Ruinus's Devastators, who had now made it onto the roof of the bunker. Meanwhile, the command squad was punching out hellfire shells into the constricting spiral of the swarm, which closed irrevocably on the bunker.

The Thunderhawk broke down through the cloud of gargoyles, spraying lasfire in all directions, its weapons systems firing automatically; it was greeted with a tremendous roar from the surviving Mantis Warriors. The gunship dropped as low as it dared above the Marines and opened its lower hatch. Meanwhile, side hatches opened on both flanks, and clutches of Marines appeared on both sides, firing fiercely into the swarm to provide cover for the extraction.

'Ruinus, get your men on board!' cried Audin as he fired a carefully placed bolter round into the neck of a snarling alien. 'Now!'

Ruinus herded his Marines towards the lower hatch, watching thankfully as powerful hands reached down and dragged the remnants of his squad up into the vehicle. Snatching up a fallen boltgun, he planted himself firmly in front of the extraction point, firing continuously into the frenzy that continued unbroken around him.

'Now you, sergeant,' called Audin from the midst of the cacophony, knowing that Ruinus would refuse to leave him without a direct order.

Still firing with his right hand, Ruinus lifted his left into the air and was pulled up into the Thunderhawk.

A sudden explosion shook the bunker – a lance of warp-energy smashed into a battling figure on the rim of the roof, but then bounced out into the swarm, annihilating a brood of hormagaunts.

'Shaidan!' cried Audin in horror. But the librarian stormed out of the blue haze with his force staff spinning into a frenzy of energy around him. He was charging towards Audin. The zoanthropes were just visible on the outside walls of the compound, pulsing with warp-taint and preparing to release another blast.

Shaidan threw himself into a dive between the enemy and Audin, as the serpents fired off their tainted pulse. The energy punched directly into his chest as he flew across the face of his captain. His force staff spluttered and spat crackles of blue lightning as the bulk of the zoanthrope's force bounced off it and back into the swarm.

The librarian slumped to the ground, supporting his weight on the staff. As he swam on the edge of consciousness, he felt a strong grip close around his wrist and then the vague sensation that he was flying. For a moment, he thought he was dead.

'WE MUST ISSUE a call for assistance,' said Audin, leaning over the vox unit in the Thunderhawk as it powered away from the surface of Herodian IV. 'This enemy is beyond us. This is no time for foolish pride or selfish dreams of glorious penitence.'

Looking down out of the viewports, Audin could see the scale of the swarm that had descended on them, like a giant, black, roiling ocean being sucked into a whirlpool around that command bunker. It was an incredible sight – something to inspire awe in the heart of any Space Marine captain. Audin pushed the tinges of doubt to the back of his mind; no Chapter could have done any more than the Mantis Warriors had done.

There was a hiss of static, but then a reply came back from the *Penitent Quest*, the Second Company's Strike Cruiser that was playing a game of cat and mouse with the tyranid in orbit around the planet.

'Help is already on its way, captain. An Imperial Navy fleet and a detachment of Deathwatch Marines is en route. We received the communiqué more than an hour ago.'

'Understood,' said Audin in barely disguised surprise.

Already on its way, thought Audin. Already? But how could they possibly know that they were needed? Are the Mantis Warriors still under such suspicion? And a Deathwatch kill-team – that would also mean an inquisitor from the Ordo Xenos.

'And the others?' asked Audin, clearing his thoughts. 'Did the others make it back to the *Quest*?'

There was a slight pause. 'Some of them, captain.'

CHAPTER TWO:
'I'

[Two Days Remaining]

FROM THE VIEW-STATIONS on the *Vanishing Star* Commander Kastor could see the battle for Herodian IV unfolding. His command ship, a bristling Gothic-class cruiser, was positioned in a mid-distant orbit, monitoring the engagement. Even from this distance, the massive lance arrays were providing formidable covering fire for the Imperial battlegroup. Nonetheless, a number of the junior officers on the command deck clenched their teeth with frustration, wanting to be closer to the action. Under their breaths they whispered curses at their cowardly commander. But Kastor was no coward.

'Concentrate all fire on the largest ship – the Razorfiend cruiser on the port side of the *Extreme Prejudice*,' commanded Kastor.

He had fought tyranids before and was well aware of their genus classifications. In fact, he had posted class descriptors to the command crews of every ship in his battlegroup, complete with notes on their capabilities and cautions to expect variations and transmogrifications of the standard design. Like the tyranids themselves, their vessels seemed to evolve and morph to fit the needs of the situation. Kastor had suspected for a long time that the vessels were actually giant tyranid organisms, and recent dispatches from the Ordo Xenos had confirmed this.

The Razorfiend was a lethal battle cruiser, heavily armed and immensely armoured. Two massive pincers protruded from its prow, tipped with cannons and it was releasing a continuous venom stream against the shields of the *Extreme Prejudice*, where the port batteries were retaliating with a tirade of lasfire. The confrontation was a standoff, effectively locking the Dictator-class cruiser out of the main battle and rendering it vulnerable to boarding actions from the flurry of brood drones that swam in shoals around the Imperial fleet.

Squadrons of Fury interceptors were flooding out of the landing bays of the *Extreme Prejudice*, desperately trying to repel the tyranid boarding action before it could really gather any momentum. Clouds of Escort Drone organisms were being spewed out of the Razorfiend craft to meet this new threat, engaging the Furies two to one.

The lance array of the *Vanishing Star* reached full charge with a resounding whine.

'Fire all beams,' commanded Kastor.

The lance of energy pushed its way through the cloud of Escort Drones and chaff-spores, detonating the mines and bleeding energy as it cut its path towards the Razorfiend organism. It punched into the starboard pincer of the tyranid vessel, sending ripples of explosions along its length. After a couple of pregnant seconds, the pincer buckled and then exploded from within, sending the Razorfiend vessel spinning out of control.

The *Extreme Prejudice* saw its chance and opened up with its torpedo banks, sending a wave of missiles plunging

into the wounded monster, where they sunk into the carapace armour before exploding with unforgiving ferocity.
Gushes of organic tissue oozed out of the wound, spilling
into the vacuum of space.

The Razorfiend spun under the impact, spiralling back
towards the bulk of the tyranid fleet that held a low orbit
around Herodian IV. As it closed with the horde, its spin
slowed and it brought itself around to face the Imperial
battlegroup once again – its grievous wound already
sealed over with grotesque scar tissue and its single pincer pointing menacingly back at the *Extreme Prejudice*,
where its Drones and Brood Ships persisted in their dog-
fights.

'Hold position here,' said Kastor calmly.

'Should we not press our advantage, sir?' asked Tactical
Officer Lopthyr.

'We have no advantage, son,' replied Kastor without
taking his gaze from the battle outside. 'The vessel has
retreated into a position with long range cover. If we
close, we move into range of the Hive Ship's fire.'

Kastor pressed his hand against the armoured glass of
the view-station and stared into the gyring clouds of
combat that surrounded the *Extreme Prejudice*; Captain
Melyus would deal with the short-range fighters for now,
but eventually the lance arrays of the *Vanishing Star*
would be needed to confront the Hive Ship. They must
not sustain any damage before then.

If he didn't know better, Kastor would have thought
that the penetrating attack by the Razorfiend was
designed to fail, in an attempt to draw the *Vanishing Star*
into the melee prematurely. He had heard of tyranids
throwing thousands of their smaller organisms into
impenetrable barrages of Imperial cannon fire just to
exhaust the batteries before launching their assault, but
he had never heard of the mindless animals launching
sacrificial raids with prize vessels like the Razorfiend.

For now, the Dictator-class *Extreme Prejudice* and the two Sword-class frigates, *Purgation* and *Strident Virtue*, would fight the war in the interval between the withdrawn *Vanishing Star* and the heavily defended tyranid Hive Ship.

Kastor turned from the view-station and walked slowly back to the elevated command throne in the centre of the circular bridge. He pushed himself deeply into the seat, propping his head on his hands as he gazed back into space. Just breaking the horizon of Herodian IV, silhouetted against a burst of eclipsed starlight and misted behind the flecks of battle in the foreground, he could see the ugly bulk of the Hive Ship. It was already in low orbit, skimming the atmosphere of the planet with its belly, sucking the planet dry of nutrients and releasing storms of toxins, spores and creatures into the air. It was only a matter of days now, perhaps hours, before the planet would be completely consumed.

THE GUNSHIP SLID effortlessly into one of the huge landing bays of the *Vanishing Star*, firing its retros into hisses of smoke and steam as it gently came to rest on the polished deck. The deck officer stood bolt upright, staring unblinkingly at the sleek lines of the unusual vessel. It seemed to bristle with armaments, yet the officer could see no signs of any at all. To the casual observer, the ship might have passed as a pleasure cruiser, but it filled the landing bay with such weight and gravitas that it could only be a gunship and an unusually lethal one at that.

Deck Officer Abett stole a glance behind him, wondering whether the guards had arrived yet. The ship had not appeared on any of the *Vanishing Star*'s scopes and it had slipped into the landing bay uninvited – virtually unnoticed. For some reason, the gun-servitors in the hanger space would not activate and the batteries encased in the mouth of the bay had not even twitched as the vessel had eased past them.

Abett's eyes scanned the hull of the ship, letting his gaze caress the graceful and unfamiliar curves. The guards were on their way, but until they arrived, there was only Abett and a handful of tech-servitors to meet, greet or simply be slaughtered by their uninvited guests. He swallowed hard and stiffened his back.

With an uncomfortable bulge of his eyes, Abett saw the ship's insignia just as the lower hatch jolted ajar, hissing as the atmosphere inside equalised. There, etched colourlessly into the gunmetal grey of the nosecone, was a tiny letter 'I'. It was simple and unadorned; no effort had been expended on drawing attention to the icon. It was as though the little symbol had enough power on its own, so that it needed no ornamentation: if you were close enough to see it, then it was already too late – a signature rather than an emblem.

The hatch lowered from the belly of the ship, clanking onto the deck with a metallic ring. Abett stepped forward, holding his breath in terror as the three figures stepped towards him, clearing the deep shadow of the vessel. He opened his mouth to speak, his eyes flicking up and down anxiously as they struggled to take in the scale of his visitors. Two of the figures were enormous – far taller than any man – and encased in shimmering black power armour. On their shoulder-plates, he noticed, was the same 'I' as was etched almost imperceptibly into their ship – except their shoulder icons were emblazoned gloriously and ostentatiously. The third figure, standing stiffly between the two Space Marines, was a delicate looking woman enrobed in a long, black cloak that spilt onto the deck behind her – her pale grey eyes burning with purpose.

'Where is Kastor?' snapped the woman before Abett managed to find any words.

The deck officer started to hyperventilate, twitching his head from side to side in the desperate hope that the guards had arrived. They had not. The woman stared at him implacably and then seemed to come to a decision. She pushed the man in the chest to move him aside and then swept past him into the interior of the *Vanishing Star*, the two Deathwatch Space Marines following at heel.

'I AM NOT accustomed to being kept waiting, commander,' said Kalypsia levelly. She sat with her back to the door as it slid open and Kastor paced into the room. She did not rise to greet the Navy officer, and she did not even turn her head to look at him.

'And I am not accustomed to having my ship violated so unceremoniously.' Kastor collected himself. 'You deprived us of our chance to welcome you properly, inquisitor, and I fear that the *Vanishing Star* might not forgive you for that.' Kastor spoke with silk shrouded fists. He was a direct man and no amount of Naval high-etiquette training could change his nature, even if it was expected of all officers of his rank. 'Nonetheless, I see that you have made yourself at home here.'

Kalypsia played casually with the stem of her wine glass, rolling it between her fingers, creating a gentle whirlpool of motion in the deep red liquid. 'Yes, thank you, commander. I am quite comfortable.'

Kastor stood in the doorway with his retinue of junior officers fanned out behind him, some of them still standing in the corridor outside the room. He was watching the back of the inquisitor's head as she spoke. Over her shoulder, he could see a flute of wine set out on the large, oval conference table, taken from his personal collection. He made a mental note to have the responsible servitor reassigned to one of the front-line vessels of the battlegroup.

It was only then that Kastor noticed the two huge, black figures standing against the polished, concave walls of the chamber. His head snapped around to face them with a barely dignified double-take. How could he have failed to notice them before?

They were absolutely motionless, with their features hidden behind the impenetrable visage of their helmets. They might have been magnificent statues, but still they were the most imposing soldiers that Kastor had ever seen. Nonetheless, somehow his gaze was drawn constantly to the small, female inquisitor at the table. It was almost as though the giant warriors did not want to be seen and as though the entire chamber was focussed irrevocably on Kalypsia. The Inquisition could have that effect.

'Are you going to come in?' asked Kalypsia without a hint of satisfaction and still sitting with her back to him.

Kastor composed himself immediately – this woman was not going to intimidate him on his own ship. He motioned silently for his guards to fan out around the wall opposite the Space Marines and then he walked evenly towards the table. 'Thank you, I don't mind if I do.'

Quite deliberately, the commander made his way to the side of the table where the giant warriors were standing. He wanted there to be no doubt in anybody's mind that he was in control. This was his ship. As he reached the chair in the middle of that side of the table, Kastor paused with his back to Kalypsia. Instead of turning to his left and taking his seat, however, he turned smartly to his right.

'Captain. It is an honour to welcome you aboard my ship. As you will be aware, there are a number of Space Marines from the Mantis Warriors Chapter temporarily stationed here. However, the Deathwatch are a particularly rare and unusual honour. Should you or your team require the use of any of our facilities, please do not hesitate to requisition them.'

There was a moment of silence in which Kastor imagined Kalypsia's deflated frustration. He had seen Space Marines before, even before he had rendezvoused with the Mantis Warriors' strike cruiser, *Penitent Quest*, earlier that day. It was true that he had never encountered the Deathwatch before, but he had heard enough stories about them to recognise them when one of their Marines was standing two feet in front of his nose. He had also heard enough stories to know that he didn't want to get on the wrong side of them.

With a sudden and abrupt movement, as though a decision had been reached, the Deathwatch captain unclasped the seal around his helmet and removed it from his head. Despite himself, Kastor took half a step back, nudging against the chair behind him. The face that looked down at him was struck through with a deep scar that ran from its left temple to the angle of the right jaw line. Short, fine hair fell loosely over its tanned forehead, partially obscuring a row of golden studs. But the eyes – the eyes shone with an ineffable blue that seemed to hold compassion and horror all at once.

'I am Captain Octavius of the Deathwatch, and I thank you for your welcome. Your ancient vessel honours us, and we shall show it every respect.'

Kastor held those eyes for a fraction of a second, searching their depths, nodding slightly in acknowledgment, before an irritated voice made him turn back to the table.

'Commander, when you are finished, we have much to discuss.'

OCTAVIUS HAD HEARD of the Mantis Warriors, and their name made him grimace inwardly. They were a mysterious Chapter, roaming the outer reaches of the galaxy on a perpetual quest to redeem themselves after their treachery during the Badab Wars. They had been stripped of their homeworld but, for some undefined reason, they had been granted the Emperor's forgiveness, on the condition that they complete a penitent crusade. Evidently, the Emperor's light found some utility in the Chapter's disgrace – but Octavius could not imagine what that might be. It was not his place to ask why. He shivered involuntarily at the thought of working alongside these renegades. Then he stiffened his back, resolving that such petty issues of politics were below the Deathwatch and below a veteran captain of the Imperial Fists such as him.

The two figures seated at the conference table before him were arguing energetically. From time to time, the Navy commander would bang his fists against the table in agitation, but the inquisitor would just lean back into her chair and sip delicately at her wine – agitating the officer even further. Octavius looked on impassively – he knew why he was here and the squabbles for jurisdiction made no difference to the Deathwatch. In the end, it would be he and his kill-team who would do the fighting, no matter who directed them to their target.

The Deathwatch were the Chamber Militant of the Ordo Xenos. In the end, no matter who claimed the theatre of war, Octavius would answer to Kalypsia. She was young and ambitious and she wore the seal of the Inquisition with a little too much ostentation, but she was nevertheless a fully fledged inquisitor. Octavius had not agreed with her stealthy approach to the *Vanishing Star* – the manner of their arrival would alienate the Naval officers unnecessarily. Far from being a subtle approach, their stealth could not have been more ostentatious had they been accompanied by an Inquisition battleship firing a broadside salute. But these were Kalypsia's methods and Octavius did not doubt for a moment that she would get what she wanted.

The Navy commander had made a good impression. He had acted with honour and dignity, even in the face of such antagonism from the inquisitor. On the approach run to the *Vanishing Star*, Octavius had taken careful note of the strategic deployment of the naval battlegroup and he had approved. Kastor was clearly a soldier and Octavius could think of nothing more praiseworthy than a good soldier. Nonetheless, he doubted that any soldier would be a match for Kalypsia.

The inquisitor had been appointed to the mission at short notice and without consultation. The Deathwatch team had paused on the Inquisition battleship *Veiled Salvation*, en route to the frontier of Segmentum Obscurus, where there were reports of a large tyranid swarm massing. Intelligence suggested that it was a splinter of the Kraken Hive, which had been scattered into deep space by the Ultramarines many years before. However, the Obscurus frontier was a long way and the Deathwatch team were on their way to the Herodian warp-gate when Inquisitor Lord Parthon on the *Veiled Salvation* had redirected their mission – appointing Kalypsia to lead them. Shortly afterwards, the call came in from the Mantis Warriors, requesting support.

The appearance of a tyranid sub-splinter so far within Segmentum Obscurus was perplexing. It was not clear whether this small force was a vanguard for the larger swarm massing on the frontier, or whether it was actually a small, independent hive. What was clear, however, was that its presence so close to the warp-gate had made the immaterium in the region too unstable to sustain traffic to the frontier. For as long as the sub-splinter remained in the Herodian system, the gate would have to be closed, which would mean that it would take months to get reinforcements and supplies to the frontier by other routes. By that time, the frontier war might already be over.

It was fortuitous that Octavius's Deathwatch team had been on hand and he was determined that they would get the gate open and get to the frontier before it was too late. All of this political posturing was just wasting time – and there was not enough of that to waste any of it.

Octavius watched Kalypsia fingering the pendant that hung around her neck – an elegant and simple vertical line, crossed three times in its centre like a mutant crucifix. It seemed to shine at her touch, glinting against the dark fabric of her body glove, delicately shrouded under the folds of a simple, black cloak. The medallion was worn on a loose chain so that it rested just above the exposed skin of her midriff. For the first time, Octavius noticed that the lights in the chamber had been gradually fading as the meeting went on. In the dim light, the icon of office seemed to radiate a steady glow, drawing all eyes to it.

Kalypsia wasn't speaking, but clearly Kastor was waiting for an answer.

Inwardly, Octavius shook his head as the audacity of the inquisitor struck him anew. She didn't even have to argue with this commander. That perfectly innocuous pendant gave her all the power she needed, like the tiny symbol on her gunship. Once you see it, it's already too late. Octavius could see this realisation gradually dawning on Kastor as he thumped the table in annoyance and threw himself back into his seat.

The scene was interrupted by a mechanical grind from the doors, which slid open to reveal a large, armoured figure standing in the sudden flood of light.

THE MANTIS WARRIOR captain bowed deeply from the doorway, acknowledging the stature of the people in the room before steeling himself to enter it. Despite the fact that he was fresh from combat on the surface of Herodian IV, Audin's armour had been polished until it resembled a shimmering emerald, adorned with sparkling gold purity seals. Without his helmet, his long black hair cascaded onto his shoulders, and piercing green eyes stared forth unflinchingly. Kastor rose to his feet and welcomed the Space Marine.

'Captain Audin, thank you for joining us. We realise that you must have a great deal to attend to on the *Penitent Quest.*'

'Thank you, Commander Kastor. Your concern is appreciated. We have just heard that our company's battle barge, the *Endless Redemption*, is entering the Herodian system. So we are waiting for its superior facilities before engaging in any serious technical work on the wounded.'

'That is excellent news, captain. Would I be correct to assume that the *Endless Redemption* is equipped with planetary bombardment cannons and the Exterminatus array?'

'Yes, commander,' answered Audin. 'The *Endless Redemption* is fully equipped in that regard. It is, however, under strength when it comes to Marines. The *Redemption* is home to two companies – my own, the Second, as well as the Fourth Company. Unfortunately, the Fourth Company's numbers are significantly depleted after an engagement with a detachment from the renegade Astral Claws in the Tenkudari nebula. As you will be aware, the Second Company has also suffered serious losses on Herodian IV.' Audin's manner was professional, crisp and formal, but the information he reported wounded him deeply. For nearly a century the Mantis Warriors had not been permitted to recruit new Marines and their numbers were now becoming perilously low.

'It is of no concern,' said Kalypsia, rising to her feet and turning to face Audin. 'The further assistance of the Mantis Warriors in this engagement will not be required.'

Octavius could see Audin's eyes narrow at the casual slight, as though he were suppressing a barrage of words that bubbled into his mouth. For his part, Kastor snapped his head round to face Kalypsia again, clearly shocked by this revelation.

'With the greatest respect,' grimaced the commander, 'the involvement of a Space Marine battle barge might make the difference between victory and defeat in this conflict, inquisitor.'

'You forget yourself, commander. The grace of the Emperor will make the difference and will bring us victory,' smiled Kalypsia as though springing a trap.

'Brother-captain. The presence of the Deathwatch in this theatre was unexpected, but most welcome. Should you or your team require our facilities, they are yours.' Audin had composed himself and turned his attention to the imposing figure of Octavius.

Octavius considered Audin for a moment, meeting his eyes. Something flickered deep inside. He nodded an unspoken acknowledgment, but then added, 'Thank you, captain. We have our own facilities.'

'Of course,' returned Audin with some discomfort, as he walked to the other side of the conference table and the others returned to their seats.

'The grace of the Emperor is forever in my soul, inquisitor, be not mistaken about that. I merely seek to facilitate its expression in the most expeditious manner possible,' retorted Kastor with some rhetorical flourish.

'Well said,' replied Kalypsia with mock admiration, 'but my instructions are clear on this point. The war will be won, but it will be won without the annihilation of a complete planet. The Imperium has moved beyond the barbarism of the Exterminatus, gentlemen. This is a more civilised day. Herodian IV will be saved, not destroyed. Besides, more important than the planet is the Herodian warp-gate and there is no telling what effect the destruction of the planet would have on the

warp signatures in this region – we may well ruin the
gate through such clumsy measures.'

With that display of snide cultivation, Kalypsia had
taken command.

'What, then, do you propose, inquisitor?' asked Kastor
through clenched teeth.

COLLIA JERKED HER Fury into a spin, diving through a
corkscrew roll that sent the stars into a dizzying spiral.
The sleek Drone flicked after her, following her twists
and turns with impossible ease. She was rocketing
through space, frantically looking back over her shoulders to track her pursuer.

'It's still with you.'

'Really! No kidding,' answered Collia as she threw her
weight forward against the stick, pushing her fighter into
a steeper dive.

From behind came the concussions of a series of impacts,
and she craned her neck round to see what had happened.
The Drone was ruined, with oozes of ichor seeping out into
space through vicious punctures along its side. It had lost all
propulsion and was just floating in space, dead. There was a
flash overhead as something overshot her position.

'You're welcome.' It was Gordus, the squadron leader.

'Thanks, Gordus,' said Collia, settling back into her seat
and gently rolling the Fury back towards the flock of
Drones that were assaulting the *Extreme Prejudice* at close
range. She could see the side batteries of the battle cruiser
working overtime, sputtering with fire and light, but the
scene was hazy and blurred, as though viewed through a
cloud. Collia strained her eyes, peering into the space
between her and her mothership, and she gasped.

'Can you see that, sir?'

There was a long hiss of static before the voice of Gordus crackled into Collia's ear. 'Yes, I can see it. But I don't
know what it is.'

The space between the squadron and the *Extreme Prejudice* was speckled with little spherical objects, which bobbed and fluttered with motion. From this distance, they appeared bunched into a cloud or a mist around the battle cruiser but, as the Furies accelerated back towards their mother vessel, the scale of the objects became apparent; they were like asteroids, spinning and darting with thunderous momentum.

Flocks of Drones seemed to flit through the bizarre asteroid field almost as though it wasn't there. Inside the cloud, Collia could see the Drones spewing venom against the armoured plating of the *Prejudice*, and she could see some Brood Ships trying to gain entry to the launch-bays.

With so many targets, the automatic laser batteries of the *Extreme Prejudice* were firing frantically, but their hit efficiency was low. They traced Drones through the void, only to be distracted by the flight path of an orbiting asteroid, then caught again by another flock of attackers.

If I didn't know better, thought Collia, I would think that the flock of Drones had lured the Furies away from the *Extreme Prejudice* in order to set up this bizarre trap.

'Should we call for supporting fire from the *Vanishing Star*?'

'Negative.' It was Gordus. 'The *Star*'s lances would punch straight through the spore-field and smash into the *Prejudice*. That would be playing into their hands, Collia.'

'They don't have any hands, sir.'

'Shut it, Collia. We need to get through that cloud and protect the *Prejudice*. All units commence their attack runs.'

The first wave of Furies was virtually annihilated. As they penetrated the cloud of mysterious orbs, they realised in an instant that the objects were not asteroids, but spore mines. Great ripples of explosions convulsed through the spore-field as proximity mines detonated. In some places, giant tendrils were fired out of the mines, weaving into massive, barbed webs that enwrapped Furies three at a time – packaging them into cocoons in which they were slowly consumed by toxins.

Collia thrashed at the control-stick wildly, sending her Fury into a haze of movement, twisting beyond the reach of spines and tendrils, ducking around mines that were drawn organically to the heat of her engines. She opened the throttle completely, punching through the spore-field at breakneck speed, putting her faith in control to get her through safely.

In a flash she was through, bursting into the tiny interval of clean space between the inner rim of the spore-field and the battle cruiser besieged at its heart. She fired the retros and pulled up sharply, fighting to avoid running her fighter into her own mothership. But as soon as she had the craft under control, she was assailed from all sides by flocks of Drones.

'COLLIA! NO!' CALLED Gordus as he watched the first wave of Furies explode impotently against the spore mines. He saw Collia's Fury twitch and dive into the fray with great bursts of energy bleeding from its rear burners. But he had no time to mourn. No sooner had the first wave been broken against the mines than the squadron's rear support units started to report.

'We're under attack from behind.'

'There're hundreds of them.'

Gordus pulled up out of his attack line and turned his Fury back towards the rear of the assembled squadrons, back towards the planet and the hulking masses of the injured Razorfiend and the Hive Ship. Sure enough, a great shoal of Drones had been unleashed against the rear lines of Furies, presumably manufactured in the depths of the Hive Ship itself. It seemed that the Fury squadrons had fallen into a trap of their own.

The lines of Furies were shattered, and pilots peeled away from their formations, dragged into desperate dog-fights with these new enemies. The frigates *Purgation* and *Strident Virtue* had moved in to support, but they were being met by the advance of two Razorfiends. The space surrounding Herodian IV was alive with motion and death. Only a single squadron was left in formation, waiting for the order to penetrate the spore-field to defend the *Extreme Prejudice*. Gordus held the line.

A searing beam flashed past the formation, cutting into the spore-field and causing thousands of mines to deto-nate, leaving a temporary tunnel carved into the roiling cloud. Without pausing to see where the beam had come from, Gordus charged into the opening with his guns blazing – *Storm Squadron* hot on his heels.

The *Sword of Contrition* was decelerating rapidly to engagement speed, having blasted its way in from the outer reaches of the Herodian system, accelerating all the way. Captain Krelian had expected to find the tyranid swarm attacking the outermost planets and then working its way in towards the more heavily populated inner worlds – as precedent suggested. Finding nothing in the outer reaches, Krelian had left the *Endless Redemption* unescorted and used the speed of the Fourth Company's Mantis strike cruiser to get to Herodian IV ahead of it. The battle barge would roll up in another day or so.

The theatre of battle had been obvious even from the most distant orbit – the blazing mess of fighters and las-fire could be seen from the very edge of the system – and Krelian had directed his ship into its heart without paus-ing to confer with the *Vanishing Star*. Veteran Sergeant Ruinus, back on the *Penitent Quest*, had explained that the Second Company was in tatters and that its strike cruiser was as much a hospital ship as a gunship at present. It was withdrawn, in the shelter of the giant Gothic-class cruiser.

'Fire one more pulse in support of the squadron in the mine field,' ordered Captain Krelian of the Mantis Warriors, 'and then we'll see what we can do to help the rest of these fighters.'

'As MOST OF you will all be aware,' continued Kalypsia, with the tone of a lecturer informing the ignorant, 'a tyranid invasion proceeds through various stages. The current incursion appears to have already reached the end of stage IV. Whilst this is more advanced than might be ideal, there is still hope.

'Having only been alerted to the threat at a relatively late stage, we don't yet have full details about how the swarm proceeded through the previous phases. In particular, it is unclear why the tyranids targeted this planet. Some of you will be aware,' she said, nodding slightly towards Octavius, 'that precedent suggests that tyranid swarms usually work their way from the outer reaches of a star system towards the interior, consuming all the organic matter they find on their way. In this case, it seems that the swarm has come straight to Herodian IV, neglecting the string of planets out to Herodian XII, some of which support small colonies of life.'

'Why did it take us so long to detect the incursion, inquisitor?' asked Octavius, his eyes darting to the Mantis Warrior captain.

Kalypsia noted the look, but answered formally. 'There are various reasons, captain. Perhaps the most significant is the relatively small size of this splinter hive. As you know, the first sign of a tyranid invasion is usually a distortion in the warp, as the hive mind moves into the vicinity. In this case, the warp shadow was not substantial enough to excite our attention, especially in comparison with the immense darkness gathering on the frontier of Segmentum Obscurus.'

'Small splinter?' interjected Audin defensively. 'With all due respect, inquisitor, there is nothing small about the scale of the tyranid invasion of Herodian IV.'

'With all due respect, captain,' answered Kalypsia, as though none were due, 'the tyranid force that took Herodian IV is tiny in comparison with the swarms that were faced by the Ultramarines in the Ultima Segmentum. Here, the horde is big enough only to assault a single planet – there they rampaged through entire systems. That said,' she added with the smallest hint of contrition, 'the warp shadow generated by this swarm has grown significantly since the hive tyrant descended to the planet's surface.'

'So, why is it here, inquisitor?' asked Kastor, leaning forward with his hands pressed against the conference table. 'Why is it here and how long have we got to get rid of it? Can you tell us, or not?'

Kalypsia turned her sharp grey eyes on Kastor and stared at him for a long moment. 'The important question for you, *commander*, is how we are going to get rid of it. My calculations suggest that we have, at most, two days in which to destroy the swarm. After that time the planet will be completely consumed and lost to us forever. This must not be allowed to happen. If the planet falls, so too falls the Herodian warp-gate. If the warp-gate is not reopened, the Obscurus frontier will be lost. Two days, gentlemen.'

'Very well,' answered Kastor with agitated resignation. '*How are we going to get rid of it?*'

Kalypsia said nothing, but rose to her feet and walked to the back of the conference room, enjoying the focus of the gazes that followed her every move. Her long black hair shimmered over her shoulders and seemed to blend into the cascades of her cloak as she walked. At an invisible signal, a screen whirred down from the ceiling, clicking into place against the back wall. Kalypsia pointed at the planetary chart. She had been building to this moment from the start.

'Building on the intelligence gathered by the esteemed Inquisitor Kryptman, who was so instrumental in the victories against the Great Devourer in the Ultima Segmentum, Inquisitor Lord Parthon of the Ordo Xenos has developed a strategy for the location of a swarm's hive tyrant. One of the key lessons learnt by Captain Bannon's Deathwatch squad during the Tarsis Ultra campaign against the tyranids–'

'–may the Emperor guard his soul,' intoned Octavius at the mention of Bannon's name. Bannon was a legendary figure in the annals of the Deathwatch – a heroic captain who gave his life so that the Ultramarines might triumph over the Great Devourer. For Octavius, Bannon was an icon of duty and honour and it pained him that their shared Chapter of origin – the Imperial Fists – would never know how their heroic captain died. Such was the nature of a secondment to the Deathwatch – it provided the warrior with matchless opportunities to prove his worth in the eyes of the Emperor, but it placed these legends into the shadowy realm of Inquisitorial records. Octavius had been called up to the Deathwatch from the Fists just after Bannon's death and he had made it his mission to be worthy of the mantel passed down from this fallen hero. When he eventually rejoined the Imperial Fists, he would make sure that Bannon's name was written large in the Chapter's history books – the Imperial Fist captain who saved the Ultramarines.

'Indeed, captain,' said Kalypsia, conscious of the honourable devotion in Octavius's interjection, but resentful of the interruption. 'As I was saying: one of the key lessons taught to us by the heroic actions of Deathwatch Captain Bannon and his team on Tarsis Ultra was that the destruction of a hive tyrant will cause critical disruption in the organisation of a tyranid swarm. Indeed, Inquisitor Lord Parthon now believes that the disruption caused in a small hive splinter, such as the one we have here, would be so great that it would tilt the balance of the battle dramatically in our favour – allowing us to wipe out the swarm with quite acceptable losses on our side. This is because a splinter of this size is likely to have only one hive tyrant – and this tyrant acts as the nerve centre for the coherence of the entire swarm.

'A swift surgical strike by an elite force led by Captain Octavius,' Kalypsia nodded an acknowledgment towards the captain, 'should be able to knock out the tyrant and give the rest of you,' she swept her hand casually across the room, taking in Kastor and Audin, 'the window required to eradicate these pests from the system. This obviates the need to utilise the crude Exterminatus on Herodian IV and thus preserves the integrity of the warpgate.'

'This is a dangerous plan, inquisitor,' said Kastor suspiciously, sharing a glance with Audin. 'If your team fails, the planet will be completely consumed and the warpgate will be utterly lost in the warp shadow. Not only that, but the tyranid swarm will have gained a significant foothold in this sector, from which it may be able to advance deeper into Imperial space – Exterminatus would prevent that, at least.'

'Mind your words, commander. Failure is not an accusation to throw at a Deathwatch captain. If it can be done, the Deathwatch will not fail,' said Octavius levelly.

'And if it cannot be done?' replied Kastor, unphased.

'We will see it done,' stated Kalypsia flatly, closing the issue.

CHAPTER THREE:
DESERT

[38 Hours Remaining]

'I TOLD THEM that we knew how to locate the hive tyrant and that the Deathwatch kill-team would be able to exterminate it,' said Kalypsia into the crackling vox unit. It hissed and cackled with interference as she waited for a response – the distance was great so there was a slight delay. Not for the first time, she cursed the tyranid swarm's warp shadow; it disrupted all psychic traffic in the area and made astropathic communication almost impossible. Hence, even the Inquisition had to rely on these crude voice-transmission devices. They were slow, cumbersome, and ugly – none of which were qualities that Kalypsia appreciated.

Inquisitor Lord Parthon's voice fizzled and sputtered. 'Excellent. I assume that you were as convincing as I have come to expect you to be. It is important that they trust you. Remember, Kalypsia, time is of the essence. In less than two days, the tyranids will have what they came for. That could be very dangerous for us, not to mention for the rest of the Imperium.'

'I understand, my lord. The mission will be accomplished in the time available to us. Have no fear of that.'

'I have no fear of time, Kalypsia, for my eternal soul does not recognise it. But I fear the Great Devourer, and I fear what it may accomplish if we do not stop it here. The Herodian system is but a stepping stone. If the tyranid master it then time will be an irrelevance – instead, I shall fear for my soul.'

'The tyranids will not succeed here, my lord. The Deathwatch will prevent this.'

'I hope you are right, young Kalypsia. And what of our heroic Captain Octavius? Does he show any signs of suspicion?'

'None, my lord,' said Kalypsia with certainty. 'I have offered no cause for suspicion, and I would not stand for it even if I inspired some. As far as he is concerned, we are hunting a hive tyrant. Octavius is a servant of the Inquisition, nothing more. He is a soldier – a tool.'

'He is a Deathwatch captain, young Kalypsia, and the champion of my old friend, the Inquisitor Lord Agustus. You would do well not to underestimate him. He has been fighting the foul xenos since before you were born. There are eldar exarchs and ork warlords who shudder at his name – you should not treat him lightly. His presence on this mission is our greatest asset, but he is not entirely our closest ally.' Parthon's voice was level and calm, despite the keen insistence in his tone.

'I will watch the honourable captain,' replied Kalypsia with the faintest hint of sarcasm. For some years now, she had been concerned that her mentor was losing his nerve as he was growing old. There was no doubt that he was a wise man and a great inquisitor. Nobody rose to the rank of inquisitor lord and made so many enemies without being ruthlessly brilliant. But his edge seemed to be dulling and Kalypsia was confident that she could sharpen his plans as she went along.

'See that you do,' said Parthon and then the vox clicked sharply before falling silent.

Kalypsia stood up from the console and stared out of the view screen into the darkness of the landing bay that enveloped her ship, *Perfect Incision*. It had been sealed and emptied of all Navy personnel – something that Deck Officer Abett had been only too pleased about.

She looked back along the length of her sleek vessel, and she could see two giant Marines, one standing on each side of the open landing ramp. They were motionless sentries, almost invisible in their black power-armour, shrouded in the shadow of the *Incision*, encased in the solid dark of the *Vanishing Star*'s landing bay.

They were something of a mystery to her, and it went against her nature to take them too seriously – military men were simple men. Her father had been in the Imperial Guard until he was shredded by a tyranid hormagaunt as his squad marched slowly forward in a straight line, firing volleys of lasfire. It was pathetic, and she hated him for being such a grunt. Of course, she also hated the vile xenos creatures that had taken her father away from her, so she was left with a complicated psychological scar – hating the aliens and hating the pathetic way that people tried to fight them. So much hate. As a confused and passionate child, she had vowed never to lapse into a crude, stupid life. She was a natural recruit for the Inquisition, and she had made it her mission to ridicule the stupidities of military personnel ever since she was appointed as an inquisitor. There was more than one way to fight the xenos creatures of the galaxy.

But she had to confess that there was something different about these Deathwatch Marines. They were dark in complex ways and filled with silence. Never wasting words where none were needed. Despite herself, she could not think of them as stupid – the fathomless blue of Octavius's eyes spoke of painful wisdom.

She had been on the *Veiled Salvation* under the tutelage of Parthon for many years, but this unexpected assignment had brought her into contact with the Deathwatch for the first time. Indeed, this was her first real contact with Space Marines of any kind. She had heard about them, of course. And she had occasionally seen them in Inquisition facilities, making reports of their various missions for the Ordo Xenos. But she had always suspected that the spectacular reports of their feats were exaggerated. The space between those stories and what she already knew of her father's time in the Imperial Guard was just too massive. These Space Marines would have to be superhuman to do the things they were rumoured to do, or her father must have been even more pathetic than she thought.

In truth, she hated Space Marines already, but she could see how useful they were: giant, super-human warriors, absolutely dedicated to service to the Emperor. Perhaps it was their dedication that she hated most – like the blind devotion that had made her father walk slowly into the talons of a tyranid swarm. To Kalypsia, the devotion of soldiers seemed like a simple and unquestioning affair – they followed orders. Thinking was done elsewhere, not within their heads but without them. And, in the spiralling bureaucracy of the Imperium, sometimes no thinking was done at all. That's where the Inquisition fitted in – it had to do the thinking for everyone. This was something to which she could be devoted.

She pushed her doubts to the back of her mind: she would do the thinking on this mission and her Deathwatch Marines, including the heroic Octavius, would do as they were told. No matter what the ageing Parthon thought of the Deathwatch, they were just like any Space Marines, just like any soldier – they were still her men.

* * *

'THERE. THAT'S OUR landing site,' pointed Kalypsia, indicating with her finger.

Octavius shook his head slowly, running his hand over the deep scar across his face. 'I'm afraid that I cannot concur, inquisitor. That location is sub-optimal.'

'But that is our target, captain. Judging by the formation of the tyranid swarm and the geological information we have about the territory in that sector, it is almost certain that this is the location of the hive tyrant.' The young inquisitor was not trying to convince Octavius, she was merely explaining why his opinion was irrelevant.

'You do not understand, inquisitor,' said Octavius carefully. 'Even if that is our target, we cannot land on that site. It is already completely overrun by the swarm. You can see here and here,' he said, pointing, 'that the site is located in a narrow valley, and that both sides of it are swimming with xenos. Our Thunderhawk would be too exposed, too vulnerable on the descent and we would suffer too many casualties before we could even deploy our forces. The Deathwatch do not throw away their lives so lightly, inquisitor.'

'But we must reach that site, captain. The lives of your team, precious as they are, are not the primary concern of this mission.'

Sitting in the corner of the room, his face hidden beneath the folds of a black hood, Deathwatch Librarian Ashok rose to his feet. Even without his power armour, the Marine was an imposing figure – more than humanly tall, with thick muscles giving the simple, heavy cloak an impressive shape. Kalypsia turned to face the unexpected movement, distracted for a moment from her engagement with Octavius. From the blackness beneath the librarian's hood shone two pearls of swirling darkness, as his black eyes burned in the shadows.

The Deathwatch do not fear to die, inquisitor. Indeed, we expect it. Ashok's voice was low and smooth, almost a whisper. Something in the tone made Kalypsia wince slightly and she shrunk back imperceptibly. Looking quickly to Octavius, she realised that he had not heard the voice – he was looking at her with some concern. He had insisted on the presence of his librarian for the meeting and now Kalypsia understood why.

Are you also ready to die, inquisitor? Ashok's voice eased directly into her mind, pushing aside her other thoughts gently but firmly. Kalypsia was not a great psyker, but she had been trained by the Inquisition to use her limited abilities to their greatest effect. She had developed a strong capacity to shield her mind from the incursions of others – which is partly why she was so suitable for the present mission; only a psyker with strong barriers would survive contact with the tyranid warp shadow without going insane. But somehow this librarian had circumvented her defences. She resolved that this would not happen again, and she slammed shut all the doors to her mind.

'We will not throw our lives away needlessly,' said Octavius, staring out of the briefing room of the *Vanishing Star*, gazing at the planet far below. Kalypsia turned back to face the captain, aware of Ashok's eyes behind her all the time.

Even from this distance, the tyranid swarm was clearly visible as a series of black clouds swirling over the golden sands of the desert planet, roiling and oozing across the surface. It was incredible to think that the shifting oceans of black were actually made up of millions of scything, taloned tyranid creatures, swarming over the planet with the single, unified purpose of the hive mind. If it were not for the vile repugnance of the xenos, the sight might even have been beautiful.

'We will land there,' said Octavius, pointing towards the planet. He walked away from the view screen and back to Kalypsia's chart where the movements of the swarm were projected onto the map. He pointed his finger to a small clearing in the swarm, just to the south of the target site. The black clouds swam and flowed around it, leaving it as a spot of light in the swirling darkness. 'This landing site is relatively clean and close enough to the target zone. It is not flanked by enemy strong points. It is a more acceptable risk, and it does not diminish the success probability of the mission.'

Kalypsia considered the site for a moment. It might have been a rock promontory or a patch of deep desert where the tyranids had found no organic matter. Whatever the reason for its clarity, it certainly looked like a fortuitously clear spot. There were one or two other such spots in the vicinity, but this was by far the closest to the target area. There also appeared to be a thin corridor of less densely occupied territory leading through the valley from the site to the target. Despite her natural inclination to dismiss the ideas of this Marine and his precious protocols, Kalypsia had to admit that this was a good landing site. 'Very well, captain, I agree. We will use your insertion point.'

THE THUNDERHAWK BUCKED and screeched as it pierced the atmosphere of Herodian IV, its machine spirit protesting against this apparent mistreatment of its hull. Deathwatch Techmarine Korpheus administered to its complaints with firm care, planet-fall was usually a routine affair, but the atmosphere of Herodian IV was now so dense with humidity and oxylene gases that the Thunderhawk could feel the alien violation of its engine vents and the air resistance blasted the vessel's armour with unusual ferocity.

The planet was changing, as the xenos Hive Ship pumped the atmosphere full of strange alien enzymes designed to accelerate the growth of all organic compounds on the surface and also to provide essential

nutrients for the tyranid swarm that swam over the
planet's crust. Everything would grow to the point of sat-
uration, and then it would lapse into a fecund decay.
Specialised organisms would consume the carrion, using
it as energy to fuel pupation and transformation into bigger, more powerful organisms. Meanwhile, the rest of the
swarm would harvest every last molecule of nutrition
and the Hive Ship would suck vast amounts of bio-mass
out of the atmosphere to replenish its energy reserves.
The tyranid – the Great Devourer. If there was enough
rich material on the planet, the Hive Ship might even
calve, giving birth to more ships for the tyranid fleet. If
things got this far, then there would be no going back for
Herodian IV.

'Are your men ready, captain?' asked Kalypsia without
concern.

'We are always ready, inquisitor,' answered Octavius.

Octavius looked around the interior of the Thunderhawk at his team, each strapped securely into their
landing braces. Only Korpheus was out of his position,
tending to the Thunderhawk itself. The others sat in
calm, almost motionless silence, their helmets secured
and their weapons held ready. Only Ashok had no helmet. Instead, his face was hidden below the folds of an
ornate, heavy shroud. He stared fixedly into the polished
floor of the Thunderhawk, never shifting his gaze nor
showing any signs of breathing. Kalypsia was sure that
she could see a faint red glow emanating from under the
Marine's hood.

Genuinely unnerved by the librarian, Kalypsia asked,
'What is wrong with him?'

'There is nothing wrong. He is simply finding his balance before the battle to come. We must all do this in our
own way. As you know, our traditions are all different,
but we must honour them all as though they were our
own,' answered Octavius quietly. Out the corner of his

eye he saw the grotesque deathmask-helmet of Chaplain Broec twitch slightly. An altitude alarm sounded, and the flash of a warning light glinted off the stark white shoulder guard of the Chaplain, revealing the highly polished black cross insignia of the Black Templars – tolerance for diversity was not his forte.

Sitting across from Broec, towering over the other members of the team, was Neleus, resplendent in the Terminator armour of the White Consuls. Since joining the Deathwatch many years before, Neleus had blackened his armour to honour the spirit of this elite division, but one of his shoulder guards still proudly displayed the blue eagle of his Chapter, set against an immaculate white background. The ancient armour of a Space Marine would not stand for its identity to be completely swamped, not even by the majestic blackness of the Deathwatch. Each Marine preserved the original insignia of their original Chapters on one shoulder.

Neleus was tapping his foot against the floor in agitation, eager to be on the ground. None of the Marines enjoyed being sealed in a Thunderhawk, with their lives in the hands of a pilot-servitor; it would not become a Space Marine to die in such a context. In any case, the White Consuls were proud of their shared origins with the Ultramarines, and Neleus was keen to be on the ground and to show that their honoured brothers were not the only Chapter who could slay tyranids.

'Are you really so different from each other?' asked Kalypsia, inherently sceptical about variation amongst soldiers, especially soldiers as manufactured as the Space Marines.

'The Deathwatch are a team, inquisitor. Our individual differences make the whole stronger.' Octavius spoke from conviction. He was proud of his eclectic team, and it had never failed him before. The awesome reputation of the Deathwatch was founded upon exactly this insight: just as the Emperor divided his essence between the Primarchs of the various Space Marine Legions, so the Deathwatch would draw on the elite of each Chapter, uniting that essence once again. The result was suitably magnificent.

A warning siren sounded, filling the compartment with a pulsing orange light.

'Brace for landing,' called Korpheus from the cockpit. 'This might be a little rough.'

A flurry of impacts smashed against the sides of the Thunderhawk as it descended. Even from within the sealed drop-chamber, Kalypsia could smell the gradual corrosion of the vessel's armoured plating.

'What's hitting us, Korpheus?' called Octavius over the rising din.

'We just dropped through a flock of gargoyles. Most of them were shredded by the automatic guns, but a few survived. They're firing on us with some kind of toxic venom. The armour will hold for now. At least until we hit the ground.'

'Understood,' replied Octavius. 'And what about the landing site? How does it look?'

'Still clean, but we're going to hit it pretty hard. If I slow our descent any more, there won't be much left of the hawk by the time we reach the ground,' said Korpheus, still ministering to the craft as it screeched through the last stages of the drop.

A sudden lurch threw the team against their restraints. There was a faint hiss that ripped into a terrible, rushing gust, and then a piercing scream thrust into the compartment through a fresh tear in the wall. In an instant, Ashok was on his feet, whilst Octavius levelled his bolt-gun at the breach. A flash of blue lightning arced from the tip of Ashok's power staff and stabbed through the gap in the ceramite. There was another shriek and a faint spluttering sound as liquid ichor rained against the hull from the outside.

The Thunderhawk rocked unstably, as though its balance had been thrown by the assault on its flank. It pitched and yawed as though adrift on a violent sea, and cracks began to appear in the walls on all sides. The Marines were all out of their harnesses now, each of them covering a different breech.

'How far to the ground, Korpheus?' asked Octavius.

'Too far for the inquisitor, captain.'

'Understood,' said Octavius, his eyes fixed on the growing cracks in the walls. 'Short bursts to minimise structural damage. This tub has got to get us down to the ground before it falls apart.'

Then the tub fell apart. With the hiss of toxins and the metallic scrape of talons, great chunks of the Thunderhawk's armour were suddenly ripped away. Air and moisture flooded into the compartment, misting as they hit the warm air inside, obscuring the creatures that clawed their way through the breeches behind.

A blaze of bolter fire erupted almost instantaneously, shredding anything that moved around the perimeter of the vessel, but also chipping away great chunks of the ship's substructure. Screams and inhuman shrieks echoed through the mists, and jets of toxic ichor splattered against the black armour of the Deathwatch Marines. Kalypsia stood her ground in the centre of the compartment, surrounded by an impenetrable wall of Space Marines. Her bolt pistol was drawn, but she could not see anything to fire at.

The Thunderhawk flashed through its descent like a meteor, shedding armoured panels and instrumentation as it went. Korpheus had now lost complete control of the machine and had joined his battle-brothers in the fight against the gargoyles.

'Ten seconds to impact, captain,' he yelled over the tumult of gunfire.

Octavius nodded his understanding as he fired off a rapid burst of bolter shells into the flapping form of a tyranid creature clawing over the Thunderhawk's wing. He turned to Kalypsia and said calmly, 'Time to leave, inquisitor.'

Wrapping one arm around her waist, he took a couple of steps towards the edge of the vessel, lowering his shoulder and crashing through the wall into the rush of air outside. As he fell, he could hear the rattle of explosions cease above him and he knew that his squad had followed him.

ASHOK STOOD UPRIGHT and looked across the sand, scanning its featureless terrain for signs of threat. Heat haze rippled across the horizon and he strained his eyes to see beyond it. How far away was the swarm, he wondered?

His mind was alive with voices and sounds, but they were utterly incoherent and deafeningly loud – he could learn nothing from the psychic utterances of the hive mind, except perhaps the location of his own insanity. And he had spent decades burying the genetic insanity of his Chapter.

He pulled his hood further down over his face, hiding his sensitive eyes from the intense glare of the local star. The texture of the shroud on his skin reassured him. The cloth had been presented to him after that terrible ordeal on Hegelian IX, when the Angels Sanguine Death Company had been sent into the catacombs to mop up the remnants of a fleeing tyranid force, but they had lost their minds to the Black Rage and had started to kill each other to slake their thirst for blood. Ashok had killed three of his own battle-brothers before he finally managed to bring his Rage under control. After that, he had spent three years strapped to the Tablet of Lestrallio in the Chapter's fortress monastery, thrashing against his nightmares. When he finally emerged, he was presented with the Shroud of Lemartes – Guardian of the Damned – as a symbol of his mastery of himself. It was then that the call had come from the Deathwatch and he had been waiting for an opportunity to confront the tyranids again ever since.

A sharp movement over to his right made Ashok spin, planting his power staff into the sand in readiness. But it was Korpheus, climbing out of the crater his landing had punched into the ground, the silver Raven insignia on his auto-reactive shoulder plate a starburst in the bright light. He kept himself low to the ground, checking the surrounding terrain for signs of the enemy before emerging from the crater.

Ashok watched the caution of his battle-brother with a hint of amusement. The Raven Guard were justly famed as covert operations specialists and Korpheus was no doubt well experienced in this kind of drop mission, but Ashok found the creeping about faintly comical. He would rather face the enemy head on, in a blaze of warp energy. Hiding from your enemy prevented you from scything through them like an angel of death – and what could be a better label for the Adeptus Astartes?

Beyond Korpheus, a scattering of other dark figures were emerging from the sand. On the rise of a small dune stood Octavius, resplendent in his magnificent armour, shining in black against the endless undulations of the yellow desert. His head was turning slowly as he scanned the horizon. Behind him, dwarfed by his inhuman size and superhuman presence, stood the delicate figure of Kalypsia, her long cloak billowing in the dusty wind.

Further into the distance, beyond Octavius, Ashok could see the towering figure of Neleus, surrounded by a clutch of other Marines, each a black smudge in the rippling heat haze. A burst of red from the shoulders of one told Ashok that the Crimson Fist Veteran Sergeant Grevius was amongst them. A blink of silver suggested that the Space Wolf, Kulac, was also there. Their guns were drawn and pointed skywards. Scattered around them

were a series of prone, smoking corpses – presumably the
remains of the gargoyles that had attacked the Thunderhawk. The Thunderhawk itself was nowhere to be seen.

'Tyranocide, mission check,' stuttered a broken signal
into Ashok's vox bead. He pressed his hand to his ear, trying to improve the signal. Perhaps the impact had
unbalanced the implant? More likely, the tyranid hive
mind was spilling into real space and disturbing communications. Ashok could remember how his Death
Company had lost communication on Hegelian IX and
there the swarm had already been broken by the Angels
Sanguine. He could remember the voices in his head, driving him into a killing frenzy – part of him knew that the
voices were not his, even then. But the Blood Angels and
their successor Chapters, like the Angels Sanguine, lived
with the constant fear of a frenzied and suppressed internal voice and thus paranoia had kicked in automatically.
Ashok was still not sure whether he had lost himself to his
own Rage on Hegelian IX, or whether he had been assailed
by the Hive Mind and driven to the point of insanity.

'Broec, check.' The chaplain's signal was strong and
clear. It was followed by a string of affirmations from the
rest of the team, each of whom appeared to have made it
down to the ground in one piece.

'Ashok, check,' added the librarian finally, completing
the squad list.

'Tyranocide proceed,' came the voice of Octavius again.
Ashok could see him on the dune, waving the dispersed
line of Marines forward to the north. 'Remain dispersed.
Hold the line. Extreme caution.' The signal was broken and
weak, but it was audible enough. Ashok swept his gaze
across the horizon once more and then set off through the
desert towards the target, one hand holding the rim of his
hood to keep the wind from blowing it off his head.

* * *

THE DESERT WAS silent. Dust and sand whipped up into eddies and sand-devils that whisked across the gently rolling landscape, occasionally being swamped by great powdery clouds that floated on gusts of wind. The footprints of the Marines vanished as soon as they were made, leaving no trace of their presence. But the sand was loose and soft and the heavy, armoured boots of the Deathwatch sunk deeply with every step – so the approach was slower and more heavy-going than Octavius had anticipated. Kalypsia, lighter on her feet than her hulking escorts, kept pace comfortably – something that she would have struggled to do had they been on firmer ground.

Scanning from left to right, Octavius could see his team progressing over the sand. They were making ground steadily and without opposition. It was too quiet. Octavius had been wondering about the gargoyles that attacked the Thunderhawk on their descent. Most of them had been killed from the air, and the immense fire power of Neleus's Terminator armour had despatched the rest after they had made landfall. But it seemed odd that nothing had come to support the ugly, flapping wretches.

Octavius shook his head mentally, trying to shake free his human preconceptions. Tyranids are animals, I should not expect them to behave like humans. For all I know, the gargoyles have no way of calling for support. It is entirely conceivable that the rest of the swarm would not care enough to give them support in any case.

However, he could not quite convince himself that the creatures were so simple. It was so very quiet, and Octavius had fought enough battles to know that silence is often the most dangerous noise of all.

'It seems that our landing site was well-chosen, captain,' said Kalypsia, pushing her way through the sand and pulling her cloak around her body to prevent the sand cutting into her exposed skin.

'So it seems, inquisitor,' replied Octavius without looking at her. His eyes were flicking across the horizon with a hint of anxiety. It was still clear – there was nothing but sand and haze. In his peripheral vision to the left, he could see that Ashok had stopped walking and had planted his staff into the sand in front of him. He stood motionlessly, as though waiting for something to happen. Some distance away, Korpheus had also stopped. The Raven Guard had dropped to one knee and was feeling the sand with his hand, apparently inspecting something on the ground.

Octavius twisted his head round to his right and saw Neleus striding onwards, followed by the rest of the squad, including the two Crimson Fists and Kulac. Just beyond them was Chaplain Broec, his Crozius Arcanum held proudly aloft, as though he were leading a crusade. A wave of reassurance washed over Octavius as he watched the confident progress of his squad.

'Ashok, Korpheus, what's wrong?' asked Octavius, the vox signal hissing badly before fading into a screech of feedback. There was no reply. Octavius punched the side of his helmet in a reflex reaction, but the vox just spluttered and crackled worldlessly.

'Inquisitor,' asked Octavius, quickly turning to face Kalypsia, 'are the tyranids capable of disrupting vox communication?'

'No, captain. They are simply animals. The presence of the Hive Mind does disrupt psychic communication, but it has no effect on conventional technologies. They are not capable of artifice, captain.' Kalypsia tried to look directly into the captain's eyes as she spoke, but they were hidden behind the deeply tinted visor of his helmet. She could not tell where he was looking and this made her uncomfortable for more than one reason. 'Is there a problem, captain?'

A burst of gunfire made them both spin round to their right. Even from that distance, they could hear the cries of pain and the orders being barked by Neleus. The Terminator had his storm bolter pointed down at the ground and was unloading an incredible discharge into the sand. The other Marines had deployed into a wide circle, their guns similarly trained on the ground at their feet. Octavius did a quick mental count – there were only three others. One was missing.

From behind him came the sound of shouts and the pounding of feet. Without turning, Octavius knew that it was Ashok and Korpheus on their way to help the rest of the squad. Octavius also broke into a run, and the three of them went storming across the desert towards their stricken comrades, leaving Kalypsia standing alone on the crest of a dune.

IT WAS GREVIUS. He had gone. Vanished into the sand. The squad had been pushing on through the desert in the wake of Neleus, their guns trained on the horizon and the sky, waiting for the first signs of an attack. There had been no sign at all. Just the gusts of desert wind and the incredible, eerie silence. Then, with a suddenness that had shocked them all, Grevius had pulled up short and let out a gasp of pain. His comrades had skidded to a halt and turned to face him, in time to watch him teeter precariously and then crash to the ground.

At the front of the column, Neleus had been the last to turn, but had been the first to reach the fallen Marine, ploughing through the sand with ease in his Terminator suit. By the time he had reached Grevius, the sergeant's leg had already stopped bleeding, as his enhanced blood rushed to clot and seal the gaping wound. Grevius had rolled over into a sitting position with his boltgun directed back towards his remaining foot. A couple of metres away, lying just were it had been severed, with blood soaking into the sand around it, was his right leg.

In a sudden flash of movement, a giant blade had darted out of the sand beneath Grevius, slicing cleanly through the armour of his shoulder and taking his left arm off in a single swipe. Neleus had opened fire instantly, but the blade vanished beneath the sand as quickly as it had appeared. The dismembered sergeant had reacted almost as quickly, firing a volley of bolter shells into the increasingly blood-soaked sand underneath him. By this time the rest of squad had formed a defensive perimeter around their sergeant, scanning the ground with their guns for the tiniest sign of movement.

The desert had seethed and started to heave around Grevius, knocking some of the Marines off balance. Only Neleus had stood firm, firing continuously into the shifting sands, but he had little effect. With a sudden rush of movement, the sand around Grevius caved in as the massive blade reappeared, thrust through the back of the sergeant, shattering his spine and punching out towards the sky. The subsidence disturbed the footing of all of the Marines, even Neleus and their swift reactions were not enough to bring down the monster that dragged the hideously disfigured sergeant below the surface of the desert. As they fired into the ground, the blood stains gradually vanished into the shifting sand and, by the time Octavius and the others arrived, there was no sign of Grevius at all.

'What was it?' asked Octavius, turning to Neleus after surveying the area.

'I'm not sure, captain,' answered the Terminator, his voice full of self-recrimination. 'But it was fast, and it came from under the sand.'

'How many?'

'Just one, as far as I could see,' conceded Neleus, biting on each word.

'Did you hit it?' asked Octavius, conscious of Neleus's discomfort, but needing to know.

'No, I don't think so.'

Octavius was shaking his head in disbelief as Kalypsia arrived at the scene.

'Something wrong, captain?'

'Yes, very wrong. Inquisitor, what kind of tyranid organism hunts under the ground?' Octavius's tone contained a hint of accusation.

'None that I am aware of, captain. However, as you know, a number of the tyranid genus are mutable. There may well be a new form here on Herodian IV, adapted for hunting in the desert. What did it look like?'

There was a slight edge to Kalypsia's voice that made Ashok turn his fathomless black eyes to study hers.

'It had two extended fore-talons, perhaps two metres long. There were four other limbs, which appeared to end in webbed claws, with which it scooped at the sand. When it ducked back below the ground, it exposed a long tail. It appeared to be scaled in yellow.' Eager to make amends, Neleus was as detailed as he could be.

'It sounds like some kind of lictor,' concluded Kalypsia. 'They are a predator species. Hunters. Extremely adaptable to hostile environments.'

'Mantis stalkers,' said Octavius, giving them their most common name. 'I have seen them before – although never like this. They exude a pheromone trail that draws the rest of the swarm after them. We need to get to some solid ground,' he added, turning his back to the squad and scanning the horizon.

'There,' said Korpheus, pointing out across the desert with his chainsword. All Space Marines had enhanced vision, but the Raven Guard's eyes were sharpest of all. A great cloud of sand drifted across the vista, parting to reveal a jagged ruin on the horizon to the north. It wasn't very big, probably no bigger than a Vindicator tank, but it was better than nothing.

In a sudden blur of motion, Ashok whipped his force staff into the air, spinning it above his head before thrusting it down into the sand at the feet of Neleus. The staff spat a bolt of blue flame, which coruscated and cracked between the grains. Neleus took a giant step backwards just in time, as the warp energy impacted with something under the surface, causing the desert to convulse. The rest of the squad dove for the ground, rolling into readiness with their weapons primed.

With a terrible keening, the creature roared out of the sand, rearing up on its hind legs and screeching into the sky. Sand cascaded down its scaled body, and bloody ichor gushed from a deep, pulsing wound in its abdomen. Its fore-talons thrashed wildly around, but the kill-team was already clear of its reach.

Neleus was the first to react, charging forward with his storm bolter a blaze of shells. By the time he launched himself bodily at the lictor, it was already a shredded, ruined mess of cracked scales and decimated tissue. The rest of the squad opened up. Neleus smashed into it, driving his power fist straight through its thorax with all the violence of vengeance, sending a shower of xenos life-blood splattering into the absorbent sand.

A gasp sounded from one of the other Marines and Neleus spun in time to see Broec driving his Crozius into the ground next to the disappearing gauntlet of one of his battle-brothers, a growing diffusion of blood spilling out into the sand around him.

Suddenly there were talons everywhere, flashing out of the sand and thrusting at the Marines from all sides. The desert shifted and flowed, rippling with vicious blades like a treacherous ocean. The team were on their feet, loosing volleys of fire into the sand all around them and fending off the talons with their own blades.

Stabbing out a couple of bolter shells, Kalypsia cast her gaze over the surrounding terrain – even she could see that the horizon was now thick with seething blackness. For a moment she thought that it was just the heat haze, but then the blurry forms began to resolve into fixed shapes. In every direction, the horizon was crammed with tyranids, scampering, leaping and charging in their direction.

THE MASSIVE SCYTHING talon swiped out of the sand just as Kalypsia caught the outstretched hand of Octavius. Her feet left the ground just in time, as the barbed blade cut through the air at her heels, finding nothing on which to bite. Octavius pulled her clear of the desert and dropped her unceremoniously onto the overturned flank of the ruined emerald green Vindicator tank, his other arm a blaze of energy as his boltgun spat shells into the incoming horde.

Kalypsia was straight up onto her feet, her bolt pistol drawn in one hand and a crackling force whip burst into life in the other. She strode to the edge of the tank, firing a hail of shells from her gun, until she was in range with her whip. Holstering the pistol, she took the whip in both hands and lashed out with it on full extension. It snapped through the dusty air with a crack of lightning that raked across the sea of protruding talons, slicing them apart in a series of small explosions.

The rumbling horizon was drawing closer, as the swarm descended on the old Mantis Warrior Vindicator tank, which had been completely ruined by a huge explosion at some point in the recent past. The armoured plates on one side had survived the blast, so presumably it had been hit by some kind of cannon on the other side, flipping it into its present position; the armoured plates now acted as a reinforced floor and the Deathwatch team were bunched together on top of it, repelling the borders.

The towering figure of Neleus in his Terminator suit occupied the stern of the vehicle. His storm bolter threw out a torrent of hellfire shells that punched, ripped and shattered their way through the advancing swarm. He was so close to the edge of the tank that he could reach out and catch some of the subterranean talons as they thrashed impotently around the armour of the ruined vehicle. Grasping one talon in the formidable grip of his power fist, Neleus dragged the lictor creature out of the sand and held it momentarily, dangling from its own fore-talon. Then, with a swift movement, he crushed the talon in his fist and launched the hapless creature in the air with a swing of his immense arm, riddling it with hellfire shells as it flew. By the time it landed back in the sea of its own kind, the creature was little more than a shredded husk.

'Korpheus! What about that vox link?' yelled Octavius over the screeches and shrieks of combat.

The Techmarine's head appeared from within the devastated interior of the Vindicator, shrouded in a gust of smoke.

'The vox amplifier is barely operational, captain. But I have sent a signal. The unit will repeat the signal until it fails,' called Korpheus as he pulled himself through the hole in the decking and readied his weapons. 'The lictors are pounding the armoured plates at the bottom of the tank. When they get through, the vox will be finished, and so will we.'

'The Emperor protects!' cried Broec, as he brandished his Crozius into the air, rattling a volley of bolter shells from the gleaming gun in his other hand. 'The vile xenos will suffer his wrath before they see the end of us!'

'You are right, Broec,' cried Ashok as he launched himself from the Vindicator in a blaze of warp-energy, taking the fight to the enemy in the best traditions of the Angels Sanguine.

'Well said, chaplain,' agreed Octavius as he cast his bolt gun aside and drew his ornate, two-handed force sword from its holster on his back. The blade was a memento of a previous campaign against the Biel-Tan eldar and it cackled with unspeakable energies as bizarre alien runes swam along its length like quick-silver. 'This is no end for a Deathwatch kill-team!'

Octavius took an epic swing with his sword, slicing it through the abdomen of the first hormagaunt that made the leap onto the Vindicator and pushing it into the mouth of another as it threw its head back to keen.

The swarm was on them now and they were besieged on all sides, with nothing but the damaged armour of the ruined tank between them and the lashing claws beneath the sand, and nothing but their blazing weapons to repel the thousands upon thousands of tyranid organisms that swarmed through the desert towards them.

Two huge explosions rocked the remains of the Vindicator, impacting in the desert just a short distance from it. A spray of liquefied tyranid sleeted across the Deathwatch team, caught in the dust-filled wind.

'THERE! THERE THEY are,' said Shaidan, leaning over the pilot-servitor of the Thunderhawk as it powered down through the atmosphere. 'Fire the lascannons on either side of their position. They need support.'

Searing lances of power fired out from the nose of the Thunderhawk, punching great craters into the sand around the Deathwatch team, showering them with debris.

From their altitude, they could see a hooded figure leap from the Vindicator, surrounded by a halo of blue light. It fought its way into one of the craters left by the lascannon fire and started to engage the tyranids at close range, carrying the fight to them rather than waiting for it to be brought to him. He was surrounded by fire and energy.

In his right arm was a force staff of some kind, spinning in a frenzy of warp-energy, spitting bolts of blue into the enveloping swarm. His left arm seemed to be coated in coruscating pulses of power and great javelins of light rushed from his fingertips, incinerating swathes of hormagaunts as they leapt for him, lashing their claws.

Slithering towards the librarian from three separate directions, Shaidan could see the familiar serpentine shapes of oscillating zoanthropes closing in. Running to the back of the Thunderhawk, he cried, 'Take us down directly over them. Hold position for emergency extraction.' Then he launched himself out of the drop-hatch.

'INQUISITOR, WHAT ARE they?' asked Octavius, nodding in the direction of one of the giant serpent creatures that were slithering their way towards Ashok. As he spoke, he swept his blade in a low arc, taking the feet away from three termagants that had just crested the Vindicator. With the back swing, he took off their heads before they could even shriek in shock.

Kalypsia turned her head, glancing quickly in the direction indicated by Octavius before resuming her work with the force whip, lashing out into the encroaching sea of claws, rending it into a mush of instantly decaying flesh and shattered bones.

'Zoanthropes!' she called over her shoulder. 'Psykers,' she added as an explanation. 'Three of them will be too much for your librarian.'

'Thunderhawk!' yelled Korpheus, struggling to make himself heard over the commotion and the roar of his own chainsword. His eyes were enhanced beyond even those of the other Marines, and he caught the glint of the Thunderhawk as it broke the cloud line. 'And something else…' But he could not tell what it was. A smaller shape, hurtling towards the ground at an incredible speed. It was not a torpedo. It looked rather like a man. A Marine.

'Neleus,' cried Korpheus in sudden realisation. 'Clear a landing site for that Marine!'

The Terminator turned his head at the call from his battle-brother and nodded his acknowledgement. Leaving the growling Space Wolf Marine, Kulac, to hold the stern, he ran the few steps towards the prow and punched the cyclone missile launcher into action. Two rockets blasted over his shoulders and smashed into the swarm just in time, clearing a large crater and filling the air with great plumes of dust, showering Ashok with slime-filled debris as he fought on nearby.

The falling Marine flicked out his arms just as he was about to hit the ground, forming a cross in the air. And he stopped, just hanging there in the air, making no mark in the sand below his feet, his emerald power-armour gleaming in the hazy desert sun. The tyranids seemed to stop momentarily, as though awestruck by the arrival of this new figure. Then they launched themselves forward, lashing at him with talons, claws and teeth. The Marine revolved his weapon, an odd looking force-staff with blades on each end, and prepared for battle.

A cry made Neleus and Korpheus turn back to the stern of the vehicle, where they saw Kulac, their battle-brother from the Space Wolves, encased in a terrible orb of purpling fire. His weapons had been scattered to the ground, and he was held in an agonising sphere about ten metres above the ground. Broec was there in an instant, pushing his Crozius into the energy field and scanning the sea of tyranids for the source of its power.

The orb of warp-energy shattered with the touch of the chaplain's holy staff of office, sending the Marine slumping to the ground. Another blast of purple fire stabbed out from the swarm, originating from one of the zoanthropes that was working its way round to Ashok's position. It was passing the stern of the Vindicator on its way.

Broec met the blast with his Crozius once again, and returned fire with a cough from his bolter. Neleus was already alongside him, and he opened up with his storm bolter, raining a torrent against the slippery creature of the sea. But the shells just seemed to bounce off, flicked aside by tiny bursts of purple energy, as it made its way round towards the librarian.

'Broec! What about Kulac?' called Octavius from the midst of a maelstrom of flashing blades.

The chaplain knelt quickly by the side of the fallen Space Wolf. 'Dead, captain,' he shouted back.

THE THUNDERHAWK ROARED down above the Deathwatch team, holding its position a few metres above their heads.

'Inquisitor, you first,' cried Octavius over the intense noise of the engines and gunfire.

Kalypsia nodded, raked her whip across the front of the swarm with a final flourish and then leapt for the hands reaching down from the Thunderhawk.

'Broec. Korpheus. Get Kulac's body into the Thunderhawk,' yelled Octavius, conscious that the Space Wolves would not forgive him were he to leave this battle-brother to be consumed by the Great Devourer. 'Neleus, cover them.'

A flare of purple fire dragged Octavius's attention back to his librarian. Ashok and the mysterious new Marine were now fighting in the same crater, repelling the boarders with incredible ferocity and skill. Huge blasts of psychic power were jetting out from both figures, and each wielded their force-staffs with formidable prowess. The Mantis Warrior was pressing into the faces of the creatures in the front line, slashing his bladed staff into the sea of claws and whirling it into a frenzied sphere of crackling energy. Ashok stood in the centre of the crater, unleashing a constant tirade of lightning from his fingers and from his staff, holding the tyranid swarm at bay. Great piles of incinerated corpses lined the rim of the crater.

Octavius glanced up at the Thunderhawk and lifted up his left arm. Neleus reached down and caught his captain's wrist. 'Take us over that crater!' ordered Octavius as he swung from the secure grip of the White Consul, his force-sword arcing and lashing at the pincers that reached desperately for his boots.

On the rim of the crater the three zoanthropes were pulsing into syncronisation, sending out oscillating streams of warp energy that smashed into the psychic defences of the two librarians. Octavius could see that Ashok was weakening in the heart of the crater and that the other librarian was fighting a losing battle to repel both the swarm and the energetic assault of the tyranid psykers at the same time. The mysterious librarian had bought Ashok some time, but it was fast running out.

The Thunderhawk swooped down over the crater, with Octavius still hanging out of the drop-hatch. He chambered his sword and reached down with his free hand, covering fire sputtering out of the hatch from Korpheus and Broec. Ashok looked up at his captain and yelled, 'For Sanguinius and the Emperor!' His eyes were burning with red fire and he turned back to the frantic battle that was gradually enveloping him.

'Ashok! This is not a fight you can win,' called Octavius calmly. 'There will be another time.'

For a few seconds the Angels Sanguine librarian appeared not to hear the words of his captain, as he released a vicious jet of crackling energy towards the zoanthropes on the crest of the crater, causing a great explosion of multi-coloured fire as it impacted on their force-shields. But then he looked back up at Octavius, his eyes gradually fading back to black, and said, 'You are right, captain. Another time.' Ashok reached up his left

hand and was pulled up into the belly of the Thunderhawk.

'Take it up!' came the roaring voice of the Mantis Warrior librarian from the crater below as he swung his
force-staff around his head in a crackle of power, clearing
a short perimeter around him. In the brief respite,
Shaidan held his staff vertically against his body and a
flickering blue fire enveloped his form. Jets of venom
spurted out of the swarm from nearby, hissing pathetically against the fire; a hormagaunt launched itself
towards him but ricocheted impotently off the energy
field.

With an explosion of power that sent shock waves
through the swarm, the Mantis Warrior slowly pushed up
into the air, dripping blue flames down into the seething
mass below his feet.

'Let's scoop him up and get out of here,' said Kalypsia
to the pilot-servitor in the Thunderhawk's cockpit.

She looked out over the scene below and was stunned
by the extent of the swarm that had descended on them
– it stretched as far as she could see in every direction.
Glancing northwards there appeared to be a slight clearing in the near distance around some kind of man-made
structure and she bit her teeth together as she realised
that they were so close to their target.

'We've seen enough of the tyranids for today,' she muttered.

CHAPTER FOUR:
VEILS OF SALVATION

[29 Hours Remaining]

THE ROILING BLACK clouds of the tyranid swarm coated large swathes of the planet's surface. The landing site was now completely swamped, black for kilometres in every direction. Octavius shook his head and turned away from the view screen.

'They knew that we were coming, inquisitor,' he said, fixing his complicated blue eyes on Kalypsia's smooth face.

'Don't be ridiculous, captain,' she countered with conviction. 'The tyranid are just animals. They would have no way of calculating our landing site.'

'Yet they laid a trap for us?'

'I am sure that it was not a trap, captain,' said Kalypsia, springing one of her own. 'It was just a poorly chosen landing site.'

Octavius did not even flinch. 'No, inquisitor, the site was strategically sound. Somehow, the tyranids knew that and they knew that it would be our site of choice. They prepared it for us.'

'That is simply not possible, captain,' retorted Kalypsia flatly.

'The captain is right,' said Korpheus, walking into the briefing room with Ashok. 'The ground was disturbed before we arrived. There were traces of movement under the desert. The lictors were waiting for us.'

Ashok studied Kalypsia's face as she responded. 'It would be quite unprecedented for the tyranids to anticipate our movements. Even if they were capable of such sophisticated thought, there is no way that they could have known that we would pick that site.'

Ashok's voice was low and barely audible, his black eyes gazing at Kalypsia featurelessly. 'It was almost as though they somehow had knowledge of Deathwatch protocols, inquisitor. That was the natural site for us to pick. It was relatively clean, and, according to you, proximal to the position of the hive tyrant. If I were a tyranid, that is where I would have laid a trap.'

'You are not a tyranid, librarian,' replied Kalypsia smoothly, 'and you would do well not to ascribe to them too many human characteristics. To do such borders on heresy.'

The librarian tilted his head slightly to one side, but Kalypsia could not tell whether it was a shrug of indifference or a motion of concentration. 'As you say, inquisitor, we all need to be wary of heresy.'

'Do you HAVE a sample?' asked Dasein.

'Yes,' answered Shaidan, handing over the talon-fragment that he had wrenched from one of the beasts on the surface.

The Techmarine reached out and took the shard, turning it over in his hand a couple of times. 'This should be enough,' he said. 'But I am not sure that I have the expertise to perform such a test. It would be better if we could wait for the *Endless Redemption* to arrive – they have superior facilities and a comprehensive Apothecarion.'

'There is no time for that,' murmured Audin. 'We need to know what we are up against, and we need to know now. By the time the *Redemption* arrives, this could all be over.'

'Perhaps the inquisitor has better facilities on board the *Perfect Incision*?' suggested Dasein.

'Yes, perhaps,' answered Audin. 'But let us see what we can discover without the inquisitor for the time being.'

Techmarine Dasein nodded and turned to leave, carrying the sample back to the *Penitent Quest*'s laboratory. 'This may take some time.'

Audin turned to Shaidan with weary eyes, the ghosts of long repressed memories flickering over his soul. 'My friend, I fear that we have unleashed something terrible. Perhaps the Mantis Warriors are truly cursed, after all.'

The librarian considered his captain in silence. He could see the pain in Audin's face, an anxiety that he had not seen for many decades – not since that fated day nearly a century before when they had realised their terrible mistake. Shaidan had seen the way his captain had lost faith in his own judgement after that evil episode, and the Chapter had also lived with the suspicions and distrust of others since their disgrace in the Badab Wars. Shaidan had seen the doubts in the eyes of Kalypsia and even Octavius when he had told them that he was going to return to the *Penitent Quest* to help patch up the wounded Mantis Warriors. Of course, they were right to mistrust him – he was lying to them. And that pained him still further. But was he also right to mistrust himself?

The recent history of the Mantis Warriors did not echo the glorious legends of the Imperial Fists or the Ultramarines. It was not a dark or secretive Chapter, like the Dark Angels or the Raven Guard. There was no reputation for reckless heroism, as there was for the Angels Sanguine or the Space Wolves. Whilst Shaidan was sure that each of those magnificent Chapters harboured secrets of their own, the Mantis Warriors were unique amongst their brethren in that they wore their worst secrets on their sleeves for all to see. Every librarian in the galaxy knew of the treachery of the Mantis Warriors – it was carved into the history of the Imperium itself.

But they had been forgiven. By the grace of the Emperor, they had been brought back into the fold. There was a place for them at the side of the forces of the Emperor in the galaxy. Whilst the Astral Claws had been banished and declared excommunicated, the Mantis Warriors had been stripped of their home-world and dispatched on a penitent crusade. Although deprived of their right to recruit new aspirants from the innumerable worlds of the Imperium, they were given the chance to prove their worthiness. The light of the Emperor must have penetrated their souls and seen something of its own magnificence within.

But they were the unforgiven. The crusade was not yet complete. The last remnants of the Astral Claws still rampaged through the fringes of the galaxy, flicking in and out of the Eye of Terror – although now they called themselves the Red Corsairs. The Mantis Warriors had not yet cleansed the galaxy of their pollution.

In its time of need, a planet of the Imperium would not call on the Mantis Warriors for help. In the last one hundred years, not a single Marine from the Chapter had been summoned for service in the Deathwatch, which could only be taken as a deliberate insult by a Chapter with such a long and distinguished tradition of service. The Chapter was on the edge of the law, teetering on the brink of oblivion and approaching the borders of extinction, fighting desperately to regain its place amongst the chosen. They were not outlaws or renegades, but they had no home in the Imperium of man.

Deep down in his soul, Shaidan was sure that the gene-seed of the Mantis Warriors was pure. He had been there when they had made their stand with the Astral Claws – he knew that their intentions had been pure, even if their judgement and understanding had failed. He was sure that the Chapter would earn its salvation. The Second Company had rushed to the aid of the Herodian system before any Imperial vessels had even heard the distress call. This had been an unambiguous chance for glory and redemption. The Mantis Warriors would cleanse their sins in the fires of battle and repel the Great Devourer from the sector.

But something had gone wrong. The tyranid swarm was more powerful than any they had encountered before. It was riddled with psyker zoanthropes for which they were not prepared. The Second Company had been pulled apart and driven back. Their glorious victory was reduced to a scrappy withdrawal. With their diminishing numbers and their dubious souls, were they just too weak to confront this enemy?

There had been a moment, near the end, before their last stand on the command bunker, when their luck had appeared to change. But this luck was stillborn, and Shaidan shared with Audin the fear that they had unleashed something terrible in those desperate moments. They had both seen the Mantis Warriors fall victim to errors of judgement before, and they prayed that history was not repeating itself.

'The light of the Emperor found good in our souls,' said Shaidan eventually, placing his hand onto his captain's shoulder. 'We will redeem ourselves before this battle is over.'

* * *

IT WAS ONLY a few days ago that it had all begun.

The voice had been broken and cracked, shrouded in the hiss of static as the weak signal broke the silence of the *Endless Redemption*'s vox-array. There were screams in the background and the speaker was on the verge of panic. He was breathing heavily to stave off the encroachment of insanity. Audin had only been able to make out one word, but it was enough: *tyranids*.

Deploying the Second Company into the rapid strike cruiser, *Penitent Quest*, Audin had set off for Herodian IV at once. The *Endless Redemption* had been prowling the outer reaches of the galaxy for nearly a hundred years, searching for opportunities for the Mantis Warriors to redeem themselves, searching for daemons, aliens and heretics to kill, searching for the renegade Space Marines of the Astral Claws, who had tripped them into their fall from grace. Here was a chance to defend the glory of the Imperium, and the Mantis Warriors would not shirk their responsibilities.

When the *Penitent Quest* blasted into the Herodian system, the fourth planet was already under attack. Its atmosphere was a rain of spores, and the surface was speckled with newly hatched organisms. The air was beginning to fill up with toxins and bio-modifiers that increased the temperature and humidity on the surface. Acidic rain peppered the already sparse vegetation on the planet, melting it into bubbling pools of raw bio-mass for consumption by the growing swarm.

The planet had only a few population centres and they were already under siege from the vanguard creatures of the hive. Flocks of winged gargoyles herded people into smaller and smaller areas, swooping and diving in concentric waves of attack to drive the indigenous life forms into dead-ends, keeping them all together in preparation for their consumption when the main tryanid force arrived.

Strange organic drop-ships were beginning to deposit the smaller foot-soldiers of the horde: six-legged termagants started to spill out over the planet's surface, squeezing out jets of bio-plasma over any motile life-forms that they encountered, melting them into the growing reservoirs of ichor-like nutrient pools. Larger, leaping hormagaunts started to bound, screeching out of their drop-spores, scything through any of the life-forms missed by their smaller cousins.

The Mantis Warriors had dropped straight down in front of an advancing tide of tyranid creatures, which was lapping through the desert on its way to the last stronghold of human resistance on the planet. The circling gargoyles were driving the few survivors towards a rockcrete bunker in the desert and the swarm was descending on this tiny facility to finish them off.

Almost the entire Second Company of the Mantis Warriors was deployed onto the planet's surface. Squads took up firing positions on all sides of the bunker, defining a defensive perimeter about two kilometres in diameter. Vindicator tanks were air-dropped into supporting positions and Predators were deployed to take the fight into the swarm.

But they could not stop the advance of the horde. Despite vicious combat, they were driven back into the rockcrete compound, wherein they found the huddled survivors of Herodian IV. The compound appeared to be some kind of research station, and the gates displayed the battered insignia of the Adeptus Mechanicus.

Librarian Shaidan had raced through the facility searching for reinforcements, weapons, or assistance of any kind, desperate to find something that might turn the tide for his battle-brothers outside. Buried in the depths of the research station, he had found a large circular chamber. Inside was a man, shrouded in a dark cloak with a hood pulled far down over his face. Even against the psychic turmoil generated by the hive mind, Shaidan could feel the power of this inquisitor, could see his eyes burning with energy beneath his hood.

The chamber also contained an intricate and beautiful machine, which the inquisitor was staring at with something like alarm. The inquisitor had turned to Shaidan, pulling his hood clear of his face to reveal gaunt and wrinkled skin – almost inhumanly old. In a single flash from those burning eyes, Shaidan had understood: this machine was a weapon that could save them all. He had watched the old inquisitor strap himself into the device, then he had turned and run back to the surface, where he rejoined the frantic, last ditch battle.

There had been a sudden and invisible blast that radiated out from the bunker at the centre of the besieged ring of Mantis Warriors. Shaidan felt it pass through his mind like an icy wave from an ocean of warp energy. For a moment, the hive mind had been silenced, and Shaidan could hear the thoughts of his comrades once again. He had yelled out with his mind, his words penetrating the souls of every Marine: *For the Mantis Warriors! For Redemption! For the Emperor!* And the Mantis Warriors had pressed forward against the swarm with new energy and power, driving it back into the desert. The tyranid creatures had been in disarray, thrashing and lashing out at each other as often as at the Marines that slaughtered them like the animals they were.

Then something had changed. The hive mind had thundered back into Shaidan's brain, smashing into his psychic defences with incredible force, like a terrible backwash from the earlier, icy blast. And with the wave of psychic force had come a renewed attack from the tyranid swarm, constricting around the last bastion of human resistance on Herodian IV. The creatures had fought with renewed strength and power, apparently being able to pre-empt the defensive strategies of the

Mantis Warriors, splintering the defenders into smaller groups which would be easier to cut off, encircle, and consume.

It was at this point that Audin had realised that the planet was lost and that the Mantis Warriors had failed. It was at this point, when the planet swam with alien life and birthed giant warrior creatures bent solely on the annihilation of the last traces of human life, that Audin had finally called for Thunderhawk extraction, abandoning the Mechanicus base and leaving the planet to die.

'THERE IS MORE to this than a tyranid invasion,' said Broec, flicking glances towards Ashok across the room. 'And someone here must know what. Perhaps the *psyker* can tell us something?' The chaplain almost spat the word in barely disguised disgust.

Ashok was standing quietly in the corner of the room, his hood pulled down over his face so that nobody could see his eyes. Without his armour, he appeared more human, although his musculature was more impressive than any normal man could hope to achieve. Unlike the other Marines, he liked to be without his armour; it seemed to confine him, to hold him in. As soon as he left a combat zone, he would remove it, respectfully cleaning each piece and praying to its spirit with all due reverence. But he was glad to be rid of it and he suspected that it was glad to be rid of him. When he was in full armour, it was a constant effort of will to reign in the violence in his soul.

'I know nothing,' he said simply, lifting his head slightly so that the ambient light fell into the depthless black of his eyes.

Broec stared back at him, his cropped white hair shimmering in the artificial light of the armoury. A row of golden studs were riveted to his forehead and a series of tattoos snaked around his neck – litanies and prayers inscribed in the cursive curls of High Gothic script.

'Ah, nothing. A useful insight from the psyker.' Broec made no secret of his disdain for psykers. They were touched by the treacherous and heretical energies of the warp and were consequently anathema to the puritan ideals of the Black Templars. The extreme intolerance of Broec marked him out even in his home Chapter, but it made him a formidable opponent of any mutation, witchery or xenos taint – and the Deathwatch valued this trait like gold dust.

'Octavius, has the inquisitor told you anything?' asked Neleus, redirecting the conversation.

'No, nothing. She denies that the tyranid are capable of constructing a trap,' answered Octavius openly.

'But do you believe her? We know nothing of this inquisitor,' asked Korpheus darkly.

'It is not our place to question the integrity of an inquisitor of the Ordo Xenos, Korpheus. Watch yourself. If Kalypsia tells us that the tyranids could not lay a trap, then that is how it is.' Octavius's voice was even and firm. 'We are the Deathwatch, battle-brothers, and it does not become us to be so suspicious of our own.'

'And what of the zoanthropes?' asked Ashok. 'I have never seen so many in such a small swarm.'

Neleus nodded his head. 'Yes, the swarm is unusually powerful for such a small splinter.'

'Yes,' agreed Octavius, 'we need to understand the nature of this swarm more fully. Its composition is unusual and its potency is great.'

There was a brief silence, and then Broec spoke again. 'And what of the Mantis Warriors? What role do they have in all this?'

All eyes turned to Octavius, waiting for a response to the question that had been in everyone's mind.

'They responded to the distress call from Herodian IV. They were the first to make planet-fall, but were unable to stem the advance of the swarm. They suffered great losses and are now considerably under-strength,' said Octavius, as though in a briefing.

'Yes,' continued Broec, 'but–'

'No buts, Chaplain Broec,' cut in Octavius. 'I know what is on your mind, but this is not the time. The Mantis Warriors are the only Space Marines within days of this planet. They have put themselves at our service, and we will treat them with respect. Understood?'

The chaplain nodded, acknowledging the authority of Octavius and the wisdom of his words. Broec's natural distrust for deviance in any form was overcome by his faith in the leadership of the Imperial Fists captain. They had served the Deathwatch together for many years, and Octavius had never yet led him wrong.

'Good,' continued Octavius. 'As it stands, the Mantis Warriors are our best source of intelligence regarding the Herodian swarm. We need them.'

'THE TYRANIDS WERE ready for us, my lord,' said Kalypsia, after checking that the auditory seals were in place around her private chambers.

The vox hissed with static. The signal was weak and broken, despite the massive amplifier arrays built into the *Perfect Incision*.

'Indeed,' came the voice of Inquisitor Lord Parthon. 'I confess that I wondered whether they might be.'

'You foresaw this?' asked Kalypsia, a little taken aback.

'No, but I thought that it might be possible, given what has happened,' replied Parthon.

'I see no reason why this should change our plan, my lord,' said Kalypsia, gathering her confidence.

'What did you tell Octavius?' asked Parthon, ignoring the young inquisitor's air of assertion.

'I told him that it would not be possible for the tyranids to lay a trap and that he must have chosen a poor insertion point.'

'And he accepted this?' Kalypsia could imagine the raised, incredulous eyebrows on Parthon's face as he asked.

'He does as he is told – according to his charge,' said Kalypsia casually.

'Do not underestimate our valiant captain, young Kalypsia, or his Deathwatch team. You may need to give them more if they are going to follow you to the end of this. You may not win their sympathy, but it is their loyalty that you need. They may give that more freely if they feel that you are being honest with them. The Deathwatch are a formidable force.'

'Understood,' said Kalypsia as she broke the connection. Again, she found herself wondering whether the old lord had lost his edge. The Deathwatch had certainly impressed her down on the surface of Herodian IV, but she had expected them to be good soldiers; they were the best that the Imperium could produce. However, she had seen nothing to convince her that they were more than just soldiers. They would follow her orders and she would give them information as and when they needed to know it. Not before. Besides, if this Octavius was really the puritan that Parthon claimed, she could not jeopardise the mission by confessing too much to him.

INQUISITOR LORD AGUSTIUS sat staring into the blackness of space, fuming inwardly. His apprentice, Interrogator Lexopher, stood silently in the corner lost in contemplation and, somewhere in the vast shadowy chamber, the death cultist Slyrian was lurking. The best security was a silent and invisible threat. The rest of Agustius's retinue had remained aboard his own gunship when he had boarded the grand Inquisition battleship – Lord Parthon had been a little too insistent about that.

The massive engines of the *Veiled Salvation* rumbled evenly through the infrastructure of the vessel, and

Agustius could feel the motion through the chassis of his wheelchair. In truth, he didn't really need the chair – his legs were strong enough to keep him standing and some simple bionics would have had him running with the youngest cadets. But Agustius would have none of it. 'I am old,' he would say, 'and old people have the right to a seat.' In fact, he simply distrusted the bionic implants. 'There is but a small step between dependency and vulnerability,' he would say. If the truth were known, he worried about all technology – he even distrusted his chair, but at least he knew he could get out of it if the need arose. And it pleased him to reflect that others tended to underestimate the apparently disabled.

Agustius had been on his way to the Obscurus frontier when the Herodian warp-gate had been closed, so he had redirected his cruiser to rendezvous with the Inquisition battleship. He had known that it was under the authority of his old friend, Brutius Parthon and this was a rare opportunity to renew the acquaintance. At the very least, he could wait for news of the warp-gate in the substantial luxury boasted by the *Veiled Salvation*.

However, the old inquisitor lord had been rather disappointed to see the amount of traffic that flooded in and out of the various landing bays of the *Veiled Salvation*. This was certainly not how he would have run such a formidable vessel. There was definitely nothing *veiled* about it and, judging by the extravagant manner in which some of the more senior personnel lived their lives, there was little in the way of *salvation* either. It seemed that the battleship was doing rather well for itself, positioned so conveniently close to the Herodian warp-gate. It was almost a trading hub – which did not strike Agustius as a particularly appropriate function for an Inquisition battleship.

According to the bridge commander, the *Veiled Salvation* had held its current position for the last few years, since Parthon had taken command of it. There was a fairly regular flow of traffic, mostly Ordo Xenos personnel, but occasionally other Imperial vessels would pause to pay their respects on their way to the gate. It was sufficiently close to the warp-gate that senior officers of the Imperial Navy would feel duty-bound to acknowledge its presence, but far enough away that they didn't feel as though it was monitoring their passage.

The bridge commander, a tall, thin man called Gregor who seemed cursed with a permanent smirk, had cheerfully confessed to Agustius that the combination of stability and constant visitors had brought the *Salvation* more commerce and wealth than was usual for an Inquisition ship. He seemed equally cheerful about the fact that pirates and raiders would sometimes coast through the system looking for prey around the gate, but that not a single raid had been launched against the battleship in the whole time that it had been there, despite the fact that it was the only permanent Imperial facility in the sector. Agustius had smarted at the use of the word 'permanent,' but had noted with some satisfaction that the reputation of the Inquisition was enough to deter would-be attackers, even out here in the forgotten reaches of the Segmentum.

Parthon had always been an ostentatious man. In this, Agustius could not have been more different from his friend, but the Inquisition itself has no rules about such things. Inquisitors are free to pursue their sacred duties in whatever manner they see fit. To Agustius, this institutional vagueness seemed dangerously lax, but he had to confess that Parthon had always proven himself to be a most able agent of the Holy Orders of the Emperor's Inquisition – even brilliant at times. Indeed, he would not have risen to the hallowed rank of inquisitor lord had his methods been suspect. Nonetheless, Agustius did not have to like the way that the *Veiled Salvation* appeared to have become a massive, super-armoured marketplace.

Reflecting on it now, Agustius could not remember why they were friends. They had nothing in common other than a profound hate for the xenos creatures that plagued the galaxy and a certainty of faith in the Emperor, of course. And their methods could not have been more different. Even during training over a century ago, Agustius had been courted by the Thorians, a puritan sect within the Inquisition. The Thorians rarely have anything to do with the Ordo Xenos. Instead, their power is concentrated within the hallowed halls of the Ordo Malleus, where the Imperium's daemonhunters work their secret arts in the defence of the realm. But Agustius had shone so brightly and the Thorians had moved quickly to assimilate his light.

At first, the high lords of the Thorian sanctum had striven to pull the youthful Agustius over into the Ordo Malleus. Such things were not unheard of, especially in the case of such an exceptional and pure young talent. The Ordo Malleus has great influence within the Inquisition, charged as it is with policing the Eye of Terror and with combating the emergence of warp-taint anywhere in the galaxy. But Agustius had stood firm – his calling was in the Ordo Xenos, fighting the foul aliens in their myriad forms – and the Thorian lords had finally conceded that he might be of use where he was. In truth, their sect was particularly weak in the Ordo Xenos, where it seemed widely accepted that alien technology could and should be used in the fight against the aliens, if possible. Indeed, for some Ordo Xenos inquisitors, the exalted alien hunters, the fabled Deathwatch, seemed to be merely artefact collectors, charged with the location and retrieval of alien technology for future use by the Inquisition in its ongoing wars against the xenos.

For various reasons, the Thorians frowned on this type of activity: the ends do not always justify the means – sometimes the means were an end in themselves. Alien hunters should hunt aliens, not assault them and steal their possessions. The Deathwatch were chosen from amongst the finest Space Marines in the Imperium, they were not thieves or archaeologists. The key issue was purity. How could the Ordo Xenos really claim to be better, cleaner, or more pure than the aliens if it craved alien technology for itself? Where should the line be drawn between hating the alien and lusting after its abilities? For the Thorians, any contact with xenos creatures or their perverse productions introduced pollution into the Inquisition – into the very heart of the Imperium – and long rituals of purification would be required to return a proper human balance to the soul.

Agustius had spent long years pondering the intricacies of Thorian mythology and he was not always convinced by it, although he made no attempt to hide his affiliation. Deep in our core of being, thought Agustius, humans are essentially different from the xenos – they are *humans*. Flirtation with alien artefacts might be distasteful, but he wasn't sure that it would cause irrevocable damage to one's soul. The most devout Thorians in the Ordo Malleus believed that the Emperor's soul could be born again into the real world of conventional space, if only a person of suitable piety, holiness and purity could be found. The last such man was Sebastian Thor, the magnificent warrior who overthrew the insane Lord Vandire and brought an end to the Age of Apostasy. Hence, any and all pollution should be avoided – be that contact with aliens, daemons or heretical teachings – so that another man of such purity might arise.

Whatever his doubts about his own faith, it was clear to Agustius that Brutius Parthon was certainly no Thorian.

Indeed, Parthon had never understood why Agustius would willingly hold himself back by subscribing to such silly superstitions. The Inquisition was supposed to explode superstition, not cultivate it. So the two men had clashed from the start, disagreeing on nearly every question of strategy or tactics, but bound together by the formidable bonds of a shared, sacred maxim – 'suffer not the alien to live.' Despite their differences, the friends respected each other's talents and never doubted their dedication to the Emperor or the Imperium of Man. It took all sorts to guard the immortal souls of men.

Sitting in his chair, staring out into the star-speckled darkness, shot through with a constant stream of traffic making its way to and from the landing bays of the *Veiled Salvation*, Agustius reflected that it may have been a mistake for him to come here. He was not the kind of man who could sit on the sidelines and let somebody else take command, especially in such a volatile situation as this – if the Herodian warp-gate was not reopened soon, then the Obscurus frontier would fall.

The inquisitor lord and his retinue had been following in the wake of his Deathwatch kill team, led by his long-time champion, Quirion Octavius. The team was to pass through the gate ahead of him and then they were to rendezvous on the frontier, where Agustius would take command of the Segmentum's defences.

Until being confronted with the gyring confusion of energies that churned and spilled out of the closed gate and thus redirecting to the nearby *Veiled Salvation*, Agustius had assumed that his team was on its way to the frontier. However, once he arrived on Parthon's battleship, he discovered that his team had been redeployed.

'They were a wasted resource,' Parthon had explained to his old friend, handing over a glass of fine red wine. 'The Deathwatch has no business sitting in comfort when there is an alien invasion underway so nearby.'

Agustius had been forced to concede this point. If there was no way for his team to make it to the front lines, they may as well be put to work here, trying to cleanse the Herodian system. But it galled him that Parthon had taken such liberties with his command in his absence. Parthon had placed his own protégé, the youthful Kalypsia, in charge of the kill-team.

What galled him even more was the fact that he could see no need for the mission at all. 'Why not just bombard the planet from space?' Agustius had asked, taking a long draw from the wine glass.

'There is really no need, my old friend.' Parthon had dismissed the idea with a casual wave of his hand. 'We have learnt how to locate the hive tyrant, and your Deathwatch team will be able to take it out. Once the tyrant is dead, the planet will be saved. Even the Mantis Warriors should be able to retake it then.'

Agustius had looked up at Parthon, watching his long cloak whipped into a whirl by the latter's ostentatious flourish of his arm. 'How do you know where the hive tyrant is, Parthon?'

Parthon had been ready for this question, it seemed. 'We learnt the location technique from Captain Bannon's interaction with the Great Devourer in the Tarsis campaign. The tyranid give away their tyrant's position themselves, through their formation.'

The two inquisitor lords had held each other's gaze for a few moments, each searching the other for doubts.

'Strange that I had not heard of this technique, Parthon.' Agustius's voice was steady and his eyes narrowed slightly.

Parthon had just laughed. He had *laughed*. 'I had assumed that the Thorians would not want to know such things.'

And that was it. Parthon had refused to launch a bombardment; he had taken control of Agustius's own

Deathwatch kill-team and sent them on a mission, the success of which depended on some spurious alien intelligence that Agustius himself had never even heard of. And Inquisitor Lord Agustius was left alone in his wheel chair, gazing into space, fuming inwardly. He would have done things differently.

CHAPTER FIVE: SUICIDE

[23 Hours Remaining]

'I'M GLAD YOU could join me, inquisitor,' said Kastor, doing Kalypsia the courtesy of rising to his feet as she entered the conference chamber, her cloak flooding out behind her in a plume of drama.

Kalypsia swept past him and sat crisply into her seat, snapping her fingers at one of the servitors that lingered nervously by the door. She pointed at the empty glass on the grand table before her and the servitor scuttled forward to dispense some wine. 'This had better not take long, commander. I have much to attend to, and there is little time.'

'About twenty hours, I imagine,' said Kastor, enjoying the inquisitor's discomfort.

'Twenty-three,' corrected Kalypsia, still able to appear officious and fierce, even now.

'Very well, twenty-three.' The exact number was of no concern to Kastor. 'I would like to talk with you about your little sortie to the planet's surface, inquisitor.'

'There is nothing to be said,' answered Kalypsia with a snap. 'The mission was not an unqualified success. We will be better prepared next time.'

'Next time?' inquired Kastor, relishing the prospect of his next sentence. 'There will be no "next time".'

The inquisitor turned her reflective grey eyes onto the commander, and he winced despite himself.

'We will be better prepared next time.' She simply repeated herself, more quietly and rather more slowly.

Kastor's face shifted. 'This is not a game, inquisitor!' He was on the verge of shouting. 'We are talking about the fate of an entire system. There is no time for your vanities now.'

'You are quite right, commander,' replied Kalypsia with unnerving calm, 'this is not a game. So I would thank you for your cooperation.'

Kastor was stunned into a disbelieving silence. His mouth opened to speak, but he didn't dare utter the words that fought for air in his vocal chords. Shutting his mouth abruptly and taking a deep breath, Kastor replied. 'Inquisitor Kalypsia, I have been in touch with Inquisitor Lord Agustius on the *Veiled Salvation* and he has instructed me that a bombardment from space would be the most suitable response in the event that your mission should fail.'

The commander noted with some satisfaction that Kalypsia's eyes widened at the mention of Agustius. But she recovered well. 'Agustius has no authority in this matter, commander. He is a guest aboard the *Veiled Salvation*, under the patronage of Inquisitor Lord Parthon, on whose authority I am acting here. In any case, commander, my mission has not failed. Even as I sit here wasting my time with this conversation, the Deathwatch are preparing for a second "sortie" to the planet's surface.'

With that, Kalypsia was back on her feet and out of the door, leaving behind only a rush of air and an untouched glass of wine. Kastor watched her go. When the door had hissed shut and he was left alone in the conference chamber, he leant forward in his chair and took Kalypsia's glass of wine from the table. Knocking it back in a single gulp, Kastor sat back into thought: what could be so important about this little planet that it would divide the inquisitor lords of the Ordo Xenos?

COLLIA THREW HER Fury into another roll as streams of venom flooded past the screen of her cockpit. She was looking desperately from side to side, trying to catch a glimpse of another member of her wing. Anyone would do, even that show-boater squadron leader, Gordus. But there was nobody. She was the only Fury from her squad who had made it through the spore-field.

Turning the Fury in a tight arc, she brought the gunsights round to bear on a bunch of Drones that came swooping out of the spores above her. Punching her right hand into a fist, she clenched the trigger and a burst of energy jabbed out of her fighter, piercing the group of tyranids and incinerating two of them completely. But it was a small victory and brought Collia little sense of triumph – she could fire randomly in any direction and hit at least a couple of targets with each shot.

The biggest challenge was avoiding the incoming fire, not producing some of her own. It was hard enough to avoid colliding with the Drones themselves – the space was thick with them, spiralling and darting like a cloud of insects around a rotten corpse. But the *Extreme Prejudice* was not a corpse yet. Its side batteries were a blaze of light and fire, cutting great swathes out of the attacking flocks of Drones. Its landing bays were buzzing with activity, but it couldn't seem to get any of its remaining fighters out into space – the tyranid vessels were pestering the launch-shoots with spore mines, which kept exploding into intricate webs of thorny tendrils, draped over the tubes, sealing them.

If only they could get some support up here, thought Collia in angst, as she spun her Fury between several new venom trails and fired off a volley of lasfire into a prowling group of tyranid organisms.

She checked back out towards the spore-field, thinking that she would have a better chance in there than out here against this kind of assault, but then she realised that this battle was not supposed to save her, it was supposed to save the *Extreme Prejudice*. So she banked again, peeling away from the Drones that had joined the pursuit and blasting her way back in towards the cruiser. She flicked her main guns to automatic and let them dump vast amounts of energy out into the boiling soup of alien life that oozed around her. Every shot would hit something.

A rattle of lasfire ripped through the increasingly ichorous space around her as she charged in towards the *Extreme Prejudice*. The flashes overshot her cockpit and smacked into the shoal of Drones that lay in wait for her, blocking her path. Collia spun her head behind her just in time to see half a squadron of Furies in a neat V formation roar over her head with their guns blazing.

'Come on, Collia, let's get those launch-shoots open.' It was Gordus.

About bloody time, thought Collia. 'I'm with you, sir.'

THE *Sword of Contrition* was taking heavy fire. It had slid itself between one of the Razorfiend cruisers and the frigate *Purgation*, which had taken a direct hit to its command tower. A strange, tentacled growth was creeping over the hull of the frigate, puncturing the armoured plates with giant barbs that dug into the vessel as though it were flesh. Although the *Purgation*'s port-side guns could still fire, its main forward-facing lances had been rendered useless and its armour was buckled and cracked. A decent hit from a venom cannon would burst through the hull and melt the frigate from the inside out.

The *Strident Virtue* was locked into a duel with another Razorfiend cruiser. Captain Krelian could see the exchange of fire out of the *Contrition*'s rear view screens. It almost obliterated his view of the planet and the Hive Ship that sat untouchably on the edge of its stratosphere. The *Virtue* had support from a couple of squadrons of Furies and Starhawks, but it still looked like an uneven match. The smaller fighters were gradually being picked off by the marauding Drones, which the Hive Ship seemed to be able to spew out in endless numbers, as it sucked the required nutrients directly out of the atmosphere of Herodian IV.

Krelian checked all the other view screens, and each contained the snowy fuzz of small, fluttering tyranid vessels, questing for prey. He could no longer see the *Vanishing Star* or his sister ship, the *Penitent Quest*, but they were on the other side of the planet, keeping it between them and the Hive Ship, holding their guns in reserve for the last push. For a moment, Krelian wondered when that push would come – he could certainly use a blast or two from the *Star*'s lance arrays about now. It seemed a little strange to him that the *Star* had been kept so far out of the theatre and yet still remained within drop-distance of the doomed planet's surface.

'Captain Ordius,' called Krelian, opening a channel to the *Purgation*. 'This is Captain Krelian of the Mantis Warriors, Fourth Company. We have to get that barbed vine off your ship and we have to do it now. The *Sword of Contrition* cannot go on shielding you much longer, and your armour will be shredded within minutes.'

'...lian, th... ks for your hel... assista... much appre... iated,' came the broken voice of Ordius.

'Your signal is weak,' said Krelian, noting that the tyranid vines had already consumed the gaint vox-amplification

modules on the side of the command tower. 'If you have
any space-worthy troops, get them out there to detach
the tendrils. I will lead a team from the *Contrition* to
assist.'

Krelian turned smartly from the vox unit, not waiting
for a response from Ordius.

'Hold us here for as long as you can,' he said, handing
the bridge over to his pilot-servitor. 'It is time for the
Mantis Warriors to be Space Marines again, not effete
Naval pilots.' Like most Space Marines, Krelian was not
keen on space battles – he preferred to meet his enemies
face-to-face.

THE MEDICAE-HALL stretched for thousands of metres
across the stern of the *Vanishing Star*. It was truly massive,
with room for perhaps half a million beds, designed to
attend to the medical needs of a fleet or an invasion
force. The ceiling was unusually low, giving the space a
vague sense of distortion, as though it had been
squashed or stretched out horizontally. Kalypsia stared
through the whimpering air and squinted her eyes
against the medical fumes that stung her corneas. The
noise was incredible. There was constant screaming, but
they were not screams of pain – they were screams of tor-
ment and nightmare. And the voices: thousands of voices
chattered and wailed; some cried out while others whispered in barely audible tones. Shaking her head to clear
the noise, she realised that the sound was compressed by
the low ceiling. She nodded to herself, impressed with
the efficient planning. The ceiling was low so that a second level could be fitted into the space of one.

A medi-servitor shuffled up to the inquisitor, looking
anxious and harried. 'Can I help you, inquisitor?' it
asked.

'Yes. I need to talk to some of the survivors.' Kalypsia cast
her eyes around the chamber, and noted with sudden

alarm that there were Adeptus Mechanicus insignia on some of the patients. She composed herself quickly. 'I need to talk to some of the Mechanicus personnel.'

'As you wish,' answered the servitor, turning to lead Kalypsia through the cluttered aisles of the great hall. 'You should be aware, inquisitor,' continued the servitor, 'that most of the survivors are heavily traumatised. Nearly all of them are suffering from extreme shock, and large numbers appear to have completely lost their minds after exposure to the hive mind on the planet's surface.'

'I understand,' said Kalypsia with something approaching relief. 'Are any of them coherent?'

'Hardly any at all, at this stage,' replied the servitor, coming to a stop at the foot of one of the thousands of metal-framed beds.

The bed's occupant was sitting bolt upright, staring into nothingness with wide eyes. A network of bandages wound their way around his head and upper body, but they had lost any hint of white. There was a deep gash in the left hand side of the man's head, and his left arm was completely missing, apparently severed at the shoulder. Judging by the fresh trail of blood down his side, a single scything talon had sliced down from his head to his waist, taking his arm and gouging deeply into the skull and ribcage. Blood had soaked through everything, and the sheets on the bed were already turning brown as it dried. The stench of human excrement surrounded the bed and threatened to overpower Kalypsia's senses.

'What's his name?' asked Kalypsia, but the servitor had already rushed off to tend to someone else.

'…endal. Xenos… nology. They're coming! Ssssh, nobody must know. Gren… tyranids are coming! Emperor save us! Use it. Turn them back. The weapon! The weapon!' The man was screaming and thrashing his legs, twisting his head from side to side and causing new rivers of blood to stream down into the thin mattress.

Kalypsia pulled a wire-frame chair up to the side of bed and sat down calmly. 'It's alright. You're safe now. Tell me what happened.'

OCTAVIUS DUCKED HIS head and stepped into the low-ceilinged hall. The air tasted poisonous and rusty, as though run through with bad blood and cheap medicine. He could feel his neuroglottis working to filter out the toxins before they could make it past the back of his mouth.

The long, low chamber had not been designed with Space Marines in mind and Octavius was not comfortable, hunched and stooped as he scanned the thousands of beds for a sign of Kalypsia.

A servitor came rushing down one of the aisles and hastened to address Octavius. 'My, we are busy today. How can I help you, captain?' it asked.

'I am looking for Inquisitor Kalypsia. She said that she might come to the medicae-hall to check on some of the survivors,' said Octavius. He swept his hand slowly across the scene. 'I had not realised that there were so many.'

'I am not sure that you can call them all survivors, captain. Many will be lost to themselves forever. But, yes, the Mantis Warriors managed to extract two hundred and seventy thousand personnel, including a handful from the Adeptus Mechanicus, it seems.' The servitor was standing proudly upright as it explained the composition of the chamber.

Ocatvius raised his eyebrow with surprise. 'Adeptus Mechanicus personnel?'

'Yes, they were few in number. One of them retained some ability to speak, despite rather serious wounds. In fact, the inquisitor was also most interested to meet that man. Would you like me to take you to him?'

'Yes, yes please,' said Octavius, his mind suddenly racing. 'How long ago was the inquisitor here?'

'She has just left, captain. Not more than half an hour ago,' answered the servitor almost cheerfully.

The servitor rushed along through the aisles without looking back over its shoulder, threading its way easily between the abandoned obstacles in its path. Octavius picked his way carefully between the beds, keeping his head down to avoid the ceiling fixtures and lifting his feet cautiously over the litter of medical equipment, supplies and discarded possessions that were strewn all over the floor, coated in a film of dirt and blood. It took him several moments to catch up with the servitor, who had stopped at the foot of a bloody bed further down the aisle.

When he arrived at the bed, the servitor was already in a state of excitement, buzzing around the bed, checking all of the equipment for faults and gasping, 'Oh my!' Octavius was confused for a moment, until he saw that the man in bed was completely motionless. Looking up and down the aisle, he noticed that this was the only man not wailing and shouting. He seemed to be dead.

'Is he dead?' asked Octavius, ready to defer to an expert opinion.

'I'm afraid so, yes, captain,' came the concerned reply, as the servitor continued to make checks and adjust settings.

There was a glint of light from under one of the blood-drenched sheets, and Octavius tugged the fabric aside. It was a blade, fallen just fractions from the right hand of the dead Mechanicus. Flicking his eyes from the dagger to the man, Octavius saw the slice across the man's throat.

'There is your answer,' said Octavius, squinting his eyes suspiciously and nodding towards the seeping wound.

'Oh my,' said the servitor, 'another suicide.'

'Perhaps,' replied Octavius as he inspected the cut. 'But this gash was made from his right to his left, which would be almost impossible for a man with only a right arm.' He was thinking out loud and suddenly thought better of it. The dagger may have been next to the dead man's hand, but it was *under* the sheet – how did the dead Mechanicus cover himself up again after slitting his own throat?

'Yes, as you say, another suicide.' Octavius turned sharply and picked his way out of the medicae-hall, leaving the servitor to clear the bed for the next man. His mind was racing with questions: what were the Adeptus Mechanicus doing on Herodian IV? If they had lost personnel, why weren't the Mechanicus here trying to resolve the situation for themselves? Who had killed this man, and why? Despite the natural reverence that the captain had for the agents of His Emperor's Inquisition, Octavius couldn't help but think that Kalypsia had some role in this.

THE SHUTTLE PUSHED smoothly out of the *Penitent Quest*, its engines humming gently for the short trip to the *Vanishing Star*. Audin was in the cockpit, watching the landing bay approach as the pilot-servitor angled for the final run. He turned and walked back into the compartment, where Shaidan was sitting quietly, his long black hair loose on his shoulders and his green eyes fixed on the small view-port in the side wall. His face was covered in an intricate network of tattoos – strange insectoid patterns that seemed to shift and crawl over his skin, curdling away as Audin watched. They were ritual markings, given to the librarian when he had been inducted into the Praying Mantidea, the Chapter's elite cadre, charged with hunting down the renegade Astral Claws and restoring honour to the Mantis Warriors.

Audin considered his battle-brother for a moment. 'Brother Shaidan, what do you suppose the inquisitor wants with us?'

The librarian looked up from his reverie, fixing his captain with steady eyes. 'I do not know, Audin. The Inquisition has kept the Mantis Warriors under some scrutiny for nearly a hundred years and we have not given them cause to intervene in our affairs during that time. I hope that our intervention here on Herodian IV was not a mistake that we will regret – despite our honourable intentions.'

'I share your fears, Shaidan. There is more to this invasion than meets the eye, and I can foresee the need for a scapegoat before the events are finished,' said Audin ruefully.

'Being a scapegoat is one thing, captain. Being guilty is another. I hope that we have not made matters worse. Perhaps the Mantis Warriors truly are cursed.' Shaidan spoke in a whisper, as though to himself, and Audin did not respond immediately. They both understood what he was talking about.

'What of the sample that you gave to Dasein?' asked Audin eventually, as the landing sirens sounded and the shuttle began to shudder slightly against the gravity of the Navy battleship.

'Techmarine Dasein discovered traces of eldar DNA, which is highly unusual in tyranid swarm organisms. It has been hypothesised before that the zoanthropes utilised eldar material to boost their psychic potency, but it is unheard of for the gaunts to share this genetic make-up,' answered Shaidan, clearing his mind of his previous thoughts and climbing to his feet for the landing.

'I see,' said Audin simply. He paused, and then turned to his friend. 'Is this because of what we did?'

KALYPSIA WAS STANDING at the far end of the chamber with her back to the door. She was staring out into space through the viewing-wall, watching Herodian IV's suffering; the scene was dominated by the roiling clouds of tyranids on the planet's surface. She did not turn when the two Mantis Warriors entered, but she spoke straight away.

'Thank you for joining me, gentlemen. I have some questions for you.' Now she turned to face them, her hair whipping around over her shoulders and her cloak-tail defining a gentle arc on the polished floor. Against the backlight emitted by the planet, which filtered through the fabric of her cape, the Mantis Warriors could see her taught, muscular body, enveloped in an armoured body-glove. There were various blades glinting from fixings down her thighs and a coiled force-whip was attached to her belt. Hanging on a chain around her neck was the faint glow of a pendant, which rested on the exposed skin of her stomach – even from the other side of the room, the Mantis Warriors could see the simple shape of an 'I.' She cut a dramatic, imposing and dangerous figure and Shaidan could not help but be impressed.

She motioned them into the room, gesturing towards two chairs that had clearly been arranged specially for this meeting. The two Space Marines responded to her bidding, sitting carefully into the ornate chairs.

'How can we help you, inquisitor?' asked Audin, affecting an impressive air of dignity.

'I have been trying to work out exactly what we are facing here,' she said, waving her graceful arm casually in the direction of the planet behind her. 'And I wondered whether you might be able to shed some light on things.'

'You must have read our report, inquisitor?' responded Audin carefully.

'Of course, but I was hoping that I could hear the story directly from you, captain. As I am sure you have been informed by the good librarian here, our expedition to the planet's surface was not entirely successful and I thought you might be able to help explain why.' Kalypsia was looking intently into Audin's green eyes, as though searching for something hidden deep within them.

'I would not presume to judge the failure of a Death-watch mission, inquisitor,' he answered, measuring his words. What was she looking for? What did she want him to say?

Kalypsia inclined her head slightly to one side, as though judging the truth of Audin's response. Then, apparently decided, she said, 'Of course not, captain. Instead, tell me about the failure of the Mantis Warriors on Herodian IV.'

Audin's back stiffened at the use of the word 'failure,' but he was prepared for this question.

'The Second Company was overpowered by the superior numbers of the alien swarm, inquisitor. We fought a tactical retreat to our point of extraction, where we fought a last stand on top of a ruined compound – the only strong point in the region. I should like to commend Librarian Shaidan, Sergeant Soron and Sergeant Ruinus for their courage and valour during this engagement. In addition, Devastator Sergeant Magnir, Company Chaplain Aegir and Terminator Sergeant Hoenir should be awarded posthumous honours – each gave his life so that we might live to fight again.' Audin paused to allow the magnitude of these great losses to sink in – but the inquisitor did not seem moved.

Shaidan took over the story. 'The tyranids seemed able to pre-empt our movements, deploying their forces to disrupt our strategic operations. It was as though they had read the Codex, inquisitor. As though they knew our range of movements before we acted.' The librarian was studying Kalypsia's face as he spoke. She gazed back at him with pale, unmoved, grey eyes.

'The tyranid cannot read, librarian. You should be careful not to humanise their memory. You do them too much honour and veer perilously close to heresy,' she said evenly.

'I meant no offence, inquisitor. I was merely trying to answer your question in the fullest manner possible.' Shaidan did not bow his head as he spoke, but kept his piercing green eyes fixed in the shallow grey of Kalypsia's. She was hiding something and he could see that she knew that he was hiding something too.

CHAPTER SIX:
WOODEN DESKS

[19 Hours Remaining]

OCTAVIUS STUDIED THE faces of the Mantis Warrior Marines lined up before him. They were fierce, noble and scarred with years of constant battle. Each had a long cascade of black hair and sparkling green eyes. Their skin was dark and inscribed with cursive and barbed tattoos that curled and flowed across their faces and necks, like heavy shadows cut into their upper bodies. Octavius understood that these were ritual markings, etched into the skin of the finest warriors of the Chapter – those charged with hunting down the cursed Astral Claws. These were the marks of the Praying Mantidae, a cadre created nearly a century before, following the fall of the Mantis Warriors in the Badab Wars – its warriors had all stood side by side with the renegades and they all had more to prove than any Marine that Octavius had come across before. The Deathwatch captain could see the passion and the pride burning in their eyes. There was almost a desperation hidden in those fiery depths, something that Octavius had rarely seen in the eyes of a Space Marine.

Behind the three Mantis Warriors were the rest of the Deathwatch team, arrayed in their immaculately polished black armour, but with their helmets off so that their eyes glinted with life in the half light of the ceremonial chamber in the *Perfect Incision*. The right shoulder plate of each Marine shone with particular splendour, as though the insignia of their home Chapters that were inscribed there had been ritually purified. Their left shoulders bore the mark of the Deathwatch: a skull set against the Inquisitorial 'I,' one eye studded with a faintly glowing red gem.

The Deathwatch line was broken, punctuated by spaces where Marines should be standing. The two Crimson Fists that had fallen during the expedition to the surface of Herodian IV were missing, as was Kulac, the heroic Space Wolf. Each had been a great hero in his own right. Each carried the pride of their ancient Chapter and the glory of the Deathwatch into the afterlife.

Octavius surveyed the line with a heavy heart. Only five of his team remained. Sergeant Grevius had fought at his side on many occasions in the past. He had been inducted into the Deathwatch by Octavius himself on a visit to the ruins of Rynn's World, the homeworld of the Crimson Fists, a successor Chapter of his own Imperial Fists, brothers in the gene-seed of Rogal Dorn himself. The Crimson Fists had a long tradition of supplying the Deathwatch with the most awesome alien hunters in the galaxy, despite their own dwindling numbers – and Grevius had more than lived up to his responsibilities. But there was nothing left of him to return to his valiant Chapter.

The only remains that had been brought back from the planet were those of Kulac, a mighty warrior in his own right to be sure and the Space Wolves would praise the

Emperor for the return of his invaluable gene-seed. But the Crimson Fists would mourn the loss of Grevius just as much – perhaps even more because of the loss of his precious progenoids. To honour the fallen Crimson Fists as much as Kulac himself, Octavius would personally ensure that every possible honour and dignity would be given to Tyrian on his passage home, symbolising his respect for each of his fallen brothers.

And then there were these Mantis Warriors, their emerald green armour polished and shimmering to the point of perfection, not sullied by a single imperfection or darkened with even a touch of black. Before the Badab Wars, the Mantis Warriors were second only to the Crimson Fists in the number of Marines that were seconded to the Deathwatch, but not a single Marine from this Chapter had ritually blackened his armour in the service of this elite force in nearly a century. Octavius shuddered inwardly at the thought that these three would have to replace the heroic Space Wolf and Crimson Fists, and he knew that the rest of the kill-team were sceptical. These Marines were an unknown quantity – none of the team had ever encountered them before.

However, Octavius's first duty was to the Emperor and to the Ordo Xenos. Although he had learnt to trust his instincts over his long decades of service, he could not let such sentiment interfere with his duty. Duty comes before everything.

The Mantis Warriors were the only Space Marine Chapter in the sector and the Deathwatch team was under strength after the loss of three battle-brothers. The maths was simple and, if he was honest with himself, Octavius had been impressed by Librarian Shaidan during the extraction of his kill-team just hours before. If these other Marines could fight like him, then they would not compromise the Deathwatch. And Captain Audin's report of the Mantis Warriors' withdrawal had praised them both highly: Assault Marine, Sergeant Soron, and Devastator Marine, Sergeant Ruinus.

In the end, no matter what else you could say about them, they were still Space Marines. Perhaps their burning eyes spoke of something pent up and great waiting to be unleashed against the Great Devourer.

Inquisitor Kalypsia had not been reticent when Octavius had explained to her the need to seconde three Mantis Warriors to support the Deathwatch kill-team. It seemed that she didn't know about their past and didn't care. 'They are soldiers, captain,' she had said with frank simplicity. Then she had paused for a moment before speaking again, as though changing the subject, 'Tell me more about this Chapter.'

Kalypsia had been clear that it would be to the team's advantage to have another librarian. She explained her theory that the Herodian swarm was actually a splinter of the Kraken Hive, which had been shattered by the Ultramarines with the assistance of the Iyanden eldar in 992.M41. The splinter had probably pursued the Iyanden craftworld through deep space, gradually absorbing eldar DNA harvested during conflicts. This explained the unusual psychic potency of the swarm and the concentration of zoanthropes.

Octavius was not entirely convinced by Kalypsia's hypothesis, but he needed no further encouragement to select Librarian Shaidan for his team. He was an impressive Marine and had already proven himself capable of dealing with the tyranid psykers.

The inquisitor was right, however, that the swarm was unusual. It did seem to be able to pre-empt the standard tactics of the Deathwatch and the tyranid creatures themselves fought with greater energy and coordination than Octavius expected from such mindless beasts. Something was different.

And then there was Kalypsia herself. Octavius had known nothing about her until they had met for the first time on the *Veiled Salvation*. The Deathwatch team had been on its way to the Herodian warp-gate, ready to make the journey to the Obscurus frontier, where they were to lead the Imperial forces against the tyranid incursion. Inquisitor Lord Agustius was to join them later and take command of the theatre, but Ordo Xenos business would mean that he would be a day behind them.

The team had been intercepted en route to the gate and escorted to the *Salvation*, where they were met by the famed Inquisitor Lord Parthon, who told them that the gate was now impassable, but that he had another mission that only the Deathwatch could complete. He praised the Emperor for their timely arrival – the nearest Deathwatch fortress being several days away and even further with the warp-gate closed. With luck, he had said, and with the hand of the Emperor to guide you, you should be finished and the gate should be reopened by the time Agustius arrives.

But the great Inquisitor Lord was not going to lead this mission himself. He protested that he was too old for such exploits now. Instead, he appointed his young protégé, Kalypsia, to head the mission against the tyranids on Herodian IV. This was her first expedition in charge of a Deathwatch kill-team, and Octavius was not totally confident in her judgement. Not only that, but he had come across Parthon before and he was not sure that the great man's methods were always sound. Although Agustius always spoke highly of his old friend, Octavius could sense that there was something unspoken between these two inquisitor lords. He was not sure that Agustius would approve of his Deathwatch team's cooption by Parthon, but it was in accordance with protocols – Parthon was the ranking inquisitor in the theatre of conflict and the team was indeed most needed on Herodian IV for the time being.

THE LONG PANELLED room seemed to stretch on forever. Dim lights glowed in dirty orbs, set into the ceiling, casting heavy shadows across the endless rows of shelves, filling the aisles with pregnant darkness. At the far end was a single desk, on which a green-shaded lamp burned warmly, shedding reading-light down onto the papers that had been left scattered on the polished wooden surface. It was another mark of the affluence of the *Veiled Salvation* that it could boast authentic wooden desks even in the lowest and most forgotten of its file-chambers.

Agustius had told them to find anything that seemed unusual. They were vague instructions, thought Slyrian as she scanned the shadows with her keen eyes. She was not a curator and, to her, a room full of files seemed unusual in itself. It was almost a waste of space. How was she supposed to know which pieces of paper were unusual and which were just normal sheets of paper?

'There, we need to see those packages,' whispered Lexopher, pointing at a column of shelves in the middle of the room. The thick dust had been disturbed and it was clear that these files had been consulted or altered recently. Lexopher had been Agustius's acolyte for nearly ten years and had learnt as much about interrogating texts as about interrogating people from his old master. In truth, Agustius doubted that the young interrogator had what it took to become a full inquisitor – he was too bookish and physically weak. In fact, he had been lucky to have been promoted from explicator to interrogator. That said, he was perfectly suited to the present task and Agustius was confident that he would find what he was looking for.

Slyrian slipped through the shadows with an unearthly grace, tracing her long fingers delicately over each shelf as she worked her way over to where Lexopher had pointed. Her feet danced lightly on the panelled wooden floor, testing each piece of wood deftly before transferring her weight onto it. Her black synthskin seemed to reflect no light and Lexopher kept losing sight of the elegant death cultist, despite the fact that she was only a few metres away from him.

There was a quiet rustling sound and then suddenly Slyrian appeared next to Lexopher again, making him start. She had a collection of files under one arm and, with the other, she gestured to the floor that led to the shelves, indicating that it was unsound.

Lexopher studied the spines of the folders in Slyrian's embrace and nodded. Those looked very promising. But they had to be sure. With a sharp gesture, the interrogator pointed at his eyes and then at the files. Slyrian nodded with a brief flick of her head, already turning to survey the little pools of yellow light that collected on the wooden aisle between them and the reading desk. That appeared to be the only way. She turned back to the interrogator, shaking her head tightly. The aisle was lit for its entire length – she was suspicious.

'Don't be ridiculous,' whispered Lexopher. 'We have to check these documents before we leave. It will be safer to check them now than to try and get back in here later on, if we have the wrong files.'

The death cultist was still unsure; she was not used to this kind of work. As part of Agustius's retinue, she was used to acting as an assassin. And she was good at that. Very good. But creeping about in the bowels of an Inquisition battleship looking for pieces of paper that might explain why an inquisitor lord was taking such a personal interest in the fate of a meaningless planet – this was not her forte. Agustius had just been concerned that the bookish Lexopher might not be able to do this on his own. Judging by the casual way that he disregarded the

danger of the aisle, Slyrian thought that Agustius was
probably right about that. She nodded slowly.

The two figures made their way down the wooden aisle
– Lexopher being careful to place his feet into exactly the
same positions as Slyrian in front of him. He knew that
the death cultist would find a safe path, avoiding the
motion sensors, weight sensors and hidden cameras. He
had confidence in her because Agustius did – his master
had explained that she was essential to this mission, but
that he, Lexopher, had to make the final decisions about
the files. The death cultist knew nothing of documents
and probably could not even read, so there was no way
that she could have done this on her own.

Sliding carefully into the seat at the desk, Lexopher
flipped open the first of the files and started to read the
yellowing manuscripts inside. Yes, this is what they had
come for. It was good stuff.

Meanwhile, Slyrian had slipped back into the shadows
between the shelves and bookcases, keeping her sensitive
eyes open and her well-trained ears to the ground. If anyone approached this chamber, she would know.

THE MASSIVE TENTACLE thrashed through the vacuum
with incredible speed, unhindered by the constraints
of air and gravity. Krelian ducked and then smashed
his huge, double-headed power axe into the sinewy tissue of the vine – the vacuum enhancing his speed. A
spray of ichor and sap jetted out of the gaping wound,
freezing instantly into a rain of tiny, razor-sharp
shards.

The small squad of Mantis Warriors were speckled
over the barbed vine that was growing all over the nose
of the *Purgation*. The hull was buckled and torn where
giant thorns punctured the armoured plates, and where
the continuous constriction of the liana crushed the substructure underneath. From the bridge of the *Sword of*

Contrition, the Space Marines looked like tiny green insects climbing over a monstrous plant.

Krelian hacked with his axe, driving it down into the tendrils with both hands, throwing his weight behind it to try and sever the organism's hold on the Naval frigate. But the lack of gravity worked against him: whilst it enabled his limbs to flash with lightning speed, it prevented him from using his considerable bulk to press his blades home.

Looking around him, he could see the other Mantis Warriors slicing and lashing their blades against the sprawling vinery. They were ducking and weaving to avoid the parries and swipes of the tendrils, leaping out into space only to catch hold of one of the barbed vines and use it to swing themselves back onto the hull of the frigate, where they would turn and slice the vine free, casting it into the void.

The squad was arranged in a rough circle, wrapped round the main lance in the nose of the *Purgation*, toiling to cut it free. Thorns and barbs were dug deeply into the array, preventing it from firing and the lashes of the tendrils bound the barrel into immobility, so there was no hope of aiming the thing, even if it could be made to fire.

In the bridge of the *Sword of Contrition*, things were not going well. The cruiser was shielding the Navy frigate, using its own flank to absorb the stream of venom being pumped out of the cannons of the prowling Razorfiend. The gun-servitors were working constantly, unleashing volleys of lasfire against the monstrous organism, but they were outclassed at this range, particularly since they were not able to manoeuvre. The *Contrition* needed to come about, and bring its frontal arrays to bear.

'Captain Krelian,' called the bridge of the *Contrition*. 'We cannot hold this position any longer. You must get your men clear of the *Purgation* now.'

'Just a few more moments,' hissed the voice of Krelian through the vox. 'We have nearly cleared away this weed.'

A series of small explosions strafed around the nose of the *Purgation* as the mines set by the Mantis Warriors detonated in the flesh of the terrible vine-organism. A flurry of axe blows later, and a huge section of the liana was detached and sent thrashing into space, its tendrils working frantically to regain some purchase on the Imperial vessel.

The lance barrel on the *Purgation* was suddenly freed, and power started to course into its systems. Captain Ordius ordered the frigate to come about, pulling the nose around to face directly at the *Sword of Contrition*, which stood between it and the Razorfiend-class cruiser on its other side.

'Now, Captain Krelian. You must leave, now!' called the pilot-servitor on the *Contrition* as its shields began to overheat.

'Many thanks, Captain Krelian,' came the voice of Captain Ordius from the bridge of the *Purgation* over the vox. 'Clear your team, and let's give that Razorfiend a taste of our lance.'

Krelian waved his team back to the extraction point – a thick wire fixing that linked the *Purgation* to the *Sword of Contrition*. It was used for rapid boarding actions, where the Marines would thread the wire through their hands and blast along its length with a burn from their jump-packs.

'Ten seconds, captain,' came the voice from the *Contrition*.

The Mantis Warriors were literally flying now, pulling themselves along the hull of the *Purgation* in zero-G with great sweeps from their powerful arms, propelling their way towards the fixing. Krelian was already there, checking each of his Marines as they arrived and slapping them on their backs to give them some extra boost as they blasted their way back towards the *Contrition*.

'Six seconds, get clear. Firing engines in four, three…'

The team were away, and Krelian reached out his hand to grasp the wire. As he did so, something constricted around his boot and held him in place against the fierce burn from his jump-pack. Looking down, Krelian saw a tendril tightening around his leg and others reaching out for him. He cut the power to his jump-pack and wielded his power axe into both hands. Letting go of the life-line, Krelian threw himself back into the tyranid liana, rending it asunder with his powerful blows.

'…one, firing engines.' The *Sword of Contrition* bucked and then parallaxed into motion, leaving a stream of green in its wake as it thrust clear of the onslaught from the Razorfiend craft.

As the *Contrition* cleared the line of sight, Captain Ordius gave the order to fire and a massive burst of power surged out of the frontal lance of the *Purgation*, smashing into the Razorfiend at close range.

At exactly the same moment, the Razorfiend released twin pulses from its pincer mounted venom-cannons. Under the impact from the *Purgation*'s fire, the Razorfiend recoiled, spinning into a haze, spilling fluids into the vacuum all around. A succession of explosions racked the organic vessel from within, sending plumes of tissue fountaining into space. Then, with a massive convulsion, the entire craft exploded, sending a fluorescent shockwave radiating from its ruins.

Meanwhile, the twin venom streams from the Razorfiend coalesced and poured against the vulnerable nose of the *Purgation*, seeping through into the lance array and eating away its heat shielding. The bridge was completely consumed, melted utterly from the frigate before any of its personnel even had the chance to scream. Then the lance overheated and its power core detonated, blowing the *Purgation* into tiny pieces and scattering its vicious shrapnel into the shoals of Drones that swam through the surrounding space like schools of fish in the ocean.

From his vantage point on the outside of the hull of the *Purgation*, Captain Krelian of the Mantis Warriors had watched the *Sword of Contrition* pull clear. He had offered up a prayer for the souls of his battle-brothers as he swung his axe for the last time and he had been vaporised by the river of venom from the Razorfiend.

IT ALL SEEMED to be there: requisition notices, transport logs, even one or two personal communiqués. There was an executive order from the Promethus sub-sector of the Ordo Xenos, confirming that the temporarily requisitioned battleship, the *Veiled Salvation*, should be kept permanently within striking distance of Herodian IV. Parthon had signed it himself. There was an Inquisitorial order requisitioning an old Adeptus Mechanicus base on the surface of the planet for the use of a certain, Derteg Grendal, again signed by Parthon. In the small print of the same document was a note stating that final control of the facility would rest with Parthon himself – the Mechanicus were cut out of the loop.

These documents had been here for years and, judging by the dust that had built up on the files, they had not been consulted much during this time. And they were all official documents. Nothing was hidden or underhand. Each manuscript had been stamped by the appropriate authorities and signed by an inquisitor lord – they had even been filed here, in the official file-chambers of the *Veiled Salvation*. Admittedly, they were not exactly on display and some effort had been needed to find them, but Parthon could have hidden them much more effectively if he had really wanted to.

Lexopher shook his head in slight disbelief – Agustius would be shocked by these revelations, but Parthon clearly thought that there was nothing to be shocked about, or he would have made some effort to prevent the documents from being found. They seemed to tell a story of a connection between Parthon and a research station on Herodian IV – obviously something rather important if it warranted the permanent positioning of an Inquisitorial battleship on its doorstep. But there was nothing criminal or heretical here. The only problem, as far as Lexopher could see, was that Parthon had not volunteered this information to Agustius himself. Then again, why would he – the Herodian system was Parthon's theatre of command and had nothing to do with Agustius. The old man was just getting nosey in his twilight years, and increasingly suspicious of his more radical old friends.

A sharp exhale of breath made him look up from his studious reveries. Slyrian was crouched on the edge of the desk, as though she had simply been there the whole time. She seemed to be staring into his eyes and Lexopher shivered as he looked back at the smooth, featureless contours of the synthskin that covered her face. It was as if she didn't have a face at all. Light just fell into her, making her almost invisible, even at this intimate distance.

She drew her finger across her throat and pointed back towards the only door to the chamber. The meaning was clear and Lexopher was thrown into a bit of a panic. Perhaps Parthon did have something to hide after all? The young interrogator snatched up the remaining papers, stuffing them into a document pouch that he had brought for exactly this purpose. Slyrian leant forward and clicked off the desk-lamp, plunging Lexopher into darkness.

'Stay,' came a delicate and seductive voice in Lexopher's ear, and he thrilled. Pushing his chair right back into the far corner of the room, he was lost in the shadows. He drew his pistol from a holster on the outside of his thigh, and sat motionlessly, waiting for something to happen.

'What now,' he whispered into the dark, but there was no reply. Slyrian was already gone.

The door on the far side of the room burst open, flooding the first few tiers of shelves with light. A plume of chemical fire rushed into the chamber, flickering and licking around the tinder-like documents that filled the room and washing across the polished wooden floor. Two tall, muscular men darted into the space cleared by their comrade with the flamer. They threw themselves to the ground, rolling elegantly into kneeling positions with their guns drawn.

One of them screeched suddenly, staggering to his feet and clutching at his throat with both hands – his gun tumbling to the ground with a loud clatter. The other turned and opened up with his firearm, its discharge resounding with bursts of light in the renewed darkness of the chamber. But he wasn't sure where to fire.

The man with the flamer advanced into the room to provide cover, engulfing the garrotted guard in another plume of fire and rendering that end of the room into a shadow show of oranges and golds. For a split second, a slender, shapely silhouette could be seen stepping into the flames. Then the flamer cut out and clanged to the ground. From his position behind the desk, Lexopher could see that the guard's gun-arm had been severed at the elbow and his head was wobbling precariously on his shoulders. With a crash, the only door to the chamber slammed shut, and the light from the corridor outside vanished.

The remaining guard was still on his knees, his gun flicking from side to side in a frantic attempt to locate a target in the shadows. He was clearly in shock and, for a moment, Lexopher even felt sorry for him. Then the row of glow-orbs in the ceiling faded, plunging the room into complete darkness, and the guard screamed.

LOOKING OUT OF the view screens in the *Perfect Incision*, Kalypsia could see the space battle unfolding on the other side of the planet. The pictures were relayed to her by a network of devices that Kastor had deployed into strategic orbits at various points around the planet. This way they could monitor events and keep clear of them at the same time.

She watched the Mantis Warrior cruiser, *Sword of Contrition*, abandon its shielding position in front of the Imperial frigate. She saw the *Purgation*'s lance burst the Razorfiend into a violent death-throw and then watched the brilliant fireball that was once the *Purgation* gradually fade into nothingness. Shaking her head, she turned away from the screen.

'Yes,' she said into the vox, as the voice of Commander Kastor came through. 'What do you want?'

'I thought that you should be aware, inquisitor, that Inquisitor Lord Agustius's gunship has just taken up a holding position in a distant orbit. His communiqués suggest that he has come to monitor the engagement.' Kastor's voice was clipped, and Kalypsia was certain that it contained a hint of satisfaction.

'Thank you for letting me know, commander,' she replied with undaunted calm. But this was indeed unexpected news and she wondered why Parthon would permit the old puritan to get involved in this affair.

CHAPTER SEVEN:
DEATHWIND

[14 Hours Remaining]

THE LIGHTS WERE perpetually dim in Parthon's private chambers. There was just a faint glow, enough to indicate that the ship's environmental sensors were aware that the rooms were occupied, but not enough for anyone else to see who was in there. Some of the underlings aboard the *Veiled Salvation* whispered that the inquisitor lord was actually allergic to bright light; none of them had ever seen him leave the battleship and make planet-fall into natural light and none had ever seen his gaunt features outside the heavy shadows that he seemed to cultivate around his ship. In fact, the ambient light automatically dropped into near-darkness when Parthon entered a room.

A clutch of explicators were continuously posted on the *Salvation*, charged with learning the ways of the Ordo Xenos from the great man himself. Amongst these junior officials, a rather more sinister explanation for Parthon's predilection for darkness had surfaced. The rumours had started back at the sector's Ordo Xenos HQ and been brought to the battleship by the various officials who paid their regular pilgrimages to the *Salvation* on their way to the Herodian warp-gate. Each successive visitor would add fuel to the fire, gossiping with the explicators about the notoriously shadowy lord of the *Veiled Salvation*. Parthon did nothing to suppress this behaviour, since he believed that a healthy veil of rumour was the best way to obscure the truth, especially if that truth were far more interesting than the rumours themselves. Hence, the old lord paid scant attention to his visitors, hardly ever even bothering to greet them when their ships docked; naturally, he had made an exception for his old friend, Agustius. In the gossip of the junior officers, Parthon's anti-social behaviour only added to the mystery of the darkness that seemed perpetually to enshroud him.

The banal conspiracy theories of the young explicators were not far from the mark, but it did not require too much imagination to realise that an inquisitor lord might think himself the target of assassination attempts. Such would simply be healthy paranoia, without which no inquisitor would survive long enough to become a lord. A truly imaginative young interrogator might come up with a better explanation for Parthon's penchant for the dark: quite simply, he doesn't need the light. There are far more efficient ways to see, if you have the skill, and depriving others of the surety of their sight is a priceless advantage.

'You should not concern yourself with this, Kalypsia,' purred Parthon with slightly forced nonchalance. 'The issue is in hand.'

The vox-unit hissed and crackled, undermining the soothing tone of the inquisitor lord's voice with bursts of grating static.

'But I cannot understand why you would let him interfere, my lord.' Kalypsia's voice was distorted and shrill, giving it an anxious and agitated edge.

'It is not my place to permit Agustius's actions or to forbid them, young Kalypsia. And it is certainly not your place to question my own actions.' The gentle pressure of his voice had hardened. 'I imagine that you have more than enough to contend with on Herodian IV without busying your imagination with events on the *Veiled Salvation*.'

There was a long pause, and Parthon smiled in the darkness as he imagined the vexed and annoyed expression that must have been cracking over Kalypsia's face.

'Of course, my lord,' she replied tersely.

'Of course,' repeated Parthon, still smiling, but trying to keep the amusement out of his voice. In truth, his amusement about his protégé's predictable response did not extend to the actions of his old friend; Parthon was far from amused by Agustius's decision to take his gunship into orbit around Herodian IV. His sparring partner had left somewhat abruptly and without any of the courtesies that might have been expected from one of his rank. Then he had placed his gunship directly into the sights of the *Vanishing Star*, as though wanting to announce to the Imperial Navy that he was there. Perhaps his position was even a deliberate suggestion that he required the protection of the Gothic-class cruiser. Whatever was in Agustius's mind, Parthon was sure that it would cause him problems before the affair on Herodian IV was concluded.

'As I said, it is in hand,' he repeated. 'Now, what is your next move, I wonder?' he continued, trying to turn Kalypsia's attention back to matters of more immediate concern for her.

There was another pause, as Kalypsia fought with the desire to press the question of Agustius. She hated to be manipulated, even when it was done elegantly, but Parthon was simply imposing rank by changing the subject so bluntly. It reminded her that the structural protocols of the Inquisition were not entirely dissimilar from those in the Imperial Guard and that was not an analogy that she cared to entertain. She was no grunt.

'Octavius has seconded three Mantis Warriors to bolster the Deathwatch kill-team, to replace the Marines who fell during our last drop-mission. Hence, the team is now effectively back at full strength and will be reinserted onto the planet's surface. This time, I will determine the landing site myself, and we will drop directly into the target zone,' explained Kalypsia formally, as though filing a report.

'Captain Octavius inducted some Mantis Warriors?' asked Parthon, his voice tinged with surprise.

'No, my lord. He merely seconded them – they have not been afforded the honour of Deathwatch markings,' replied Kalypsia, faintly amused by the inquisitor lord's concerns.

'Very good,' continued Parthon, recovering his purpose. 'Time is running short. You are right to adopt a direct approach.'

Parthon was about to cut the connection when another thought struck him. 'Did any of the survivors recovered by the Mantis Warriors have any revealing information about events prior to the fall of the planet?'

Kalypsia's answer was swift and precisely worded. 'None of the survivors have any information of that kind, my lord.'

'I see,' replied Parthon evenly. 'Very well then.' The tone of his voice was lost in the static as the connection died.

KALYPSIA JUST STARED at the fourteen tonne, adamantium teardrop held in its harness in the deck of the pod launch bay of the *Vanishing Star*. As far as she could see, it was simply a hollow lump of metal with retro-burners grafted onto its surface in haphazard places. Here and there, Kalypsia could see the barrels of boltguns protruding from the shell, but they appeared to be fixed in place, without any range of movement – they looked as though they had simply been welded onto the shell as afterthoughts. The pod was about six metres in diameter and perhaps eight in height, although it was difficult to judge precisely because it was half inset into a custom pit in the deck. The launch bay held about fifty of these drop-pods, each sunk into the deck like giant armoured eggs in a cardboard crate. Five of them had been painted Deathwatch black, and Techmarine Korpheus had been administering to them for the last couple of hours. The black ones did look slightly different from the others, so Kalypsia was aware that his administrations might also have included some modifications.

'Are you sure that we can't just use another Thunderhawk?' she asked again, hoping that Octavius would finally relent.

'Certain,' stated the Deathwatch captain bluntly. 'If you are determined to make our insertion directly into the swarm, then a Thunderhawk is out of the question. You saw what happened to it last time and that was when the landing site was relatively clean. Given your choice of insertion point this time, there is no way that a vehicle the size of a hawk would make it to the ground, and there is even less of a chance that we would survive without a drop-ship's armour if we had to free-fall a hundred metres as we did last time. You, inquisitor, would certainly die the instant the hawk broke apart. If we're going to go in next to the hive tyrant itself, we're going to go in hard and we're going to go in fast. We take the pods, and that's it.'

Octavius looked down at the inquisitor as she studied the craft in front of her. Lord Parthon had certainly thrown her in the deep end with this mission. The captain was fairly sure that this was the first time that Kalypsia had come across the Deathwatch and it was more than likely that she had never been in a drop-pod before. However, it was of no consequence to him; his job was to ensure the success of the mission and, if possible, to ensure the preservation of his team. If that meant strapping the inquisitor into a drop-pod and smashing her into the ground at several times the speed of sound, then so be it. She may not like it, but it was unlikely that she would be seriously damaged.

The two of them had studied the roiling and curdling swarm from the viewing station for over an hour, watching the way in which the currents shifted and flowed, pouring tyranids around the planet's surface like a tide of oil over a drowning man. They had searched for patterns, but Octavius had not been able to identify any, despite Kalypsia's insistence that there was one that they could exploit to discover the hive tyrant. Their previous landing site was now utterly black and swamped by the teeming swarm and, although a couple of other areas of clarity had opened up near Kalypsia's target point, there was now an unspoken distrust of those sites, despite the fact that the Codex insisted they should be the favoured insertion points.

In the end, suspicion, the pressures of time and Kalypsia's insistence had overwhelmed Octavius's strategic good sense; they could no longer afford the luxury of a soft landing, even if those clearings really offered one.

Because of the speeds and impacts involved, drop-pods were usually only used by Space Marines, but this time the inquisitor would have to take her chances with her team; she had insisted that she had to be included in the landing party, despite assurances from Octavius that his team could operate without her on the ground. She was unusually determined to get her feet back onto the planet, reflected Octavius, but he put it down to over-compensation for her understandable anxiety about her first mission with a Deathwatch kill-team. Besides, determination was something that Octavius understood well enough and they would need as much of it as possible to see them through the day.

'After you, inquisitor,' said Octavius, punching the release on the pod's entry-panel. There was a hiss of steam as the side of the pod cracked open and the entire panel lowered itself mechanically down to the deck like a ramp.

'She's not the *Perfect Incision*, but she'll get us down to the ground,' called Techmarine Korpheus as he strode up behind the other two.

Kalypsia turned as she stepped up onto the ramp, casting her eyes behind her as the rest of the Deathwatch team and the Mantis Warriors entered the launch bay and marched wordlessly towards the pods, their heavy boots clattering solidly against the deck. Korpheus, Ashok and Broec headed directly for her, while the other four split into pairs and approached two separate pods. Whilst drop-pods could usually carry up to five Marines, Neleus and Soron required a specially modified unit that could accommodate the bulk of Terminator armour and Soron's jump-pack. They more than filled a pod on their own. Besides, planet-fall in a pod was a tricky business, and Octavius had been keen to spread the risk between three rather than two drop-pods.

'I have no doubt of the capacity of a drop-pod to drop, Marine,' said Kalypsia, smiling with slightly false bravado as she strode up the ramp and jumped inside.

The inside of the pod was little more than a hollow shell with harnesses bolted into the curving walls. There were five spaces for Space Marines, but one of them had been hastily converted into a custom harness for Kalypsia. When she saw all the extra straps and padding, the true difference between her physique and those of these Marines hit her as though for the first time. Perhaps these were no ordinary soldiers, after all.

* * *

THE LASGUNS ON the Furies chattered and tracked, shredding flocks of Drone Escort organisms and perforating the sinews of liana that were creeping all over the launch bays of the *Extreme Prejudice*. The gun batteries of the beleaguered battle cruiser were a constant blaze of fire, but even the awesome power of an Imperial Dictator-class cruiser couldn't hold off the onslaught.

A warning siren sounded and Collia thumbed the override – she had no time to worry about faults in her fighter as she spun it like a corkscrew straight through a school of prowling drone ships. The heat gauge on her weapons' systems had maxed out nearly ten minutes before, but the lasguns were still firing, and that was good enough for her.

The formation of Furies had been shattered by the density of combat and Collia could only just catch glimpses of the surviving members of her squadron as their Furies flashed through the clouds of organic detritus and stalking drones. Lasfire strafed through the soupy space around them, exploding chains of chaff-spores into splattering rains of toxic alien ichor. The outside of Collia's cockpit was coated in a spotted film of gunk. The screens were cracked into lattices and scarred where venom streams had fizzed and etched a path across them. Even if she were able to see clearly through the clouds of xenos organisms that swam in tides around her, Collia would still have found it almost impossible to see her comrades through the ruined screens of her Fury.

She had already given up trying to aim her guns and they simply chattered away on automatic, spewing gouts of lasfire in incredible quantities. Without fail, each burst found a target, but there was not enough fire in the entire fleet to deal with the thousands of marks that flooded the space around the *Prejudice*.

'Gordus?' yelled Collia, banking hard and braking as she pulled her fighter into a low run along the surface of the battle cruiser. Her guns strafed fire across the deck, picking off the vines and alien forna that were forcing their way between the armoured plates and splintering them off into space.

A loud hiss cackled through the vox, blasting Collia with a shriek of feedback and making her swear. 'Emperor damn it, Gordus! Where the hell are you?'

There was no reply, but the rear burners of another Fury dropped into view in front of her. The fighter must have been within spitting distance of Collia for her to see it so clearly amongst all the crap floating around out there and she recognised the ostentatious paint-job immediately: a huge red, smiling skull had been sprayed onto the back of the fighter, with the afterburner flaring in the midst of the vicious grin. Etched into one of the eye sockets in brilliant white was the word *Storm*, in the other was *Squadron* and sprawled through the giant mouth like bloody, rickety teeth was the word *Rules*.

'Damn you, Gordus,' said Collia to herself, shaking her head as she realised that his vox must have been knocked out of action. 'If you weren't such a blasted good pilot, I'd have to kill you myself.'

As though in response, the backend of the Fury bucked in front of her, flicking its rear as though it were flirting.

'Yeah, yeah,' muttered Collia, gunning her engines to pull up alongside her squadron leader. 'You have me already.'

As she drew up next to Gordus's Fury, she could see that it was in an even worse state than hers. The main, nose-mounted lascannon had been completely melted away, and Collia could just about make out the faint sheen of toxic sludge still clinging to the edges of the wound; the metal was smoking with gradual chemical erosion. There were scars and scrapes all over the fuse-lage, and the proud graffiti that Gordus had sprayed onto his bird was all but erased under the film of hissing, alien sludge. Worst of all, one of the tyranid bio-weapons had latched onto the side stabiliser and its creeping tentacles were already thoroughly entwined around the bank of missile bays on that side.

Despite herself and the frenzy that raged around her, Collia gasped as she realised that the vile xenos creatures had even got to Gordus. As she stared across at the ruined mess of Gordus's fighter, another Fury pulled up on the other side of her, its lascannons flaring with light. It too was similarly damaged and Collia wondered what her own craft looked like from the outside; she couldn't see much of it through the smeared and cracked screens, and the bird's sensor arrays had failed ages ago. It was quite possible, she realised, that she looked just as bad as the others.

WHEN THE POD had dropped out of the launch bay of the *Vanishing Star*, Kalypsia had felt the sudden levity of weightlessness as it floated momentarily in the shadow of the huge Gothic-class cruiser. An instant later, the retro-burners fired and the pod abruptly accelerated into the gravitational pull of Herodian IV. That's when the deafening roar had begun and it had become increasingly loud as the pod had blasted through the planet's fiery atmosphere and screamed down through the dense air beyond.

As soon as the pod broke through the stratosphere, Kalypsia heard the report and chatter of the boltguns that Korpheus had fixed to the shell. There were no portals or view screens in the pod, so she couldn't see what the makeshift defences were shooting at and she was shocked to realise that there were tyranid creatures so high up in the atmosphere. In truth, even if there had been a view screen for her to use, there would have been no way that she could have moved her head to check it – the murderous negative G-forces kept her rigid in her harness, teetering on the edge of consciousness.

With her eyes bulging in their sockets, she chanced a glance around the interior of the pod. Octavius was seated quietly next to her, studying her features carefully. He looked concerned, and then nodded faintly when she looked at him before turning his attention back to his helmet, which was sitting in his lap. He appeared to be making some last minute administrations.

Korpheus was not even in his harness, but was crouched up against one of the walls, running a series of checks against a bank of flashing lights and dials. Ashok sat silently opposite Kalypsia, his un-helmeted head bowed to the ground with his eyes delicately held half-closed. A faint red light seemed to slip out from between his eye-lids and his mouth was working inaudibly in a mutter of litanies. And finally there was Broec, whose elaborate deathmask obscured his face completely. He had planted his Crozius onto the deck between his feet and he had it gripped with both hands in front of himself. His eyes glowed with a fierce blue energy as he stared straight ahead, absolutely motionless.

If she could have moved, Kalypsia would have shaken her head in disbelief. The Marines could have been anywhere; they showed no signs of experiencing the intense discomfort from which she was suffering. From the look of him, it wouldn't even have surprised Kalypsia if Ashok had been asleep – although she knew that Space Marines didn't really need sleep and she was also wary of that red glow under the librarian's hood.

A flurry of heavier impacts punched into the base of the pod, shaking it unevenly and rattling Kalypsia in her modified harness. Had she been unsecured, the impacts would probably have slammed her into a bloody pulp against the floor or one of the interior walls. The Marines swayed slightly, but otherwise showed no sign of having noticed.

But the impacts continued and grew more rapid, as
though they were screeching down through an increasingly dense layer of pulpy, flying obstructions – which
they probably were, she reflected as images of the flapping gargoyles raced back into her mind.

With an abrupt mechanical clunk, the retro-burners on
the bottom of the pod all fired at once, instantly revers-
ing the crushing G-forces in the compartment and
attempting to push Kalypsia's brain down through her
neck. At exactly the moment that she thought her entrails
were going to start seeping out of her toes, the pod
smashed down into the ground with an earth-shattering
crash. The harness holding her into the specially cus-
tomised seat sprang open instantly and Kalypsia
slumped unceremoniously to the ground.

Struggling against the shock and the weight of her own
limbs, Kalypsia looked up from the floor with a trickle of
blood running down from her nose and the corner of
each eye. A blast of humid air gushed into her face as the
exit-ramp dropped out of the wall and she could see the
black boots of the Marines storming down it. A wave of
sound crashed against her, as the cackling, braying and
screeching of the tyranid swarm pierced the suddenly
decompressed pod and the blaze of fire from the Marines
on the exit-ramp erupted into an immediate cacophony
of violence.

A firm grip closed around her shoulder and lifted her
smoothly off the deck, dropping her down onto her feet.

'Are you alright?' asked Octavius from within his helmet, his hand resting for a moment on her shoulder.

She blinked the blood out of her eyes, but the ruptured capillaries kept spilling it like tears. In place of a
reply, she pulled her bolt pistol from its holster and
unclipped her force whip with her other hand. Nodding
curtly, she pushed past the captain and strode out onto
the ramp.

'Let's try not to fail this time, captain,' she called over her shoulder as she stepped outside.

The view that greeted her made her gasp. She had never seen anything like it. The sky was thick with green, noxious clouds which were weeping with toxic rain. It was riddled with the flapping, swooping and cawing forms of gargoyles. But it was the ground that really took her breath away: it was seething with organisms from the base of the ramp all the way out to the horizon. It was a sea of flashing talons, swiping claws and glinting teeth. Scything hormagaunts leapt and sprang in the midst of the swarm, while termagants shrieked and brayed all around them.

Only about a hundred metres away, Kalypsia could see what looked like a rockcrete compound, but it was barely visible, swamped beneath the tyranid ocean. And right in front of her, the three Deathwatch Marines from the pod had ensconced themselves, holding back the almost infinite xenos tide. As she watched them, Octavius stepped past her and vaulted down into the fray, drawing his great two-handed sword as he crashed down onto the backs of a couple of hideous beasts, crushing them under his weight and sweeping his blade into an arc through the thoraxes of three others.

Kalypsia flourished her force whip and levelled her bolt pistol, squeezing off a spray of shells into the swarm to support the Marines. As she did so, an explosion of fire in the sky caught her attention. A second Deathwatch drop-pod came screaming through the cloud layer, its makeshift bolter guns flaring with fire as its bulk splattered through the flapping gargoyles. After a fraction of a second, its retro-burners fired and its flight jolted, slowing fractionally but not enough to prevent a meteoric impact. The pod smashed into the sea of tyranids like an asteroid striking an ocean. The impact shook the ground, liquefying hundreds of tyranids in the explosion of heat and sending the mutilated xenos fluids fountaining into the air.

There was a brief moment of calm as the pod settled into the sand, but then the tyranid swarm recovered and flooded down into the impact crater, scraping and clawing at the adamantium shell.

For about a second, Kalypsia was suddenly concerned that the Marines had not survived the impact, but then hatches sprung open all around it and lashes of autocannon fire sprayed out into the swarm. This was one of the two unmanned Deathwind pods that Korpheus had prepared. He had fitted one with autocannons and the other with frag-missile launchers. They would simply blaze away indiscriminately until they ran out of ammunition – but in the mean time they would certainly help to thin out this swarm.

As she watched, another pod slammed into the seething desert. Immediately, the hatch sprung open and a great gout of flame plumed down the ramp. The hulking form of Neleus stormed through the flames into the swarm of tyranids, rattling shots from his storm bolter and lashing out with his powerfist. Roaring into the sky above him, the sparkling green Assault Marine Soron was already raining frag-grenades and chemical flames into the hive, clearing a passage for the awesome figure of the Terminator below him. A debt of gratitude was certainly owed to Korpheus for getting those two warriors down in one piece.

In rapid succession, two more pods splashed down into the swarming sea. From the first streaked flurries of missiles, arcing out over the braying gaunts and exploding them into fountains of shredded mush. And from the ramp of the second came great gouts of flame and then the glittering figure of Shaidan, who stormed forth with his Mantis Staff spitting with lethal energy, carving a trench through the pressing mass of tyranids as he headed for the rendezvous. As the plume of flame died down, Kalypsia could see the figure of Ruinus standing at the top of the pod's ramp with a smoking flamer in one hand and a coughing bolter in the other.

THROUGH THE SOUP of alien filament that coated the outside of his Fury, Gordus could faintly see the shapes of the other two fighters pulling up alongside him. He had no way of communicating with them and it looked as though they were in no fit state to follow his orders anyway. They seemed to be defying the laws of physics just by hanging together as their oversized engines poured flames into the curdling vacuum behind them.

Most of the members of *Storm Squadron* had covered their Furies in paint, sprawling obscenities from one end to the other or composing crude frescoes depicting the slaughter of the Emperor's enemies. Even through the murky suspension of fluids in the space between them, Gordus could see that the Fury next to him had no such markings and he smiled. Collia had never gone in for all that glitz and rugged glamour. If he had to die today – and it looked like he probably would – he was glad to meet his end with Collia by his side.

Twitching the control stick, Gordus bucked his fighter, flicking a salute to his surviving comrades and gritting his teeth against the anxiety that his bird would fall apart as he did it. The others showed no sign of acknowledgement, but Gordus figured that they were simply being more sensible about the frailty of their crumbling fighters.

'Right,' said Gordus confidently, as though broadcasting to the entire squadron. 'We're going to go in fast, and we're going to go in with everything we've got. Chances are, we won't be coming out again, so let's make this count. We have to get those launch bays open…'

He trailed off as the mock bravado began to grate even on him. In truth, he had rehearsed several speeches for such moments of desperate heroism – he had harboured a secret desire to go down in a blaze of glory. But now, with nobody to hear his gallant last words, he realised that there was a vast chasm between show-boating, heroic speeches and actual heroic acts. With a shiver of fear and self-knowledge, he fought the desire to pull his Fury out of the engagement.

The decision was wrenched out of his hands as Collia's fighter roared away from him, forward along the fuselage of the *Extreme Prejudice*, heading directly for the lattice of liana that stretched over the huge cruiser's launch bays like giant webs, her lascannons pumping out streams of fire into the mire of tyranid organisms in her path.

'Yeah! I'm with you, Collia,' shouted Gordus, gathering his courage into her backwash and kicking his afterburners into life. If they were going to die here, he was sure as hell that she wasn't going to go first.

The three Furies screamed across the body of the *Extreme Prejudice*, with Collia's nose just ahead of the other two, strafing their guns along the tentacles that enwrapped the cruiser below them, powering towards the sealed launch bays. As the range closed, Gordus flicked the switches that activated his missile bays; a chorus of warnings echoed around the cockpit and a pulsing red light started to flash on his control panel. He just laughed – every time he pulled a lever in that decrepit bird something threatened to fall off. This was not the time for automatic caution.

As they banked round the starboard side, rolling their fighters upside down to bring the belly of the *Prejudice* up over their heads, the cavernous launch bays dropped into view in front of them, like the yawning mouths of whales drawing in the space detritus in constant and aching hunger. Like colossal retainers, huge webs of barbed tentacles reached out across the bay mouths, preventing anything from getting off the deck inside. The lascannon batteries that ran around the perimeter of the bays, like venomous fangs, spluttered and spat lasfire in random patterns in front of them, but the angles were all wrong and they could not be turned all the way back into the bay mouths that they were supposed to defend. The cruiser's defences had been designed with a full-on assault in mind, not with the creeping menace of tyranid tentacles and foul, toxic, xenos liana.

Collia found the angle first and Gordus watched the missiles streak out of the banks on both sides of her Fury, leaving spiralling trails as they homed in on the alien foliage ahead of them. After a few hypersonic seconds, the missiles punched into the xenos web, detonating instantly and sending huge plumes of flame spraying out of the impacts. A second later, another flurry of missiles slammed home, loosed from the fighter on the other side of Collia.

Even from this distance, and even through the smeary mess of his viewer, Gordus could see that the missiles had not broken through. The vines had thinned, burnt and recoiled from the impacts, but the bays were still effectively sealed. This was his chance for glory.

He held the aiming reticule steady and then punched the missile release, letting out a yell of fatalistic satisfaction.

But nothing happened.

He thumbed the trigger again and again, but still there was nothing. Looking out the side of his cockpit, he saw one of the Furies peeling away from him. The other seemed to hesitate for a second, but then it tipped its nose in salute before diving out of sight. Collia was saying goodbye, realised Gordus.

He snapped his head back to the other side, craning his neck to see the missile bays that ran along the length of the portside stabilisers. Even through the muck he could see the flames dancing around the warheads. Evidently, his warning sirens had been right this time.

Shrugging a smirk onto his face, Gordus teased the last bit of power out of the Fury's engine and gunned it towards the hastily recovering web of vines and tentacles. He imagined the broad, grinning smile that blazed from the back of his Fury as it roared towards its death. At least somebody was going to see this, he thought, as his fighter ploughed into the sinuous foliage and the missiles detonated.

THE KILL-TEAM had to wade through the pulped remains of dead creatures as they drove forwards towards their rendezvous point. The desert was soaked with alien blood and a trail of corpses crunched under their feet as they hacked and blasted their way through the pressing horde. There was nowhere else for the dead to fall other than under the feet of the living and the dying and the sodden ground was all but invisible beneath them.

Ashok and Shaidan fought side by side at the head of the team, great sheets of warp energy jousting from their fingers and staffs. Ruinus and Octavius flanked Kalypsia on both sides, fending off the gnashing fangs and swiping talons of the mass. And at the rear came Broec and Korpheus, crackling with energy and lashing out into the horde as it closed in behind the little Deathwatch bubble. The scale of the opposition was astronomical, but the team ploughed on as though undaunted, taking each talon, tooth and claw in turn. They were a burning ring of blue fire in a sea of shimmering scales and the glints of soulless, evil eyes.

Wading through the arachnid sea from the east came the striding figure of Neleus, crushing termagants under his immense boots and smashing through the skulls of leaping hormagaunts with his powerfist, his storm bolter coughing a continuous barrage. Roaring over his head, spraying fire down into the roiling sea and raining grenades into the seething mass, hovered Soron with his jump-pack flaring gloriously against the dirty green sky.

The two groups converged as they reached the outer perimeter of the rockcrete compound and they rapidly fanned out into a cresent with Kalypsia sheltered in the middle, shielded between the Marines and the wall. Soron poured flames around her as he hovered above. The inquisitor was flashing her head from side to side, as though looking for something.

'Where to?' called Octavius over the din, as he fended off waves of talons with his great sword.

Kalypsia hesitated.

'Where to, inquisitor?' Ashok repeated the captain's question and turned his burning eyes to face her, without letting up his assault against the swarm. 'Where is your hive tyrant?'

Kalypsia could not meet the librarian's gaze. 'Inside!' she yelled, cracking her whip between Ruinus and Broec, shattering the carapace of a leaping gaunt. 'We need to get inside this compound.'

Octavius nodded briskly, scanning it, looking for some sign of an entrance into the rockcrete edifice. There was something strangely familiar about the structure and for a moment he found it odd that Kalypsia had not mentioned its presence before the drop. He couldn't see anything through the jungle of claws and bony limbs.

'Soron,' hissed Octavius through the crackling and intermittent vox. 'Do you have a visual on an entrance?'

His own voice echoed back into his ear-piece, broken and spluttering as though it came from the throat of a dying man. Then a sharp whine made him wince and the voice of Soron burst loudly into his helmet.

'West side. Completely overrun. Breach in the wall.'

As the Assault Marine spoke, his jump-pack burned brighter and he roared off towards the breach, raining grenades into the swarm around the wall as he went, clearing the suggestion of a path for the rest of the team. Neleus responded at once, stepping out of the crescent formation and smashing his way into the brief clearing created by the first blast, holding it open long enough for the others to fall in behind him and then ploughing forward with his powerfist buzzing and his stormbolter raging.

Octavius swung his blade in a steep upward arc, slicing an alien creature vertically in two. Then, following the line of his blade, he saw Soron blazing in the sky like an emerald angel of death. He had run out of frag-grenades and his flamer had died. Instead, he was holding a spluttering chainsword in both hands and was hacking it into the scrambling talons of the gargoyles that swooped and pestered him from all sides. He spun and rolled in the air, as though defying gravity itself in his determination to fulfil his duty to the Emperor.

'Something's coming,' hissed the voice of Korpheus, making Octavius drop his gaze back into the organic sea. 'Something big.'

But Octavius could see nothing other than the endless swarm of glinting xenos animals covering the desert.

'There,' said Korpheus, tapping the captain on his shoulder and pointing back up into the sky.

It couldn't have been much more than a speck when Korpheus's razor-eyes had spotted it, but it was growing steadily and rapidly larger as it sped towards them.

'What is it?' asked Octavius, straining his eyes into the dark cloud as it grew inexorably nearer.

'Zoanthropes!' yelled Kalypsia, pointing out into the sea of ground-gaunts to the south, and dragging Octavius's attention away from the sky for a moment.

'I'll take care of them,' said Ashok calmly, incinerating a brood of termagants with a javelin of power from his hand and thrusting his staff through the throat of another.

About a hundred metres away, three slithering, serpentine zoanthropes were sliding through the bristling and jagged sea towards them, coruscating with power and crackling with purple lightning. They were pulsing unevenly, but there appeared to be some kind of orchestration behind their movements, as though they shared a common purpose.

Before even Ashok could act, Shaidan spun his Mantis Staff into a blur of energy, decapitating a line of gaunts with its bayonet-blades and then levelled it at one of the tyranid psykers. A bolt of warp energy lashed out of the staff and flashed across the sea, ramming into the lead zoanthrope with an explosion of light.

Meanwhile, the dark cloud in the sky had closed on them, and Korpheus could clearly see that it was made up of dozens of gargoyles. They were flapping and swooping in a dizzying mist around a huge winged beast in their midst; its belly was writhing with hideous clusters of the smaller creatures, which seemed to have hooked in between its chitinous armoured plates.

With a great screech, the soaring harridan dipped its huge head and dove down towards the kill-team, monstrous scythes dropping down from the underside of its wings as it shrieked and cawed, leaving the flock of gargoyles flapping in wild excitement in the sky behind it.

Korpheus was the first to react, lifting the bulk of his heavy bolter and loosing a stream of inferno bolts directly into the path of the plunging beast. The shells burst into flames as they impacted against the harridan's scales and it brayed defiantly, ploughing through the fire with its glowering red eyes burning.

'Incoming!' yelled the Techmarine, planting his feet and driving the powered ammunition feed through his weapon's chamber, spraying a continuous inferno into the diving monster.

Behind him, the rest of the team were too busy to react to his warnings: triple streams of warp energy gushed out of the zoanthropes and smashed against the blazing forms of Shaidan and Ashok, while Broec and Ruinus fended off the pressing tide. Octavius had joined Neleus in the vanguard, hacking a path towards the breach through the cackling gaunts and Kalypsia stood just behind them, cracking her whip and punching out bolter shells into anything that threatened to break through their advance.

The harridan shrieked as it swooped down and glided towards them, its huge scything talons dragging great gouges out of the swarm below it, churning up the desert as it approached. As the range closed, two bio-cannons suspended under its forty metre wingspan spluttered into life, vomiting streams of venom towards the Marines.

And Korpheus's inferno shells just burst impotently off the beast's scaly armour. He yelled in defiance, willing his weapon into frenzies of destructive power, but it was no good. The harridan was less than twenty metres away, and it would devastate the already stretched team.

Despite the ineffectiveness of his weapon, Korpheus refused to back down. Dropping the heavy bolter to the ground, he tugged his chainsword free of its holster and ripped it into life, setting his feet ready to meet the inrushing creature. As he did so, a ball of fire rocketed down out of the sky and pummelled into the back of the harridan, smashing it out of its flight path and sending it tumbling into the sea of gaunts.

As Korpheus watched, he saw the figure of Soron stand out of the crash with his chainsword held high, like an emerald beacon in the alien ocean. He yelled something inaudible and then plunged his sword down into the back of the giant creature, which flapped and struggled under the onslaught, squealing and screeching with pain and frustration. After a couple of seconds, the flapping stopped, and Soron stood majestically with his arms stretched out by his sides. His jump-pack had been ruined by the impact and his chainsword was lost somewhere in the interior of the dead harridan. After a dramatic second, a brood of gargoyles dove down at him, spraying him with bio-plasma and hacking at his armour with their claws. He fought them with his hands until they overwhelmed him with strength of numbers, lifting him off his feet and hauling him into the air like carrion in the clutches of vultures.

A few seconds later, high up in the sky, as the cloud of gargoyles gathered around the harridan-slayer, Soron unclipped his last weapon, a plasma-grenade, from his belt and thumbed its detonator. The air convulsed into a sphere of superheated energy, exploding outwards and incinerating all organic matter within a hundred metre radius, leaving a miniature star hanging in the air where the Mantis Warrior had just been.

CHAPTER EIGHT:
CATACOMBS

[10 Hours Remaining]

NELEUS CRUNCHED HIS powerfist into the mouth of a hormagaunt that stabbed through the crack between the closing doors, shattering its skull and throwing its weight back into the path of the tyranids that pressed up behind it. Simultaneously, Korpheus punched the door release again and the last residue of the brilliant white light from Soron's plasma sphere was finally shut out. The heavy adamantium doors crashed together, shaking the rockcrete floor and silencing the ravenous horde outside. After less than a second, however, the frantic scraping and scratching of claws against metal could be heard.

'It will not hold them forever, captain,' conceded Korpheus, turning to Octavius in the cramped, near-darkness of the service tunnel. 'And I am sure that there must be other ways into this place.'

It had been Kalypsia who had spotted the reinforced door-panel in the exterior wall of the compound. The team had ground to a halt in the mass of foul xenos organisms outside; the numbers were just too great, even for the Deathwatch and for a few moments it had looked as though they were not going to make it. But in the sudden light of Soron's heroic end, Kalypsia had seen the glint of metal under layers of corrosive slime and ichor in the rockcrete wall. Korpheus had found a way to break the seal and the team had dived for cover just as their resistance had threatened to be overwhelmed.

'It will hold them for now, Korpheus,' muttered Octavius as he scanned the passageway for possible threats. 'And that will be enough.' He seemed to spot something in the darkness, and he stalked off into the tunnel to check it out, flicking a sign over his shoulder that the others should hold their positions.

'It was most fortunate that this bunker was here, wasn't it, inquisitor?' hissed Ashok. His eyes shimmered with a fathomless black in the darkness, framed with wisps of red flame.

Again, Kalypsia did not meet his gaze. 'Indeed,' she said, holstering her pistol and looking around.

'Korpheus,' called Octavius from further down the tunnel. 'What do you make of this?'

As the Techmarine strode off towards Octavius, Ashok dropped his voice into a whisper. 'You knew this place was here, inquisitor – is there anything else that you should be telling us? I have never heard of a hive tyrant hiding out in a rockcrete bunker.'

'This is an unusual hive-splinter, librarian. It has not behaved according to precedent yet. Why should we assume that it will start now?' replied Kalypsia with elegantly controlled anger. She took a couple of steps towards him and stared straight up into his face. 'The Inquisition sees to it that I know more than you, soldier. That's why I am in command. The pattern of the hive points here, so here we are.'

Ashok's eyes narrowed slightly, contracting the miniature black holes that stared down at the inquisitor. 'You
are in command,' he repeated ambiguously.

FURTHER DOWN THE corridor, almost invisible in their black
armour, except for the bursts of colour on their shoulder
plates, Octavius and Korpheus were inspecting the way
forward; they had found a structural flaw in the wall.

'Any idea what this place is, Korpheus?' asked Octavius.

'Did the Mantis Warriors or the inquisitor say anything
about an Imperial facility on Herodian IV?'

'Imperial facility?' Octavius raised an eyebrow in his
helmet.

'Yes, those doors had an old Imperial imprint on the
lock, and this corridor was constructed out of standard
fixtures,' explained the Techmarine. 'It's a pretty old pattern, but it looks like a small Imperial compound to me.'

'We need to know what we're dealing with here,' sighed
Octavius. 'Things are taxing enough already.'

The captain ran his hand over the uneven wall-panel
thoughtfully. Then, suddenly taking hold of the corner of
the loose panel with his gauntlet, Octavius pulled. The
metal buckled and began to tear and the Deathwatch
captain ripped it clear with a sweep of his arm, throwing
it clattering to the ground in the corridor. Beneath the
panel was a scratched and beaten section of wall, with an
atrophied icon still faintly visible in the dim light.

Octavius and Korpheus exchanged glances.

Pressing his fingers up against the textured image,
Octavius traced the uneven shape. It was roughly circular
and about the size and shape of a cog-wheel. Inset in the
middle was the impression of a head; half of it looked
vaguely like a skull while the other half was covered in
augmentations and cybernetics. It had been scraped clear
of colour and the metal was cracked, but it was clearly the
insignia of the Adeptus Mechanicus.

'Mechanicus?' asked Korpheus, studying the image over Octavius's shoulder.

'So it seems,' replied the captain softly, casting his eyes back along the corridor to where the rest of the team were waiting. Ashok was looming over Kalypsia, and she seemed to be whispering something to him. The two surviving Mantis Warriors appeared to be muttering to each other while Neleus stood guard at the doorway and Broec stood broodingly against the wall, surveying the others through the gleaming visor of his deathmask.

'There were a few Mechanicus survivors on the *Vanishing Star*, Korpheus,' murmured Octavius, keeping his voice low.

'Have the Mechanicus been informed?' asked Korpheus.

'Not as far as I'm aware.'

Octavius stared at the icon as his thoughts slipped back to the huge medicae-hall on the *Vanishing Star*. He could clearly see the mutilated body and face of the dead Mechanicus 'survivor' to whom the pottering servitor had led him. 'Another suicide,' had been her words when she had seen the gash across the man's throat and the dagger lying on the sheets next to his hand. But that dagger had been left *under* the sheets. Something was not right here, and Octavius did not like to be kept in the dark.

'Keep your eyes open, Korpheus,' said Octavius, turning to face the Techmarine directly and laying a gauntlet onto his shoulder. 'I don't like this at all.' Without turning, the captain raised his arm and beckoned to the others at the end of the corridor.

THE PASSAGEWAYS ECHOED with metallic footfalls as the team pushed forwards into the compound. The service tunnel was narrow and cramped, clearly not designed with the bulk of Space Marines in mind. Neleus, in his ancient Terminator armour, was constantly hunching and stooping to avoid ventilation shafts and power fixtures on the ceiling, but he kept time with the rest of the group, protecting its rear with his bulk and the promise of awesome weaponry. Raven Guard Korpheus had disappeared off ahead, scouting through the labyrinthine corridors for signs of the enemy.

Since the adamantium doors had crashed closed, they had not seen even a single tyranid. The interior of the compound appeared to be completely deserted, and it echoed as though it had been empty for years. After the frenzy of the scene outside, the eerie quiet of the shadowy corridors put everyone on edge – everyone except Kalypsia. She had pushed to the front of the team, elbowing Ashok and Shaidan aside to take up a position next to Octavius; her force whip was coiled and clipped to her belt and, although it was drawn, her bolt pistol hung casually at her side.

Octavius held his arm out to the side to stop Kalypsia as the team neared the end of the service tunnel. Up ahead, the passageway spilled out into a large chamber, which appeared to be a junction room of some kind; five or six other tunnels emptied into the space from other directions. There was a sequence of glow orbs set into the walls between the mouths of the corridors and each glowed faintly, pulsing slightly as though they were running on the last remnants of emergency power.

Silently, Octavius edged towards the end of the tunnel, pressing himself up against the sidewall to minimise the line of sight from the chamber ahead. Peering round the corner, he could see that the large, circular room was basically empty. It contained some metal crates stacked up against the walls, with some strewn haphazardly across the floor, as though thrown down in a hurry – perhaps to provide cover. The walls themselves were pock-marked with bullet holes and streaked with venom scars and a couple of craters yawned in the floor where grenades had detonated.

But there were no bodies – neither human nor tyranid. There was not even any blood. There had clearly been a fire-fight here – and a big one, if the structural damage was anything to go by – but there was no sign of any casualties. It was as though the place had been licked clean after the combat.

Before Octavius could decide how to proceed, Kalypsia pushed past him into the chamber, striding confidently into its heart and scanning the mouths of the other corridors for some sign of where to go next. Following after her, Ashok drew up to the captain's shoulder and then paused, realising that he should not overstep Octavius.

'We're in a bit of a hurry, captain,' Kalypsia called back over her shoulder. 'No time for cow…' she trailed off, thinking better of using the first word that came to mind. 'No time for such caution,' she said, smirking.

'It is better to be cautious than dead,' retorted Octavius levelly, as he walked into the chamber, holstering his sword with a flourish.

'But it is better to be dead than to fail,' nodded Ashok, staring at the inquisitor with his unblinking eyes. For the first time that day, he found himself agreeing with her. It wasn't his way to creep around in the shadows like an assassin or a Raven Guard.

'It is better not to fail,' countered Broec, glaring at the Angels Sanguine librarian, his whispered voice amplified through the array in his deathmask. 'The Emperor protects the righteous, not the foolhardy.'

A sound in one of the corridors made the team spin, bracing their weapons instantly and dropping into a disciplined defensive formation. Behind the team loomed Neleus, with his storm bolter trained on the tunnel mouth. Ruinus stood at his shoulder with his flamer in one hand and bolter in the other. Alongside Broec, Ashok drove the end of his staff into the ground, sending up little sparks of preparedness, while Octavius stepped up to the edge of the tunnel with his sword held vertically in both hands at his shoulder.

Something shifted in the darkness of the corridor, and the team bristled in readiness for the alien onslaught. Octavius lifted his blade and waited for something to stick its head out, poised to make the first kill. It had been too quiet to be true, after all. He could hear the faint shuffle of movement and he started to bring his blade down in a smooth arc, timing his blow to coincide with the emergence of the first beast.

The ancient force sword flashed through the darkness, leaving a trail of shimmering energy in its wake, and then it stopped dead, poised less than a millimetre from the neck of Korpheus as the Techmarine froze on the point of springing out of the passageway. He looked up into the barrels of the Deathwatch guns and saw the cackling energy dancing around the menacing figures of Ashok and Broec.

'I'm glad you are on my side,' he said, unclasping his helmet and standing to his feet. 'Is my vox-unit the only one that doesn't work, or have you had problems too?' He dug his hand into the helmet and started to prod around inside, pre-empting questions about why he hadn't made contact from the tunnel.

The team rechambered their weapons, but the energy field that danced around Ashok lingered for a few seconds, as his burning red eyes gradually faded back to black.

Nobody had tried their ear-beads since entering the compound, and a quick check revealed that they had all failed. There had been a constant chatter and hiss in their heads since they made planet-fall and they suddenly realised that this had been a disturbance in their minds, not in their voxes; the hive mind had been licking at the edges of their consciousness before they had even noticed.

'It's the hive,' said Shaidan from the other side of the chamber.

Octavius realised for the first time that the Mantis Warrior librarian had not been part of their defensive formation when Korpheus had leapt into the room. He turned to find him standing alone on the far side of the wide chamber, his helmet already discarded on the ground next to him and his long black hair glinting in the faint light.

'The hive cannot disrupt conventional technologies, only psychic communication,' snapped Kalypsia curtly. 'I have told you this before.' She narrowed her eyes and took a couple of steps towards the librarian. 'What are you doing over there on your own, soldier?'

The other Marines followed her gaze but said nothing. They all wanted to know the answer to her question. None of them had worked with Mantis Warriors before, and they had so far suppressed their unspoken suspicions.

'You're wrong, inquisitor,' said Shaidan, unperturbed. 'This hive is different. I don't know how it does it, but it can block our communications. Perhaps its psychic shadow works on the communication centres in our brains, or perhaps it simply has control over some kind of blocking technology.'

'They're just animals–' began Kalypsia, ready with her standard response.

'How do you know this, librarian?' asked Broec, cutting in and spitting that last word with more than his usual disdain. He was weighing up the balance: would it be worse if this Mantis Warrior was lying to them, or if he was telling the truth?

'Because... because I have been here before,' confessed Shaidan.

* * *

KALYPSIA RAISED AN eyebrow and walked slowly towards the librarian. 'What did you say?' she hissed, her voice full of venom. 'You've been *in here* before?' He had not mentioned that to her in the debriefing.

Shaidan just stared back at her, his bright green eyes blinking in a sudden gust of moist wind that blew into the chamber and his long hair wavering delicately. As the inquisitor advanced, his eyes seemed to lose their focus on her. Slowly, he revolved his Mantis Staff from one side to the other, spinning it naturally in his hands as though it were merely an extension of his limbs. As he did so, he caught the sudden suggestion of readiness from the rest of the Deathwatch, as though they feared that he would strike Kalypsia, perhaps driven mad by the constant background chattering of the hive mind that they had all been subconsciously fighting to shut out since they made planet-fall. Even his battle-brother Ruinus twitched his bolter in an instinctive reaction.

The trace of an ironic smile crept onto Shaidan's face as he realised that the Deathwatch team still didn't really trust the Mantis Warriors. Since the briefing aboard the *Vanishing Star*, he had known that Kalypsia had some reservations, but he had hoped that the Marines would be above such things. Had they not seen Soron's end?

Another breath of humid air caressed his face.

A piercing scream echoed around the metallic chamber and an intense javelin of blue flame lanced out of Shaidan's staff, streaking across the room and singeing Kalypsia's cloak as she dropped to the ground. The energy blast smashed straight into the abdomen of a monstrous, shrieking serpent, catching it in mid-flight and throwing it back into the mouth of the passage from which it had just emerged. Its two huge foretalons thrashed against the metal walls and its elongated tail flailed wildly as it struggled to rear its ugly head, bringing its fangs to bear with a saliva-drenched hiss. With another twitch of its tail, the creature lurched forward again at lightning speed, its snake-like body jerking and flashing so fast that the Marines could hardly see it.

Another huge pulse of blue energy smashed into the ravener-creature, sending power coruscating through its writhing body and lighting it up like an x-ray. After a fraction of a second, the rest of the Deathwatch team turned and opened up with their weapons, riddling the beast with bolter shells from close range, but Shaidan was already upon it. Holding his staff out in front of him, pumping out a continuous stream of energy that held the ravener suspended off the ground, he charged forward and vaulted over the prone form of Kalypsia, slamming into the beast and driving the bayonet blade on his Mantis Staff straight down through the top of the creature's skull.

Marine and ravener careened to the ground in a blaze of flickering blue. The unnatural fire gradually flashed and faded, leaving Shaidan to stand away from the smoking remains of the dead tyranid, wiping the creature's toxic blood from his dripping staff.

'Raveners,' said Octavius, already scanning the other passages for signs of more. 'These things rarely hunt alone. We need to get moving. Which way, inquisitor?'

Kalypsia said nothing; she was looking around the chamber as though trying to orientate herself. She didn't know which way to go.

'Which way?' insisted Octavius. With no reply, he turned to Korpheus. 'What did you see down there?' He pointed down the passage from which the ravener had slithered – the same corridor from which Korpheus had emerged earlier.

'Nothing, captain. Just empty corridors. Much the same as these,' replied Korpheus, casting his arm around the chamber to indicate what he meant. 'Certainly no sign of a hive tyrant.'

'Well, there is something going on down here,' intoned Ashok, slowly moving his glance from Kalypsia to Shaidan and back again.

'Which way?' said Octavius again, this time turning to Shaidan. They may not know why the librarian had been in the compound before, but right now they just needed to know where the hell they were going.

'The centre of the compound is this way,' replied the Mantis Warrior librarian, already breaking into a run towards a corridor on the far side. 'If the inquisitor is right and the tyranids are using this place as a brood-nest, that's where we'll find our tyrant.'

Just as Shaidan reached the other side of the chamber, a cacophony of shrill calls bounced and echoed their way through the feeder corridors. The caustic scraping of claws and scales on metal rang through the air, and the Deathwatch team snapped into motion, dashing off in the wake of Shaidan. Neleus and Ruinus held the rear guard, stalking backwards through the chamber and scanning their weapons through the space, waiting for anything to move.

The team were all in the corridor by the time the raveners poured into the circular chamber. There must have been twenty of them, flicking and flashing around the space, shattering the crates as their tails thrashed in frustration. Neleus opened up with his storm bolter and Ruinus flooded the chamber with chemical fire from the tunnel's entrance.

As one, the heads of the raveners snapped round to face the two Deathwatch Marines, spotting them for the first time. Like huge armoured water-snakes, the creatures flicked their tails and lurched towards them, beady eyes simmering with bestial rage, sliding through the hail of fire that the Marines pumped in their direction.

Ruinus dropped his overheated flamer to the ground and threw his bolter out into the writhing advance. He unclasped his helmet and placed it at his feet, shaking out his long black hair. Then he reached down to his belt and unclipped a chain of krak-grenades in one hand and a chain of frag-grenades in the other. Running his fingers along the lengths of each chain, he primed them all at once.

'Get out of here, Neleus,' he said calmly, pushing his way in front of the huge Terminator, cutting off his firing line. 'I will have my redemption in the fires of hell.' Without redemption, even the precious gene-seed of the Mantis Warriors was worthless.

Neleus hesitated for a moment. Then, resolute, he nodded and turned.

'For Redemption! For the Mantis Warriors! For the Emperor!' cried Ruinus as he launched the grenades into the seething chamber of charging raveners. There was a faint clink and clatter as they hit the ground, and then a colossal explosion as they detonated, filling the chamber with flames and monomolecular shrapnel-fragments. The concussion wave blew outwards from the centre of the room, blasting plumes of fire and heat down each of the feeder passages, chasing at the heels of the storming Neleus.

For a brief instant, Ruinus could see the serpentine aliens bucking and thrashing in the inferno. But then Ruinus's discarded bolter reached critical temperature and its remaining shells detonated randomly, spraying the chamber with a fury of explosive shells, riddling the already lacerated and melting raveners with lashes of lethal ballistics.

OCTAVIUS STEPPED BEHIND Kalypsia and lifted her off her feet, shielding her from the flood of fire that roared down through the corridor behind them. The flames washed around the shimmering black armour of the Deathwatch Marines, bathing them in oranging light.

As the flames dissipated, Neleus came striding up through the corridor, the thudding of his heavy boots announcing his arrival long before he got there.

'Ruinus?' asked Octavius, placing the inquisitor back on the ground as he turned to face the huge White Consul.

Neleus shook his head minutely, expressing efficient remorse for the lost warrior. Then the huge Marine turned to Shaidan and, without a word, he held out his hand. He was holding the blackened helmet of Ruinus, a battle-brother of the Praying Mantidae.

The librarian stared at it for a moment, his mind suddenly flooded with memories of the Devastator Marine. He had known both Soron and Ruinus for decades. They had been seconded into the Praying Mantidae at the same time, shortly after the confusions of the badab Wars, and had subsequently been promoted into the Second Company together. With Captain Audin himself, they were amongst the most decorated Marines in the Mantis Warriors and now they were both gone. None were more deserving of the Emperor's forgiveness, and none could have given more in his service.

Shaidan took the helmet from Neleus and touched it to his forehead, muttering a whispered prayer under his breath. Then he set it carefully on the ground at his feet. Taking half a step back, he suddenly yelled out and stamped forward, bringing his Mantis Staff down onto the crest of the helmet, shattering it in a burst of blue fire and incinerating the fragments before they could even scatter.

'May the Emperor grant your redemption,' he said finally, bowing his head for a moment and hiding his eyes under a cascade of black hair.

While the others watched in silence, Neleus stepped forward and laid a heavy gauntlet on Shaidan's shoulder. 'He died well.'

Despite himself, Chaplain Broec felt obliged to say something. He had no love for this psyker and his puritan's heart was full of suspicion about the integrity of the Mantis Warriors, but both Ruinus and Soron had died like true warriors and he was not such a fool that he could not recognise that.

'The Emperor's light is everywhere. He will see that they died for him,' he murmured, his voice hissing through the sub-amplifier in his deathmask.

'They will be commended, when we get out of here,' said Octavius, conscious that they were wasting time. 'But first we have to find this hive tyrant.' The captain took a couple of purposeful steps further down the passageway, trying to draw the team onwards.

'Where's your librarian?' asked Kalypsia, looking up the corridor past Octavius and then back in the direction of the chamber from which they'd just come. There was no sign of Ashok.

Abruptly, Shaidan flicked his head round and stared up the passageway. His emerald green eyes were running with blood and his pale face had turned completely white. The intricate tattoos around his neck snaked and swam, as though they were alive. In revulsion, Broec recoiled from the Mantis Warrior, bringing his Crozius up between them as though fending off a vampire.

An explosion sounded up ahead, and a gust of light blew down through the corridor. The air smelled burnt and decaying, and it prickled as it caressed Kalypsia's skin. The Marines felt the sphincter implants in their tracheas kick in, redirecting the toxic air to their third-lungs, where the toxins would be filtered out of the air before they could poison their blood. But there was a chattering of voices suspended in the breeze that no organs could silence.

'That's Ashok,' said Shaidan, nodding his head along the corridor as a wave of nausea crashed into his mind.

Octavius drew his sword and started to pound down the passage towards the sounds of battle, shutting his mind to the chattering insanity that picked at his brain, louder and more forceful than ever before. The others drew in behind him, leaving Shaidan and Kalypsia standing in the corridor in their wake.

'What's going on here?' asked Shaidan, turning his bloody eyes on Kalypsia as he shifted his staff into his other hand, ready to leave.

The inquisitor looked up at the librarian with blood pouring down out of her own pale grey eyes. 'You tell me, Mantis Warrior. You're the one who's been here before.'

As Octavius sprinted through the corridors, their character began to change. The sparse, dry and almost clinically clean passageways of the outer reaches of the compound rapidly gave way to humid, dank spaces further within. At first the metal floors started to become slippery, as moisture condensed and settled onto their smooth surfaces and sheened them into ice-like channels. Further in, thick and ichorous substances started to weep down the walls, oozing in treacle like globules. All the time, the temperature and humidity was rising steadily, as though Octavius was ploughing his way deeper into a rainforest.

Here and there, strewn erratically throughout the corridors, Octavius could see the twitching forms of dismembered limbs, cracked talons and rotting tyranid organisms. Ashok had clearly blazed his way through these passages as though possessed. As he drew closer to the riotous sounds of combat up ahead, Octavius had to start kicking his way through piles of detritus and charred xenos flesh.

Pounding around a corner, Octavius skidded to a halt in a short but wide chamber. It must have been a form of observation room; the far wall appeared to be made of glass – although it was now smeared with ichor and xenos resin – and on the other side of it Octavius could see a laboratory of some kind. However, in the middle of the room was the glowing figure of Ashok. His staff was a whirl of blue fire as he swirled his body and spun his weapon with passionate intensity. Surrounding him on three sides where the slippery shapes of zoanthropes, spitting gouts of warp energy and hissing through bared teeth.

Ashok didn't even seem to notice the arrival of the Deathwatch captain and even from the entranceway Octavius could see the brilliant red fires burning in the librarian's eyes. The Angel Sanguine was lost in the rage of battle.

The zoanthropes cackled and keened, ducking under the blows from the librarian's staff and sliding around his blasts of psychic energy. They peppered him with bouts of purple fire, but he sliced through each flame with elegant parries from his weapon, dissipating the chaotic forces before they could reach him.

One of the tyranid sorcerers spluttered and coughed, then started to scream through its jagged teeth. The sound instantly filled the narrow room, echoing and ric-ocheting off the treacle-coated metal walls, amplifying itself in the enclosed acoustic space. At once, the other two zoanthropes joined the first, hacking out their screams whilst spluttering rains of warp blasts at the fren-zied figure of Ashok in their midst.

Octavius had only just had time to digest the events in the room and was on the point of launching himself into the fray when the screams pierced his head, scraping against the inside of his mind like talons through his flesh. He reeled, staggering backwards under the unex-pected and invisible onslaught, reaching up to his head with one hand in a reflex reaction. As he tripped, two strong hands caught him from behind and held him up.

Ashok himself faltered for only a fraction of a second, then shook his head rapidly, as though to throw out the invading sounds and ploughed back into the melee. But now he was not alone. Shaidan paused for a second to make sure that Octavius was conscious and then charged into the battle. Somehow he had caught and overtaken the other members of the Deathwatch kill-team who had set off before him, streaking past them in the slippery corridors as though his feet did not even touch the ground. He had felt the keening of the zoanthropes before the others and he had known that not even Ashok could stand against them alone for long. As their psychic screams had crashed down the corridor, breaking against the sprinting Marines, only Shaidan and Kalypsia had been unaffected, as they closed their sanctioned, trained minds to the horrors of the hive. The hive mind threatened psykers more than anyone else, since the attuned mind was more vulnerable to attack, but it would take more than an alien shriek to send a Deathwatch librarian staggering into insanity.

Shaidan dropped the tip of his Mantis Staff against the floor, letting a pulse of blue energy arc out through the metal panels and singe the belly of one of the zoanthropes. When the beast turned to see him, he was already in the air. He flipped his weight over his staff, using it to pole-vault through the intervening space, dragging it up behind him and thrusting it out like a lance. The zoanthrope turned just in time to see Shaidan push the bayonet-tipped staff straight through its face, exploding its head in a fountain of psychic fire.

The remaining creatures brayed hideously, lashing their tails and snarling at the two librarians, but an immense bank of firepower punched into the side of one of them, shredding it under the concentrated tirade. The rest of the Deathwatch team fanned out from the entranceway of the corridor, their weapons blazing at the ruined zoanthrope.

Meanwhile, Ashok slammed his staff against the side of the last beast's head, stunning it momentarily. He stepped in, closing the distance, before smashing his fist into its face and then springing around behind it. He clung his arms around its head and let out a war-cry that the others had never heard before. A visible convulsion of power pulsed through his body and burst out of his arms, exploding the creature's head and its upper body into a hissing rain of molten flesh.

The Angels Sanguine librarian crashed to the ground on top of the horrendously disfigured corpse, driving his fists into its remains and reducing them to a pulp. He pounded the putrid flesh over and over, as though in a frenzy.

'It's over, Ashok,' said Octavius, reaching out to calm the librarian while the rest of the team secured the chamber. But Ashok did not respond.

'Ashok!' called Octavius, standing over his crouching battle-brother.

With a sudden movement that Octavius could do nothing about, Ashok sprang to his feet, revolving his staff in a tight circle at his side and bringing its tip arcing down towards the captain's head. In a flash, Shaidan's staff intercepted Ashok's and Broec leapt forward to separate the Angel Sanguine from Octavius.

There was a long moment as Ashok struggled to free his staff from the binds of Shaidan's and his flaming red eyes stared uncomprehendingly at the elaborate death-mask of the chaplain. Octavius stood his ground, unflinching, watching the insatiable fires in Ashok's soul gradually relent, as his eyes began to fade and return to black. After a couple of seconds the others could see the tension drop out of Ashok; he closed his eyes, withdrew his staff and bowed his head, hiding his features under the deep shade of his hood.

'Captain,' called Korpheus from the entrance to the laboratory on the other side of the glass wall. 'You should take a look at this.'

THE LABORATORY WAS circular, with pristine, concave metal walls. It was almost devoid of features; there were no work benches and the walls were smooth and virtually featureless. The entire room shone with the gleam of clean metal, cutting the squalid, ichor-filled corridors outside into sharp relief.

The only object in the laboratory was an elaborate and delicate-looking chair in the very centre. It was a confusion of pipes and tubes, wires and lights, claws and teeth. Half submerged beneath the curving enclosures that rose out of the chair's arms and back, a broken, haggard, and emaciated man sat slouched, with his face contorted in what might have been agony. A jumble of dark cloth was wrapped round his shoulders, but his head had slumped forward out of the cloak's heavy hood. His eyes were closed, and there was no sign of life.

Although the surrounding corridors had been thick with ichor, decay and xenos pheromones, there was no sign that the tyranids had been in this room – not even the faintest trace of their noxious breath in the air. Nonetheless, the Deathwatch team fanned out around the perimeter of the room, securing the space as Kalypsia strode in from the viewing chamber outside.

Despite herself, the inquisitor gasped slightly when she saw the old man in the ornate chair. Her eyes narrowed and the faintest hint of a smile licked at her lips. She walked up to the complicated structure and circled around it, enjoying being at the centre of everyone's attention once again.

After walking around the artefact a couple of times, peering into its labyrinthine structure, Kalypsia paused in front of the man and reached out her hand. Gingerly, as though not entirely sure that the man was dead, she touched her fingers to his neck. His skin was cold and clammy, and her touch seemed to penetrate all the way through to his spinal column, as though there was no flesh under the skin, but there was the faintest hint of a pulse. He was still alive. As she withdrew her hand, she caught the edge of the cloak that was draped around the man's shoulders and it fell into his lap, revealing two talon-like spikes piercing through his collar bones. The tips of the spikes were gleaming and white, as though they had been polished and there was no hint of blood around the wounds. It seemed as though the slumped man was held upright by those grotesque hooks.

'Inquisitor?' prompted Octavius.

'We must recover this artefact,' she said, turning to face the Deathwatch captain.

Octavius said nothing for a moment. 'The hive tyrant must surely be our priority, inquisitor?'

Kalypsia seemed to ignore the captain's objection. 'Techmarine,' she said, directing her orders to Korpheus. 'Remove the corpse from the machine. We have no need for the excess dead weight.'

Korpheus nodded to Kalypsia and glanced over at Octavius, waiting for some kind of confirmation from his captain. Octavius nodded almost imperceptibly, and Korpheus knelt down to inspect the fixings on the chair.

'Neleus, Shaidan – cover the entrance,' said the captain decisively. 'We may be here for a little while yet.'

Octavius looked over at Ashok, who was kneeling silently on the far side of the laboratory, his hood pulled deeply down over his face. Broec stood a short distance away from him, facing away, but Octavius could tell that he was fighting with himself about approaching the meditating librarian. The two Marines had always kept their distance from each other in the past, but the events in the viewing chamber outside had brought them head-to-head. They needed some time to deal with their issues and Octavius was experienced enough to know that this moment of relative calm might be the only chance they would get. Although he had no doubt that the two would fight alongside each other when confronted by the tyranid swarm outside, he could not afford for them to hold anything back. He needed each member of his team at full capacity if they were going to complete their mission.

The Angels Sanguine librarian was a mysterious figure in his team, and Octavius had sensed his discomfort in the past. Although Ashok seemed to have no concern for his popularity, Octavius knew that his self-imposed isolation made the others suspicious of him. He was certainly a magnificent warrior – perhaps the most powerful librarian that Octavius had ever encountered – but his tactics sometimes bordered on those of the berserker. In the heat of battle, his eyes would burn with an arcane red thirst and it would take a real effort of will for him to disengage with a defeated enemy, or to withdraw from a hopeless situation. Korpheus, the cautious and disciplined Raven Guard, so accustomed to stealthy missions behind enemy lines, had voiced his concern about Ashok's conduct on a number of occasions already, and Octavius was sure that he would lodge another objection after Ashok's recent solo rampage – magnificent though it was.

However, Octavius knew that the different Chapters of the Adeptus Astartes had different traditions and different practices and he was reluctant to judge the divergences amongst his own team. They were each from amongst the finest representatives of their brotherhoods; they would not be here if they weren't. In the final analysis, even the borderline-renegade Mantis Warriors were Space Marines.

As a captain in the Deathwatch, Octavius was privy to a great deal of Ordo Xenos intelligence and he had been in this service for many years. He made it his business to know a little something about the backgrounds of each of the Chapters that he would command. Some of that information – such as the dubious history of the Mantis Warriors – worried him, but he rarely had cause to doubt the integrity of individual Marines. Most Chapters had their secrets and Octavius was always aware that the most important aspects of a Chapter's past were precisely those that nobody outside the Chapter knew. Not all of them could be as pristine and flawless as the Imperial Fists, after all.

Of the Angels Sanguine, Octavius knew very little. He knew that they shared the gene-seed of the glorious Blood Angels, sired by the great Primarch Sanguinius himself. He knew that they shared the latter's intense passion for combat, bordering on the berserk at times. But he also knew that the Chapter's chaplains played an important role in the spiritual life of the Angels Sanguine and he was sure that Ashok was missing the presence of a more sympathetic chaplain. Broec was a fierce warrior and a devout Marine, but he had little time or sympathy for the problems of psykers, whom he distrusted ardently. That said, the Black Templar was a dutiful and spiritual man – even puritanically so – and Octavius was quietly confident that he would offer his hand to his troubled battle-brother when the time came.

CHAPTER NINE:
REVELATIONS

[6 Hours Remaining]

THE FURY EXPLODED into a ball of flame that rippled out through the lattice of alien liana that stretched across the launch bays of the *Extreme Prejudice*. The tentacles seemed to writhe in the fire, twisting and twining, detaching from the hull of the battle cruiser and floating into space, thrashing and lashing with vines that tried to regain some purchase.

Collia banked her fighter back round towards the landing bays, shutting out her sense of loss as the last of the debris from Gordus's Fury rattled against her cockpit, spiralling out into the thick soup of the surrounding space. She flicked her lascannons back onto manual and started to pick off the straggling tentacles that reached back towards the *Prejudice*. She was not going to let that web haul itself back into place, not after its removal had already claimed Gordus.

Her lascannons were faltering now, firing intermittently and not always when she thumbed the triggers.

They were overheated and rapidly losing charge, but she had already exhausted all the missiles, so they were all she had left.

Checking around her, she could catch no sight of the other surviving Fury and she realised that she was on her own again. Just as the realisation began to sink in, and the cold despair of loneliness started to press into her soul, another explosion erupted in the mouth of the launch bays, finally detaching the last of the alien forna. Another chain of explosions followed, strafing through the now free floating vines and incinerating them in bursts of superheated plasma.

As the web fell away, the huge form of a Space Marine strike cruiser roared through the space beneath her, its gun batteries blazing in every direction at once, vaporising broods of drone ships and spore mines. Its main frontal cannons were focussed on the withered and ruined weeds that fell away from the immense battleship above them.

A new sense of hope seeped back into Collia's mind as the *Sword of Contrition* ploughed through the soupy suspension, shredding the little tyranid drones as though they were insects. Then, as she looked back to the *Prejudice*, she could see squadrons of Furies streaming out of the cleared launch bays, peeling off into offensive formations that started to sweep out from the battle cruiser, clearing away the tyranid scum that polluted the surrounding space.

With a grin tugging at the corners of her mouth, Collia realised that she had succeeded. The launch bays were open and the *Extreme Prejudice* could now discharge its squadrons into the battle. The battle was still far from over, but at least the Imperial Navy could now join it properly.

'Storm Squadron Fury,' hissed an official voice through her spluttering vox. 'This is the *Sword of Contrition*. You look terrible–'

'Storm Squadron Fury,' cut in another voice, 'this is Captain Melyus of the *Extreme Prejudice*. Are you receiving?'

Collia shook her head in disbelief. Space Marines and battle cruiser captains were calling her – if only Gordus could see her now.

'Captain Melyus, this is Storm Squadron Fury II. What can I do for you, sir?'

'You have done more than enough, pilot. Bring your bird in for repairs and let the *Prejudice* battle group take things from here.'

With a relieved and weary smile, Collia dropped her speed and angled for an approach. 'I'm coming in now, sir. Thank you, sir,' she said as a mindless, tumbling spore mine smashed into the side of her Fury and incinerated it in a ball of bio-plasma.

As HIS SLEEK gunship slid through the Herodian system on route to an orbit in the shadow of the huge Gothic-class cruiser, *Vanishing Star*, Agustius witnessed the full extent of the space battle for the first time. He saw the immense shape of the *Extreme Prejudice* enshrouded behind a cloud of xenos organisms, which flashed and burst with fire as the pilots of the Imperial Navy strove to exterminate the tyranid drones. In the extreme distance, he could just about make out the gargantuan form of the Hive Ship, skimming into the upper reaches of Herodian IV's atmosphere. There was no sign of the venerable frigate *Purgation*, and the Sword-class *Strident Virtue* was alone, locked in a desperate fight with two ghastly Krakens. Broods of drone ships swam through the intervening space, providing support and reinforcements whenever and wherever the tyranid fleet required them.

Agustius turned his wheelchair away from the view-screen, shaking his head in frustrated incomprehension.

'I cannot understand this battle,' he said, half to himself. 'Parthon could have just killed the planet.'

Lexopher nodded wordlessly from his seat at the huge wooden table that dominated the oval chamber. The tabletop was strewn with papers and document folders, and the interrogator was poring over them in avid concentration. He had hardly even noticed that Agustius had spoken.

'So?' prompted Agustius. 'What exactly do we have there?' He waved his hand casually to indicate the spread of documents that Lexopher and Slyrian had 'borrowed' from the vaults of the *Veiled Salvation*.

'It seems to me,' began Lexopher, lifting his gaze from the papers and resting back into his chair. He looked exhausted, as though he had been working on the documents for hours, which he had. 'It seems to me,' he repeated, still collecting his thoughts, 'that Inquisitor Lord Parthon requisitioned an Ordo Mechanicus research station on Herodian IV many years ago. He installed a certain Derteg Grendal – evidently an inquisitor of considerable psychic potential – and then effectively shielded the facility from any outside interest by positioning his battle ship within striking distance of the system. It looks as though he has been using the Herodian warp gate to bring research materials from all over the galaxy.'

'What kind of materials?' asked Agustius, nodding along with the narrative and waiting for the key information that would condemn his radical friend.

'It looks decidedly like a weapons programme, my lord,' replied Lexopher with some satisfaction. 'However, this is a programme unlike any I have seen before.'

'How so, Lexopher?'

'Well, it appears that the inquisitor lord has been shipping in alien artefacts, my lord. In particular, there has been fairly regular traffic to the planet from Ichar IV. You will recall the Battle of Ichar IV in 993.M41, in which the Ultramarines defeated the Kraken splinter of the tyranid Hive Fleet Behemoth that had plagued the Realm of Ultramar two hundred years earlier?'

'I am familiar with this history, of course.'

'My apologies, my lord,' stuttered Lexopher, his stride suddenly broken. 'Anyway, it seems that Lord Parthon has been importing tyranid remains from the Kraken splinter. However, he has not stopped with Ichar IV. You will be aware, of course, that the eldar craftworld of Iyanden was also involved in the confrontation with the Kraken fleet. The craftword vanished into deep space after the encounter, allegedly ruined by the conflict with the tyranids. It was sighted occasionally, wandering in the outer reaches of Ultima Segmentum and then Segmentum Obscurus – near the Obscurus frontier.

'According to these records, Parthon has been receiving samples of tyranid tissue and DNA from a number of the systems in which the Iyanden eldar have been sighted since 993.M41.'

'Have you reached any conclusions?' asked Agustius, studying the concentration on his apprentice's face.

'Two tentative conclusions, my lord,' said Lexopher, grimacing slightly at the prospect of laying himself bare in front of his master. 'First, it seems that the Kraken fleet must have been pursuing the Iyanden craftworld since the battles of Ichar. Hence, it seems likely that this particular splinter of the Kraken tyranids will have absorbed considerable quantities of eldar DNA, making them unusually potent psykers. I can imagine that this would be of more than passing interest to Lord Parthon, especially if he is attempting to use the harvested tyranid material to fashion some form of weapon.'

'Excellent,' said Agustius, smiling at the logic of the interrogator. 'And what about your second conclusion?'

'Second,' replied Lexopher, hesitating slightly. 'Second, it would seem likely that Lord Parthon is in communication with the Iyanden craftworld – otherwise how could he possibly know where the eldar were going to appear?'

'Interesting. Let's call that a hypothesis rather than a conclusion, shall we?' smiled Agustius. 'So, what should be done about this?' The inquisitor lord was enjoying testing his student and, secretly, he was impressed by the youngster's imagination.

'It is difficult to say, my lord, since these actions are not technically illegal. The Ordo Xenos is not proscribed from exploiting alien technology for the benefit of the Imperium. We must presume that Parthon's weapons programme aims to produce a weapon for the use of the Inquisition. Hence, no matter how distasteful we may find his methods, he has not actually done anything wrong.' Lexopher looked trepidatiously at Agustius, expecting that the Thorian inquisitor lord would want a stronger response.

'You are right, my young interrogator. And you are wrong,' responded Agustius, wheeling himself up to the table and casting his eyes casually over the papers. 'We *must* assume that Parthon's intentions are good – that is true. Since, if his intentions are anything else, this is a crisis for the Ordo Xenos and the Imperium itself. You are also right that his methods – no matter how egregious they may seem to more reasonable men – are not technically forbidden. That said, no matter what his intentions and no matter what his methods, you have overlooked perhaps the most important aspect of this affair: the consequences of his actions.

'In an attempt to protect his pet research project on this planet, Parthon is jeopardising the lives of an Imperial Navy battle group and a company of Space Marines, not to mention the lives of my Deathwatch kill-team and the integrity of the Herodian warp-gate. The correct response to this tyranid assault should simply have been an aerial bombardment – something that Commander Kastor would have been all too pleased to perform. It would have been over by now. Instead, the tyranid are now well entrenched on Herodian IV and their shadow in the warp is growing all the time.

'So, Interrogator Lexopher, I have only one conclusion: this must end, now.'

KNEELING AT THE side of the laboratory, images flickered and flashed behind Ashok's eyelids, spilling flecks of blood-drenched remembrances out into the shadows under his hood. The Shroud of Lemartes hung heavily over his face, hiding his gritted teeth and the bunched muscles around his jaw.

His mind was flooded with images of death and slaughter, as his memories of the hideous Hegelian IX campaign swam through his consciousness, curdling and stirring themselves into his awareness of Herodian IV. His thoughts raced through the catacombs of that infested planet, which the Death Company of the Angels Sanguine had purged of the tyranid menace all those years before. As he watched, the catacombs twisted and morphed into the metal tunnels and passageways of the Imperial compound on Herodian IV. Hiding under his thoughts, like sharks patrolling just under the surface of the ocean, waiting for the unwary to test the water, there was the constant chatter of the hive mind. It taunted him, prodding his rage and tipping his sanity close to the precipice.

Hegelian IX had been one of the most transformative moments in his life, paralleling even the moment at which he had first put on the power armour of an Angels Sanguine librarian.

The Death Company was not made up of the best Marines in the Chapter, but rather of those Marines who floated closest to the edge of their sanity. Together with awesome combat prowess and an unimpeachable sense of loyalty, the Angels Sanguine had inherited a genetic defect from the Blood Angels – a thirst for blood and a rage – the Black Rage – that teetered on the brink of a berserk combat frenzy. The Death Company contained those Marines lost to the Rage. They brought death to the enemies of the Emperor, but more often than not they also brought death to each other and to themselves.

Ashok had rampaged through the catacombs of Hegelian IX, carving through the tyranids and, when they were all slaughtered, he had turned on his own battle-brothers of the Death Company. Every time he closed his eyes, even now, he could see the broken and mutilated forms of the three Angels Sanguine who had met their ends under the power of his force staff. As he knelt at the side of the laboratory, buried deep under the surface of a tyranid infested desert on Herodian IV, Ashok could think of little else.

Once or twice in a generation, a member of the Death Company would plunge through his Rage, sating it and drenching it in the blood that it craved, before emerging out the other side, mastering it as a weapon to be wielded in combat. In the aftermath of Hegelian IX, Ashok had been taken back to the fortress monastery and strapped into the Tablet of Lestrallio – named after Chaplain Lestrallio of the Blood Angels themselves, who first designed and died on the tablet – where he had ranted and screamed his nightmares into the darkness of the Apothecarion. Three years later, still alive, his eyes had cleared and he was released. Presented with the Shroud of Lemartes as a symbol of his remarkable journey, Ashok suddenly became one of the most celebrated librarians in his Chapter. But it was the shadows, not renown, that he craved, as a constant battle raged in his mind between his self-control and his insatiable thirst.

Just as he had lost control on Hegelian IX, with the hive mind chattering into his subconscious, nudging his mind out of balance and luring him into the darkest recesses of his own soul, so it nattered and whistled now, besieging his sanity with a barbed and constricting wall of alien screeches and mutterings. It required a superhuman effort of will to hold his purpose together, suspending it like an orb of pristine light in the heart of his mind.

As the Deathwatch team had pressed deeper and deeper into the compound, the shrieks of the hive mind had grown louder and louder, increasing the psychic pressure – even Shaidan's and Kalypsia's eyes had ruptured with blood under the strain. For Ashok, this was a greater test of will than he had confronted since joining the Deathwatch. He had stumbled, but he would be damned if he was going to fall again in another subterranean tyranid cesspool.

His eyes flicked open suddenly, burning with red fire, and he sprang to his feet. He strode forward, brushing past the back of Chaplain Broec, and headed for the entrance-way to the laboratory. As he marched past the rest of the team, still stooped around the bizarre and elaborate chair in the centre of the room, the entrance suddenly filled with writhing shapes and crackling purple energy. It was instantly and completely blocked by a wall of zoanthropes. They roiled and pulsed, but did not attack or move forward. They appeared content merely to block the only exit.

Scanning the glass viewing wall, peering through the slime and ichor that coated the other side, Ashok could see that the xenos psykers formed an unbroken ring around the entire room. None of them were attacking – they were simply coruscating with power and emanating an implacable menace.

'Octavius,' growled Ashok, drawing his voice from the pit of his stomach. 'We have a problem.'

'WHAT DO WE know about this Derteg Grendal?' asked Agustius, shuffling through the papers on the table. 'Is there anything about him here?'

'Hardly anything, my lord. There are some references to a long relationship with Parthon himself and a strong political affinity. He is a relatively senior inquisitor, but was never made a lord – evidently Parthon took him under his wing and hand-picked him for this position on Herodian IV. According to these notes, one of the reasons that he was considered so suitable was because he was such a potent psyker – perhaps even more powerful than Parthon himself. His physical frailty seems to have prevented his rise within the mainstream of the Inquisition,' reported Lexopher.

Agustius nodded and pushed the papers away, turning his chair and wheeling back towards the view screen. Outside he could see the *Vanishing Star* looming menacingly off to his right, and over to the left was the planet of Herodian IV itself, engulfed in the roiling black clouds of the tyranid swarm.

He sighed. 'He lied to me, Lexopher. He lied to my face.'

'My lord?'

'Parthon. He lied to me – he told me that my Death-watch team were going to be used to take out the hive tyrant. He told me that he had learnt how to locate the cursed creatures from Kryptman. I thought that it was odd at the time, but I never thought that he had the audacity to lie to my face: he doesn't know where the hive tyrant is, he just wants my team to recover his science project.' Agustius was shaking his head sadly; despite their different ideological beliefs, he had always viewed Parthon as a brother.

'What about the Deathwatch team, my lord? How will they respond to this mission?' asked Lexopher.

The inquisitor lord turned his chair back to face the interrogator and one eyebrow raised in faint amusement. 'Ah yes, our valiant Captain Octavius – he will do his duty,' he said, cultivating the ambiguity with a wry smile.

As he spoke, a red warning light started to pulse above the only door into the room. It was an intruder alarm.

After a second, the door hissed open to reveal the darkness outside and then clunked closed again. Lexopher jumped to his feet, fumbling around his belt for his sidearm. Although he hadn't see anyone enter the room, he knew better than to assume that this meant they were still alone.

'Ah, Slyrian,' said Agustius, still sitting calmly.

Lexopher had finally found his weapon, and he was flicking it from side to side, searching for any would-be intruders. For an instant, he remembered the figure of the guard in the vault of the *Veiled Salvation*, snapping his gun around and then screaming in the darkness as Slyrian sliced him in half. He lowered his weapon slowly and looked over to Agustius. Slyrian was sitting cross-legged on the table in front of the inquisitor lord.

'What news, my beautiful Slyrian?' asked Agustius, reaching out and cupping her synthskin-covered cheek in his hand.

'Intruders,' she purred. 'Two dead crew already. Pilot has sealed the bridge.'

'Very good, Slyrian,' replied Agustius. 'Time to go hunting.' He smiled at the lithe lethality of the death cultist in front of him, and then shook his head in disappointment. Parthon was getting sloppy – leaving an incriminating paper trail, lying to a fellow inquisitor lord and then sending assassins to silence him. He had gone too far this time.

'Lexopher, tell the pilot to turn us around – take us back to the *Veiled Salvation*. And Slyrian, time for you to work, my dear.'

As ASHOK STRODE past him, heading for the door, Korpheus looked up from his inspection of the unusual chair in the heart of the laboratory. He followed Ashok with his eyes and jumped to his feet when he saw the brood of zoanthropes that blocked the librarian's exit. The other Deathwatch Marines also spun, bracing their weapons to confront the threat, but the zoanthropes showed no signs of entering the room. Only Kalypsia seemed unphased by their appearance.

'Well, Marine?' she asked, holding out her hands in an interrogative shrug, nodding over towards the chair. Her eyes were still weeping with blood and streams of red lined her cheeks.

Korpheus reluctantly drew his eyes away from the coiled and writhing xenos creatures at the door, leaving his bolter trained on them, and turned his attention to the inquisitor.

'It seems that the human has become organically fused with the machine, inquisitor.' As he spoke, Korpheus remained distracted by the looming menace of the zoanthropes, but his conclusions were interesting enough to draw curious glances from Octavius and Broec. 'It looks as though the man strapped himself into the machine voluntarily – there is no sign of resistance – and that the machine itself subsequently grew into his flesh. Those spikes through his shoulders are covered in tiny feelers, which have grown into the man's spinal column, meshing themselves into his nervous system. And the seat itself is coated in a complicated network of capillaries, which seem to have grown out of the chair, broken through the man's skin and infiltrated his blood vessels.'

'This is all very interesting, Marine,' snapped Kalypsia, as though she didn't really think it was, 'but I merely asked you to detach the corpse from the machine. Can you do that or not?'

Finally, Korpheus turned away from the strangely passive zoanthropes in the doorway, and faced the inquisitor. 'This is not a corpse, inquisitor. The man is still alive. His pulse is incredibly weak, but it persists. I suspect that the chair is actually keeping him alive. Bizarrely,' he continued, 'I also think that he is keeping the chair alive – it is feeding on him. Most of his soft tissue has already been drained from his body.'

'You still haven't answered my question, Marine,' said Kalypsia dryly. 'Can you remove him, or not?'

'Yes, I can, but the man will certainly die–' began Korpeus.

'So be it – he is little more than a vegetable at this point in any case,' interrupted Kalypsia. 'If the machine has been draining his soft tissues, then it must also have been consuming his brain.' Her conclusion was a little too decisive, and it made Octavius lower his ornate eldar force sword and walk over to join the conversation.

Korpheus had also noticed the inquisitor's tone. 'It is also likely that the machine will be irreparably damaged if its food source is abruptly cut off.'

Kalypsia hesitated for a moment.

'Have you seen this?' asked Octavius, inspecting the emaciated form of the man in the chair. He reached down and tugged at a fine chain that was looped around the man's neck, pulling a delicate pendent out from under the folds of his tunic. 'This man is an inquisitor, Kalypsia,' said Octavius, dangling the Imperial insignia on the medallion from his gauntlet.

Looking between the two Deathwatch Marines, Kalypsia's bloody eyes seemed to narrow with annoyance.

'Very well,' she said, her tone full of frustration rather than surprise, 'we will recover the entire thing – including its occupant.'

'As you wish,' responded Octavius, dropping the medallion into a pouch in his belt. 'But first we have to find a way out of here.'

As the Deathwatch captain spoke, a sizzling crack sounded behind him, and he turned to see the hooded figure of Ashok testing the resolve of the zonathropes in the doorway with a couple of gouts of energy from his staff. Shaidan stood next to him, the tip of his own staff resting lightly on the ground in front of him while trickles of blood coursed out of his eyes and down his face, mingling with the intricate web of tattoos around his neck. Neleus towered over them both with his storm bolter levelled and quiet in his hand.

The serpentine psykers in the exit writhed under the impacts from Ashok, but they repelled his tentative attack, falling into synchronisation with each other and simply absorbing the energy as though it were food. The blue flares from Ashok's staff seemed to dissipate as they struck the zoanthropes, streaming off in threads across the roiling forms of the other creatures as though they were sharing the pressure between them.

But no counter-strike came back at the librarian; the zoanthropes simply continued to pulse and slither, as though nothing had happened, absorbing the punishment implacably. Ashok growled, starting to pace up and down in front of the aliens, leaving crackling images of blue energy in his wake, his eyes simmering and red in the heavy shadow of his hood. He prowled restlessly, muttering litanies under his breath.

THE SERVITOR WAS lying on its face in the corridor with a pool of blood puddling out under its face. There was a single entry wound in the back of its head; it had clearly been shot by a skilled marksman. Slyrian smiled invisibly, relishing the thought of a worthy opponent.

The death cultist crouched down and dropped a fingertip into the bullet hole, feeling the warmth inside the servitor's head as the brain tissue cloyed against the synthskin membrane that coated her body. A trickle of corrosive chemicals also soaked into the synthetic skin, and Slyrian withdrew her finger as the metallic taste began to seep into her mouth, carried through the capillary action of her membranous armour. Whoever was on Agustius's gunship had toxin tipped ammunition; this killer certainly meant business.

'What news, Slyrian?' asked Agustius, his voice hissing quietly in the vox-bead implanted in her ear.

'Four crew dead,' she purred, stalking along the corridor in the direction of the bridge. 'The assassin is Ordo Xenos.' She said it simply, as though merely placing the intruder into a category for the sake of convenience. Whether or not she understood the terrible significance of her words, Agustius could not tell. And it didn't really matter – one of the wonderful qualities of Slyrian was that she had no interest whatsoever in the identity of her targets. Her universe was comprised of three different kinds of people: the dead, the marked and the irrelevant. Agustius had often amused himself to think that he himself was more-or-less irrelevant to the death cultist, and he always whispered a prayer of thanks to the Emperor that he should remain in that category.

'Ordo Xenos?' asked Agustius from the safety of his oval viewing station, where Lexopher sat with his pistol pointing at the sealed doorway. As he spoke, he saw the head of the young interrogator twitch slightly, obviously intrigued or horrified by what he was hearing.

'Yes, the bullets are tipped with tyranid bio-plasma toxins,' confirmed Slyrian as she made her way round a sweeping bend in the long passageway. There was a sudden and abrupt hiss over the vox-channel and then it fell silent.

'It would seem,' said Agustius, addressing his remarks to Lexopher, 'that the honourable Lord Parthon is aware that he may have gone too far this time. And this realisation has made him go even further.' Agustius had heard of experiments to use alien ichor to poison the tips of projectiles and he had assumed that such technologies would appeal to radicals like Parthon, but he had never thought to find himself on the receiving end of such things.

The inquisitor lord rolled his chair back over to the huge viewing screens set into the wall of the chamber, and studied the shimmering black menace that roiled and curdled over the surface of Herodian IV. He sighed and shook his head, his soul heavy with disappointment in his old friend.

While he watched, the planet jerked and slid off the side of the screen and the stars started to draw out into lines as the gunship began to accelerate back towards the *Veiled Salvation*.

Meanwhile, out in the labyrinthine corridors of his gunship, Slyrian was stalking her prey. She could hear the stuttering echoes of a gunfight up ahead, in front of the main blast-doors that blocked the route into the bridge, and she quickened her pace. She was not particularly concerned with saving the lives of the hapless guards who stood sentry on either side of the doors, but she would have been sorely disappointed if, in a moment of blind good fortune, those guards had actually managed to make her kill before she got there.

As she rounded the corner that led to the blast-doors, she vaulted lightly into the air, gripping hold of one of the ventilation pipes that ran overhead and flipping herself around onto the top of it, vanishing into the shadows of the ceiling cavity. She strode silently along the metal tube, touching her feet down as lightly as if they were hands.

Down in the corridor, she could see the faint reports of needle guns from an area of cover behind some container-caskets. Opposite the caskets were the blast-doors themselves and three guards were standing in front of them loosing volleys of laser shells from their standard-issue laspistols. The shots were pinging harmlessly off the crates, but were succeeding in keeping the intruders pinned in place.

Needle guns were not very effective in a fire-fight, and it looked as though the guards might eventually overpower their assailants. Slyrian shook her head in disappointment as she pulled an elaborate short sword from a holster on her back. The blade was made out of a rare, black alloy that was utterly non-reflective and she could hardly see it herself in the shadows above the ventilation system.

The would-be assassins must have taken up those positions in the cover of the containers in order to dispense with the guards silently – picking each one off with a needle of venom from their precision weapons. Clearly their plan had failed, which made Slyrian think that they were hardly worth her time; if they couldn't even shoot three human sentries standing twenty metres away from them, they were hardly the worthy opponents that she had longed for.

Still, she reflected, a kill is a kill: these were marks, soon to be converted into deads. The guards were definitely irrelevants.

She took another couple of steps towards the conflict and then sprang off the top of the pipe, turning a tight somersault before landing lightly on another pipe, directly above the intruders' position.

Looking down, she could see that there were three of them, all men and all dressed in black from head to toe. She almost laughed. They didn't look like assassins at all, just like regular guardsmen dressed up as assassins. It was almost as though Parthon didn't really care whether they succeeded or not. But it was of no concern to her why the radical inquisitor lord might send boys to do a man's job – or a woman's job, reflected Slyrian with a smile. They were simply the marks; she would erase them and try her best to enjoy it.

With a graceful movement, Slyrian stood to her full height and then fell forward off the ventilation pipe. As she dropped towards the ground, her body revolved slowly so that her feet replaced her head just as she reached the floor. She landed into a crouch, with her blade drawn and held horizontally in front of her eyes. To the three startled intruders, the lightless metal of her short sword looked like a gash in the fabric of space, slicing through her head.

One of them turned his needle gun towards her and pulled at the trigger. When nothing happened, he tried again and again, watching in horror as the death cultist walked slowly towards him with the tip of her blade dragging casually along the metal deck at her feet. Finally, his fearful eyes bulged as he looked down frantically and realised that his gun wasn't there – he didn't even have an arm. Turning, he saw that he had left his neatly severed arm in a pool of blood next to the crate behind which he had been sheltering. His needle gun was still grasped in its hand.

Too scared to turn back to face the death cultist, he simply froze on the spot, staring at his lost limb, waiting for the death blow to strike him in the back.

But it never came. Instead, he heard a rattle of shots from one of his comrades and then a brief, aborted scream. A fraction of a second later, he felt the toxic needles from his partner's momentary frenzy riddle his own body, fizzing into his blood stream and perforating his abdomen. As he collapsed to the ground in convulsions of agony, he lived just long enough to see the head of his other comrade roll past him, an expression of abject horror contorting his features.

CHAPTER TEN:
TYRANOCIDE

[4 Hours Remaining]

THE SPRAY OF bolter shells just impacted against the chitinous skin of the zoanthropes, exploding into bursts of flame but not dispersing the line of aliens that blocked the exit. While Broec fired repeatedly into the writhing xenos creatures, Ashok prowled backwards and forwards in front of them, muttering litanies of hate and self-restraint at the same time. The aliens did not shift.

In the end, it was Broec that snapped first, his indignation finally overcoming his self-control – as a devoted servant of the Emperor, he should not have to suffer the sight of twice-damned, foul tyranid psykers.

'What's going on here, inquisitor?' He spun on the spot, turning his bolter with his gaze, inadvertently bringing it to bear on Kalypsia as he yelled at her. 'You need to tell us what you know, or we will all die here and now!' The chaplain was an immaculate puritan, and he could smell taint when it wafted into the air.

Kalypsia recoiled from the hissing, amplified tone of Broec's voice, as it bellowed out of the pre-amp in his macabre deathmask. She stared at the barrel of his bolter, as though daring him to shoot at her, but he quickly withdrew his gun when he realised what he was doing.

In a second she had recovered her composure, and she looked over to Octavius to see what the captain was going to do about this breach of military discipline. If Broec had been an Imperial Guardsman, she would simply have shot him herself for gross insubordination; pointing a weapon at an agent of the Emperor's Holy Inquisition, even accidentally and yelling abuse at her was certainly an executable offence.

However, Octavius seemed unmoved by his chaplain's conduct. If anything, the Deathwatch captain appeared to be waiting for her to answer the question. He was standing with his arms folded and his head cocked slightly to one side, watching Kalypsia's reaction.

Meanwhile, Ashok had stopped pacing and had turned his fathomless eyes onto the inquisitor. He was searching her features for signs, and probing at the edges of her mind for a way in. But Kalypsia was ready for his advances this time, and her mind was sealed shut like an escape pod falling through a space battle. The chattering sounds of the hive mind ricocheted off her defences and Ashok had to narrow his eyes to protect himself from the backwash.

With a faint hiss, Octavius unclasped his helmet. He rolled his neck casually to loosen up the powerful muscles that bunched around his broad shoulders, and then looked back at Kalypsia, gazing at her with his pain-ridden blue eyes. The gold service studs in his forehead glinted as though polished, but the old, deep scar across his face looked raw and fresh.

'Well?' he said, folding his arms across his massive, armoured chest. Things had gone far enough, he thought. 'What is this place, inquisitor?'

Kalypsia just stared at the captain, her mind racing with a mixture of indignation and terror. She couldn't believe that these soldiers were interrogating her – *they* were interrogating *her*! This was not how soldiers were supposed to behave – and it was certainly not how her father had behaved when he was a guardsman. He had died without ever asking any questions, and certainly without pointing his weapon at an inquisitor.

The worst thing, however, was not the fact that they were questioning her, but the fact that they appeared to have seen through her. They knew what to ask. They seemed to know that she was hiding something from them. For a moment, she even wondered whether they already knew what she was hiding – after all, that ridiculous Mantis Warrior librarian had suddenly claimed to have been in the facility before. Perhaps he had already told the Deathwatch team everything, and they were simply testing her.

Her mind was racing and her own thoughts seemed barbed, as though they were cutting at the inside of her head. As she stared at the Marines, her eyes gushed with blood once again and the chittering, chattering confusion of the hive mind grated against her consciousness like glass-paper.

She shut her eyes, trying to blink out the blood, but the capillaries in her eyes were ruptured beyond such simple measures and the crimson tears continued to stream down her face. The pressure in her head was building and she could feel the blood bubbling through her corneas, rendering the scleras into sheens of red around her pale grey irises.

'It is a weapons laboratory.'

The voice made everyone turn. Almost in shock, Kalypsia spun on her heels to see Shaidan standing against the wall, away from all the other Marines. His face was pointed at the ground and his long, black hair hid it from the prying eyes of the rest of the team. His voice was low and smooth, as though he were making a confession.

'I have been in here before,' he admitted, lifting his head to meet Octavius's eyes with the bloodshot emeralds of his own. 'During the last stand of the Mantis Warriors' Second Company on the top of this compound, I came down into this facility and discovered this chamber. I was drawn here. There was no choice. The inquisitor brought me here,' he said, nodding towards the incumbent of the ghastly chair.

Kalypsia had screwed up her face with concentration as her mind danced around this new development; Shaidan may have just saved her neck.

'And when were you going to tell us this, Mantis Warrior?' she sneered, spitting the name of his Chapter as though it were an indictment in itself. The other Marines shifted their positions, fanning out around the circular room as though surrounding Shaidan.

'I am telling you now, in the hope that the information will be of use – in the hope that it is not too late. You will understand, perhaps, my reluctance to implicate the Mantis Warriors in this affair earlier on, without evidence that our involvement was meaningful or relevant. I am fully aware that my valiant battle-brothers in the Deathwatch have precious little trust in the warriors of my Chapter as it is. To undermine it further may have jeopardised the mission itself.' As he spoke, Shaidan's eyes glittered with earnestness and Octavius nodded faintly, acknowledging the librarian's reasoning without approving of it.

'Do you really think that we will trust you more now?' asked Kalypsia, finding her stride again at last. 'Perhaps the light of the Emperor was mistaken when it showed redemption in the future of your renegade Chapter, Mantis Warrior?'

Shaidan bristled visibly, forcing himself not to respond to the public slight against his brethren. He was fully aware that the other Marines would already know the history of the Badab War – it was part of the official history of the Imperium, not merely part of the secret narratives of the Chapter itself – but he had never thought that anyone would have the audacity to throw it in his face. He had been there himself. He had actually stood on the burning deck of a Fire Hawks' strike cruiser. He had clashed blades with the Marines Errant. But he had also been one of the first to realise the folly and to turn his Mantis Staff against Huron and his cursed Astral Claws. How many Space Marines could really say that they had faced a genuine choice and that they had chosen the light – blind duty is a shield for the weak minded. This was the stuff of the Great Heresy itself.

Octavius saw that Chaplain Broec was startled by the inquisitor's words, and he realised that it was because she had questioned the judgement of the Imperial will. That was blasphemy. Perhaps there was more to her attack on Shaidan than concern for the mission? Certainly she had misjudged her company if she thought that such words would turn them against the librarian.

'The Mantis Warriors came to the aid of Herodian IV,' said Shaidan firmly. 'We were overwhelmed by the forces of the Great Devourer and driven back to this compound. Once here, we discovered the existence of this weapon,' he continued, indicating the machine, 'and, although we knew nothing of its origins or technology, we sought to employ it against the tyranid swarm. It was our last hope – the Mantis Warriors can ill-afford defeats. At first everything went well and the swarm appeared to lose its sense of purpose – we started to drive it back. But then something shifted in the psychic realm and broods of tyranids crashed back against the remnants of our forces, penetrating into the compound itself. When the Thunderhawks finally came for us, we abandoned the facility and left the inquisitor, assuming that he was already dead.'

'You abandoned one of the Emperor's inquisitors?' said Octavius, genuinely shocked by this part of the story. The Imperial Fists would never leave anyone behind. However, Octavius also realised that it was extremely unlikely that Kalypsia would have been unaware that there had been an Inquisitorial presence on Herodian IV before the invasion, and he watched her carefully.

Shaidan nodded silently.

Broec took a step towards the librarian, his amplifier array hissing. 'We must all be wary of new technologies, Librarian Shaidan, even at times of great need. It is the purity of our souls that will win the day, not some fancy inquisitorial weapon.'

'We should destroy the machine and get out of here,' confirmed Korpheus, his distrust for untested technology matching that of the chaplain.

'No!' interrupted Ashok, stalking over from the doorway, where the zoanthropes continued to writhe and squirm. 'We should use this weapon ourselves. If it can turn back the tide of the swarm even for a moment, it may be our best chance of completing our mission. Any and all means are sanctioned in the battle against the alien hordes.'

'The decision is not yours to make, Marines,' said Kalypsia, reining in the discussion before it became a fully fledged debate. 'We must recover the weapon – it must not be destroyed,' she said, flicking her eyes towards Broec and Korpheus. 'And we cannot use it ourselves, librarian, since Inquisitor Grendal is organically fused into it.'

Octavius raised an eyebrow at Kalypsia's immediate decisiveness. It made sense that she would want to retain the device if possible, especially since there appeared to be a living inquisitor strapped into it. The researchers at the Ordo Xenos would be interested to see the machine and the investigators of the Ordo Hereticus may well be interested in knowing what the Mantis Warriors had done with it. But Octavius also noted that Kalypsia had given the emaciated inquisitor a name – Grendal – and he was pretty sure that nobody had mentioned it before.

'Based on what the Techmarine has told me,' continued Kalypsia, indicating Korpheus, 'it seems likely that Grendal's living tissues have been drained by the machine and somehow converted into psychic resonances. It is conceivable that the tyranids of this splinter hive have been able to exploit these signatures in order to assimilate an understanding of our protocols and procedures. As we are all aware, this hive seems unusually potent in psychic terms – perhaps because of the assimilation of eldar DNA on its way here.'

'Are you suggesting that the hive mind has been able to assimilate this inquisitor's knowledge of the strategies of the Ordo Xenos, the Deathwatch and even the Codex Astartes?' asked Octavius, some of the pieces of the puzzle beginning to fall into place. 'Is that how the nids were able to lay a trap for us at our first landing site?'

'It is possible,' said Kalypsia. 'Inquisitor Grendal was a high ranking officer of the Inquisition with almost unrestricted access to such information. If this weapon were to fail whilst he was strapped into it, it does not seem implausible that it could have been exploited by the aliens after it was abandoned by the Mantis Warriors.'

'It is bad enough,' bellowed Broec, 'that this experiment was used in the first place. But to have the experiments of the Imperium exploited by the aliens that it was designed to annihilate is insufferable. We must destroy this abomination before it can cause any further damage to the Emperor's chosen!'

Octavius could see that the other Marines shared Broec's outrage, but he was also aware that Kalypsia seemed to know much more about this weapon than she was letting on. Despite her attempts to point the finger at Shaidan, she had revealed the name of the inquisitor and she appeared to know quite a lot about him. She also seemed to have a well developed theory on how the weapon actually worked.

'Would I be correct to assume that the hive tyrant would position itself close to this weapon, inquisitor?' asked Octavius, trying to steer the conversation back around to the declared purpose of the mission.

A blank look flashed across Kalypsia's face as she struggled to recall why Octavius might be talking about hive tyrants. 'Yes,' she said abruptly. 'The strong defences and the presence of this artefact do indicate that the hive tyrant should be near by.' As she said the words, she realised that they were probably true.

'Then we should leave the question of this weapon to one side for now and press on with the mission, should we not?' asked the Deathwatch captain, peering into Kalypsia's face as he spoke.

The inquisitor hesitated a little too long, and Ashok slowly turned his own gaze onto her, waiting for her to respond. But the pregnant pause was suddenly shattered by an immense chorus of shrieks from behind them. The Deathwatch Marines spun in time to see the zoanthropes spilling in through the doorway, screaming and braying with flashes of warp energy bursting out from their coruscating forms.

They poured into the chamber as though driven by a single purpose, screaming into the minds of the Marines. But there was something else pulsing through the broiling mess of psychic energy: a deeper and still more primordial scream of horror that washed through the laboratory like the icy undercurrents of an ancient ocean.

The Marines opened fire at once, holding a perimeter around the Grendal-device in the centre of the laboratory,

shielding it from the advance of the slithering zoanthropes. They all assumed that the strange weapon
needed to be protected from the aliens, although it made
as much sense to suppose that the xenos creatures were
actually trying to protect it from them.

Ashok launched himself into the fray with a blood-cur-
dling cry of release, as his eyes flashed with fire and his
staff lashed blue flames into the thrashing and writhing
serpents. He immediately broke the defensive line, leaping in amongst the enemy so as to singe and burn their
chitinous flesh with his energised hands.

The others held their formation, tracking their bolters
across the serpentine advance and hacking their blades
against anything that strayed too close.

The laboratory was hardly big enough to contain the
battle, and the energy release from the Marines' weapons
and from the vile, psychic aliens started to rattle the
walls. With a high-pitched shriek, the glass viewing-wall
was shattered, opening up that entire side of the lab,
effectively joining the viewing-chamber and the laboratory into a single space. As the wall collapsed into lethal
shards, a great wave of psychic force crashed against the
Deathwatch team from the bank of zoanthropes that had
been pressed up against it on the other side.

Octavius turned to meet the new threat, brandishing
his long force-sword and hacking it against the coruscating scales of the sickly beasts. It was clear that the team
was utterly surrounded. They needed to get to a more
defensible position.

'We have to get out of here!' cried the captain. 'Neleus,
cut us a path towards the corridor – if we can reduce the
width of the engagement zone, we will reduce the advantage of their greater numbers.'

The huge White Consul crashed forward, stamping
down with the full strength of the servos in his ancient
Terminator armour, shattering the shifting carapace of a

zoanthrope under his boots. He punched out with his powerfist, smashing into the relatively soft exposed neck of a braying alien and ripping out its throat. He stepped again, raking hellfire shells from his storm bolter and crunching down with his feet.

Octavius threw himself into the gap behind the glorious figure of Neleus, working his sword through the writhing bodies of the tyranids to keep the space from closing behind the hulking Terminator.

Behind them, Korpheus and Kalypsia had bound the Grendal-device into a burden that the Techmarine could heft onto his back, and now they were struggling forward with their bolters coughing and Kalypsia's force whip lashing with cracks of lightning. Librarian Shaidan was a blur of action around them, fending off the attacks of the zoanthropes with parries from his Mantis Staff and dispensing jousts of warp energy from his fingertips.

On the far side of Korpheus was Broec, with his glowing Crozius held proudly aloft in one hand while the other sprayed bolter shells from his gun, his terrible deathmask even more horrifying than the ugly monstrosities that keened and screeched all around him. He was the rear guard, dealing with the aliens that had worked their way around to the back of the team, encircling them.

As the Deathwatch edged their way towards the mouth of the corridor, hacking and blasting their path one alien at a time, a sudden convulsion shook the room and a chill wind roared through their minds. A thunderous crack ripped into the rear wall of the laboratory, and a gargantuan scythed talon thrust straight through the sheet metal. After a fraction of a second, another identical talon pierced the wall further along, and then the whole wall panel was ripped out of position and tossed aside like paper. Standing in the jagged hole was the biggest xenos organism that they had ever seen.

SHAIDAN WAS THE first to react, sweeping his Mantis Staff into a horizontal circle around his head, cutting into the pulsing tyranid flesh that pressed in towards him, and then vaulting into the air. He turned a slow somersault, clearing the embattled figures of Korpheus and Kalypsia before crunching into the ground next to Broec. Without pausing to rally any support, the Mantis Warrior librarian ploughed on into the line of zoanthropes that thrashed between him and the immense hive tyrant.

Every other thought was blocked out of his mind; all he wanted to do was slay the hive tyrant. Shaidan was determined that it should be a Mantis Warrior who should kill the beast. After the events of the last couple of days, he was still not sure that the actions of his Chapter were really to blame for the mess on Herodian IV, but it did not seem impossible. Good intentions did not always produce good results, as he knew well. And if there was even the slightest chance that the Mantis Warriors could be blamed – even erroneously blamed – then it was absolutely imperative that he should be the one to complete the Deathwatch mission successfully. Honour had to be restored or, at worst, a little honour should be salvaged from the wreckage.

During the special training of the Praying Mantidae, the elite cadre charged with the pursuit and destruction of the renegade Astral Claws, Shaidan had been taught how to enter a battle-haze. It was not the blood thirsty mist of a berserker, but rather a state of mind that actually contracted the Marine's perception of time.

Legend had it that the battle-haze had been discovered by the infamous Captain Maetrus in the years before the Badab Wars. The great captain had been a native of Mordriana III, a planet that floated in the tears of the Eye of

Terror, where the local tribes gloried in a perpetual state of internecine war. The Mantis Warriors themselves were birthed from the Mordriana system in the ancient and forgotten past, and the founders of the Chapter had hardened their minds and bodies in the fires of a system stuck in vicious, constant war. Some librarians in the Chapter hypothesised that such origins, so close to the influence of the Eye of Terror, was an ill-omen from the very start and that the Mantis Warriors' quest for redemption might as well be a mask for a more profound quest for salvation. Shaidan was not such a librarian.

Maetrus, who had later founded the order of the Praying Mantidae itself, had been the first to discover that for some reason the Chapter's gene-seed was incompatible with the proper functioning of the preomnor implant that all Space Marines receive as part of their initial, surgical transformation into a Marine. The result was that certain frames of mind could actually trigger neurochemical changes in a fully developed Mantis Warrior. The key mindset was an attitude of deepest devotion and penitence.

If a Mantis Warrior were to fall or force himself into such a frame of mind, the preomnor organ would transmute it into a potent neurotoxic-chemical that would actually alter the Marine's perception of space and time in such a way that it permitted him to obliterate his consciousness of all things outside of his field of perception and thus perceive the immediate reality in an incredibly concentrated and efficient manner. The most obvious use of this state of mind was to assist the Mantis Warrior in focussing his will to do the service of the Emperor – the efficiency of his perception acted to increase his strength and the speed of his reflexes, almost to the extent that the Marine would appear to have a mild sense of precognition. It was a reward for the most pious – and piety with devotion marked the Praying Mantidea out above all others.

The process had a terrible side-effect on the Marine in question – his perception would never return to normal and he would be trapped in a narrow world of tunnel vision until he died. He would become useless to the Chapter in all but his close combative functions, and each Company of the Mantis Warriors had a special squad of Mantis Religiosa, filled with Marines who had sacrificed their will to the devotional imperatives of their purified wills and thus sacrificed their very identities for the greater glory of the Emperor. Maetrus himself was rumoured to have fallen into this state in the last great battle of the Badab Wars; when the Astral Claws had been broken and their forces were fleeing, Maetrus had plunged after them into the Eye of Terror with single-minded determination, never to be seen or heard from again.

In practice, hardly any of the Mantis Warriors would ever approach this state of mind, but all the Praying Mantidae were subjecteded to a special hypnotherapy that enabled them to feel the humiliation and desperation of their Chapter in the most acute way. In cases of extreme need, when death in battle was a virtual certainty or the Chapter's redemption was at stake, the Marine could lapse into this battle-haze and be certain that his duty would be fulfilled. Soron and Ruinus were both trained in this unique skill for the penitent and the desperate.

As he lashed his Mantis Staff through the sliding abdomen of a cackling zoanthrope, Shaidan felt the dart pierce his chest. This battle would see the end of him, but his end would see the destruction of this hive tyrant. The Mantis Warriors would suffer no shame in the annals of the Deathwatch because of him. 'For Redemption! For the Mantis Warriors! For the Emperor!' he yelled as the neuro-toxins permeated his blood and coursed into his brain.

For a moment, Shaidan moved as though in a dream: a slithering creature snapped its viciously toothed mouth out towards his head, like a striking cobra, but he stepped around the lightning strike as though it were the most pedestrian attack he had ever faced. Then, with slightly startled ease, he plunged the bayonet on his staff up through the underside of the beast's jaw, skewering its brain and killing it instantly.

That's when he realised what was happening. He could make out no changes in his own metabolism, but the entire outside world appeared to have been dropped into treacle. Suddenly, the aliens slithered and writhed as though their bodies were slightly too heavy for their muscles – they laboured as they thrashed in the thick, humid air, as though they were used to less gravity and a thinner atmosphere. As soon as they died, they simply vanished in front of his eyes; the irrelevant and the non-existent suddenly becoming the same thing. After a few more strikes and parries, he couldn't see anything except the looming colossus of the hive tyrant in front of him. Everything else had vanished from his consciousness, even the other Deathwatch Marines behind him. He was focussed irrevocably and utterly on enacting the Emperor's will, as though driven on by the Astronomicon itself.

CAUGHT IN A moment of hesitation, Chaplain Broec felt the wall being ripped to shreds behind him as he strode forward to support Korpheus and Kalypsia. He paused, snapping his head round to see Shaidan drop out of the air into the writhing brood of zoanthropes that blocked the way towards the gargantuan monstrosity that stood behind the ragged breach in the lab's wall.

Ahead of him, Korpheus was labouring under the weight of the Grendal-device, but Kalypsia was fighting alongside him, her whip snapping in a blur of motion.

The two of them were just about to reach the mouth of the corridor, where Neleus stood magnificently, dousing the aliens with hellfire shells. And scything towards them from the side came Ashok, ducking and leaping and spinning with his staff, scattering gouts of warp energy like a post-critical centrifuge.

With a gruff snort of determination, Broec turned on his heel and thrust his Crozius into the air, making it spark and radiate with the pure light of sanctity. He dropped his bolter to the ground and drew his chainsword, letting it whir and then splutter into life, as though thirsty for blood.

For a long moment he watched the elegant emerald figure of Shaidan dancing with the foul creatures. He seemed to slide around the serpents as though he were one of them, slipping past their gnashing fangs and thrashing tails with an ineffable and graceful ease. His double-bladed staff was a perpetual blur of power, spinning and thrusting through the roiling brood.

Although he hated to admit it, Broec was struck by a niggling sense of admiration for the slippery, untrustworthy, Mantis Warrior psyker. He was a magnificent warrior, and he was ploughing into the vile xenos creatures with the kind of impassioned intensity that even a Black Templar would be proud of. No matter what role the Mantis Warriors had played in this affair, the heroic Librarian Shaidan did not deserve to die alone.

Besides, the colossal tryanid on the other side of the ruined wall looked like a hive tyrant to Broec and, as far as he knew, killing the hive tyrant was still the goal of this Deathwatch mission. The others could escort the inquisitor out with the sullied experiment. He would ensure the destruction of the tyrant and, in the process, he would slay those hideous offences to the grace of the Emperor that lay before him.

'No pity! No remorse! No fear!' he yelled, amplifying his voice into a bellowing echo as he circled his Crozius in one hand and his chainsword in the other, striding forward into the melee.

FROM THE MOUTH of the corridor, Octavius saw the rear wall of the laboratory ripped apart by the huge hive tyrant. In the foreground, Korpheus and Kalypsia were battling towards him with the perverse Grendal-weapon strapped to the back of the Techmarine. Over to one side, the blazing figure of Ashok was carving his way through the brood towards him. Behind Korpheus, Octavius could see the Crozius of Broec held high like a standard. Then he saw his chaplain pause and turn away, plunging back into the frenzy of zoanthropes.

Beyond Broec, through the roiling mass of aliens, Octavius could just about make out the flashes of Shaidan's staff and the odd glint off the glittering green plates of his armour. The Mantis Warrior was moving with incredible speed and precision and the captain found himself recollecting the first time that he had seen the librarian in battle – when he had free fallen out of a Thunderhawk into the braying swarm of tyranids to assist the extraction of his Deathwatch team. Octavius was still not sure what role the Mantis Warriors had played in the events on Herodian IV, but he silently vowed that the name of Shaidan would be spoken with reverence hereafter.

Briefly touching his sword blade to his forehead in a salute, Octavius nodded his admiration towards the two Marines. 'Suffer not the alien to live,' he muttered under his breath, whispering the hallowed mantra of the Deathwatch as an honourable farewell.

'We have to leave, now,' he said as the others finally made it into the corridor. 'Shaidan and Broec are buying us some time – we must not permit them to sell themselves cheaply.'

Without waiting for responses from any of the others, Neleus turned away from the laboratory and strode deeper into the corridor, crunching through the thinner resistance with the power of his servo-assisted power armour. His storm bolter sprayed shells through the passageway, shredding the gaunts that lay in wait for the retreating team.

Octavius joined Neleus at the front and Korpheus and Kalypsia fell in behind them. At the rear of the group, holding off the zoanthropes pressing in behind them, was Ashok, his eyes still burning with red fire and his staff flaring with blue lightning.

AFTER ONLY A few seconds of furious fighting, Shaidan and Broec found themselves back to back in the xenos mire. They had pushed their way out of the laboratory and through the torn breach in the metal wall, finding themselves suddenly within reach of the huge scything talons of the hive tyrant.

A flash of deep green and red lashed out from the colossal beast, scything down towards the Marines. Broec dropped to the ground and Shaidan sprang into the air, letting the huge talon sweep horizontally through the space between them. As he jumped, Shaidan thrust one of the bayonets on his staff down against the bony blade, scraping it across the ceramic surface in a cascade of sparks and fire.

The great beast screeched in pain, thrashing its talon wildly as streams of noxious fluid ran from the gash left by the sting of the Mantis Staff. As the talon recoiled, swinging back towards the Marines, it cut cleanly through the necks of two zoanthropes, neatly severing them in half. Shaidan and Broec tumbled to the ground, careening out of the lethal trajectory of the claw.

Rolling back up onto his feet, Broec stared up at the vast alien, the eye sockets in his deathmask burning with bright blue light. He had never seen such a huge tyranid before – it towered over the two Marines, dwarfing them utterly and riddling their minds with javelins of fear.

The chaplain could feel the insidious effects of the tyrant's psychic presence, drilling and lashing against the edges of his consciousness. It chattered and shrieked directly into his mind, pushing him towards insanity. The psychic assault battered him from within, while the terrifying visage of the beast itself assailed him from without. Its vast scaled head was crested with sheaths of blood-red barbs and spiked plumes, whilst its burning green eyes fixed the chaplain and rivers of hissing saliva gushed out of its fang-encrusted mouth.

'No pity! No remorse! No fear!' cried Broec, spinning the blazing Crozius Arcanum in one hand and his spluttering chainsword in the other. He kept chanting the motto of the Black Templars, ducking under the savage swipes of the tyrant and smashing his weapons against its immense talons. The mantra drove him on, feeding his soul with the light of the Emperor and strengthening his arm with hate and disgust towards the vile monstrosity that assailed his senses and insulted the Imperium through its very existence.

Meanwhile, Librarian Shaidan was a blur of movement, working his way round behind the gigantic creature, leaping over its thrashing tail and hacking into it with the glowing blades of his Mantis Staff. The beast's back was ridden with spines and spikes in a line from the crest of its head to the tip of its barbed tail, and its chitinous, armoured scales seemed to repel everything that Shaidan threw at them. The huge talons that protruded out of its main forelimbs seemed able to twist and thrust out behind it, precisely directed without even a backward glance from the monstrous head.

Stepping inside a vicious sweep from one of the scything talons, Broec drove his chainsword forward into the belly of the beast. The whirring teeth on the blade spun and churned as they crackled against the thick scales, but the chaplain's blade failed to penetrate the alien's grotesque body.

With a deafening howl, the tyrant jerked its body into a turn, thrashing its tail into a wide arc, smashing Shaidan off his feet and battering a brood of zoanthropes into pulp as it reeled. Using the momentum of its swinging tail, the tyrant pivoted on the spot, punching out with one of its shorter forelimbs and catching Broec full in the face.

As the chaplain crashed to the ground, the tyrant stabbed down at him with a rending claw, jabbing it into the Marine's abdomen and shattering the armoured panel that protected his stomach. At the same time, lashes of sinuous muscle spasmed out of the huge beast, entangling the chaplain in writhing, living ropes, and lifting him off the ground.

The tyrant's lash whips held Broec in the air, binding his limbs into inaction as it turned its face to inspect its prey. The deeply smouldering green eyes drew close to Broec's face, and multiple rows of dripping fangs and jagged teeth sneered at the helpless chaplain. Broec growled his defiance into the jaws of the beast, returning its bestial glare with the brilliant light of his own pristine gaze.

The tyrant's mouth gushed with corrosive saliva as it widened its jaws. But just as it was about to bite down through the Marine, its lascivious snarl was transformed into a shriek of pain. Its head snapped round to see Shaidan thrusting the tip of his Mantis Staff up into the fleshy area under the monstrous beast's primary shoulder. A spray of acid blood jetted out of the wound and rained down onto the librarian, who quickly withdrew his staff and danced away.

The beady green eyes of the hive tyrant glowed suddenly and a burst of warp fire jousted out of them towards the librarian. With a swift movement, Shaidan swept his staff into a vertical arc, smashing the warp blast with a shimmering bayonet, sending it ricocheting off into the slithering form of one of the surviving zoan-thropes.

In response, the tyrant brayed and screamed in frustra-tion, turning its attention back to the chaplain still held immobile in its lash whips. It smashed the Marine against the wall, beating Broec's deathmask against the metal panels until his neck fell limp. Then, with a burst of fury from its eyes, it spat a gout of warp fire into the chaplain's face.

Shaidan was just in time, vaulting up from the ground and severing the sinews of the beast's grip around Broec. The chaplain tumbled out of his binds and crashed to the ground. Staring up from where he lay, he saw the flames of warp energy engulf the Mantis Warrior, throwing him back against the wall, where he slumped down to the ground next to Broec.

With a gargantuan effort of will, the two Marines strug-gled back to their feet. Their armour was cracked and shattered, and their enhanced metabolisms were begin-ning to fail. The tyrant's lair was awash with the broken and ruined bodies of zoanthropes, leaving the floor and walls slick with ichor and blood. The tyrant itself glared at them with emerald hate burning in its eyes and streams of hissing blood coursing over its scales.

For a fraction of a second, the two Marines shared a glance with each other, bolstering their shared resolve and brotherhood. At that moment, no matter what their differences had been in the past, they were both proud to make their last stand together. They were Adeptus Astartes and they would bring death to this foul xenos offence.

'Suffer not the alien to live,' they muttered, prowling off in different directions, keeping the braying tyrant between them. Then, as though driven by a unity of purpose, they both charged forward with their weapons blazing.

CHAPTER ELEVEN:
ALIEN EYES

[3 Hours Remaining]

THE GUNSHIP SLID silently into one of the landing bays of the *Veiled Salvation*, touching down delicately onto the well polished deck. From the bridge, Agustius looked out at the reception committee that had collected to greet him and he smiled sadly. Just as he had requested, there was an armed inquisitorial retinue fanned out across the deck, resplendent in the official finery of the Ordo Xenos. There was no way that Parthon could squirm his way out of this.

The inquisitor lord turned his wheelchair and nodded to Lexopher. 'This is a sad day,' he said simply, and he meant it. It was certainly no secret that Agustius and Parthon did not agree on a number of points of philosophy, but the two old inquisitors had known each other for a long time; there was more to their relationship than the bitterness of ideological opposition. Indeed, they had grown to trust each other over their long years of service and, despite their differing methods, neither had ever had cause to doubt the commitment or devotion of the other. They had a friendship of the kind that only decades of arduous service and common purpose could forge.

It did not please Agustius to be the cause of Parthon's downfall, but it gave him a sense of satisfaction to know that he himself remained sufficiently pure of purpose that he could prosecute corruption even in those he held dear; the light of the Emperor shines on everything and everyone without exception. Not even the scheming Brutius Parthon was exempt from the justice of the Inquisition.

The evidence against hid old friend was severe, despite the fact that he had done everything he could to keep his machinations within the parameters of Imperial law. In fact, the problem was not even with what he had done; no matter how distasteful Agustius may have found the research project on Herodian IV, it was not technically illegal. The problem was rooted in the way in which the radical inquisitor had sought to protect his pet project. The problem was the cost that he was willing to pay to keep his ambitions alive.

Shaking his head slowly, Agustius looked into Lexopher's eyes for a moment, sharing some Thorian wisdom with his young interrogator. 'Remember, Lexopher, the alien is an insidious foe – it is an idea as much as a creature, and ideas are much harder things to kill. Once one takes root in your mind, it starts to blur the edges of your will. It is better not to have anything to do with the xenos species, than to awake one morning and find your soul swimming in their vile, heretical obsessions. Once the alien ceases to seem alien to you, it is already too late. It only takes a single wrong step to fall into the abyss.'

The interrogator nodded dutifully. His master's words made sense, and he could see the great man's emotion in his eyes as he spoke. This was not the empty rhetoric of a man whose convictions had never been tested. These were the words of man about to act on his courage.

A PULSE RIPPLED through the metallic floor panels, rocking the Deathwatch team as it emerged from the compound onto the roof of the bunker. The sky was awash with the fluttering and flapping forms of gargoyles and the air was thick with curdling toxins. As Octavius stood on the rockcrete roof, he could see the ocean of tyranid gaunts still ebbing and flowing all the way out to the horizon. When they caught his scent on the breeze, a great keening erupted from the xenos broods and the swarm poured forward towards the top of the bunker once again, shrieking and cackling like braying animals.

Another shock wave rocked the bunker, rendering cracks into the already scarred rockcrete and making the Marines stagger. Korpheus struggled to keep upright under the weight of the Grendal-device as the ground rolled and convulsed below him, but the others rode the stone tide with relative ease. They were uniformly pleased to be out of the restrictive spaces of the compound, although the sight that greeted them might even have been worse than the one they left behind. Nonetheless, Neleus for one was relieved to be able to stand straight once again and Ashok felt the release from the claustrophobic confines of the catacomb-like corridors as a breath of fresh air. But there was no fresh air.

If they were going to die on Herodian IV, then they would all rather do it out in the open, where they could do credit to the Deathwatch and their own Chapters in an all-out battle.

On the top of the bunker, Octavius could see deep channels that had been eroded into the rockcrete by trails of bio-plasma. There were the thermal imprints of detonations, and part of the edge of the roof had simply been melted away by some kind of chemical explosion. Here and there were the spent shells of boltguns, and there were even the corroded remains of a couple of weapons left strewn against the stone.

He nodded his head with understanding as he realised that this had been the point of the Mantis Warriors' last stand two days before. Surveying the pressing tide of alien organisms that were rushing and leaping towards them like an organic avalanche, he understood that the failure of the Mantis Warriors had not been shameful. Perhaps even the Imperial Fists could not have stood alone against this foe. He was certain a small knot of Deathwatch Marines and an inquisitor stood no chance at all.

Holding his ancient force sword into the air with both hands, he levelled it towards the rolling advance of the aliens. 'Suffer not the alien to live,' he muttered under his breath.

As the team braced themselves for the assault, another shock wracked the bunker, this time more violent than the last. Great chunks of masonry cracked off the edges of the roofline and tumbled down into the broods of braying gaunts that leapt and scraped up the walls, crunching them under slabs of rockcrete. Then a huge explosion erupted from the lower levels of the bunker, blowing out the side walls in all directions and scattering hunks of masonry and sprays of shrapnel into the swarm, obliterating a ring of tryanids and flattening thousands of others. In the wake of the debris rumbled a slow shock wave, pulsing through the sand of the desert and under-cutting the hooves and claws of the xenos creatures.

Without any walls to support it, the roof of the bunker cracked horrendously and collapsed down into the wreckage of the compound below, squashing the crea-tures within into a mulch of reds and greens that seeped out around the edges of the ruins, bleeding into the sand.

The surviving Deathwatch Marines tumbled down with the masonry from the roof, crashing into the ruins of the old Mechanicus compound. In an instant, Octavius, Neleus and Ashok were back up on their feet, their weapons braced and ready for combat. Korpheus lay pinned under the weight of the Grendal-machine, still alive but moving more slowly than his battle-brothers, while Kalypsia had dashed her head against a fragment of stone and had passed out.

As the dust settled around him, Octavius scanned the scene. For about a hundred metres in every direction there was nothing moving. Thousands of the tyranids had been shredded in the explosion, others had been flattened by chunks of masonry or cooked in the heat of the blast-wave. Beyond that ring of destruction the ocean of tyranids was still there, but it was somehow changed. The creatures were not tasting the air for the hint of organic life and they were not rampaging over their dead towards the ruined bunker. They looked stunned and confused.

'What's going on?' asked Neleus, standing defiantly with his storm bolter trained on the distant enemy. He was sweeping it across the scene, waiting for something to make a move towards him. Nothing did.

'It's the hive tyrant,' hissed Ashok, planting his staff into the rubble and leaning his weight against it. In the midst of the huge explosion, there had been a terrible psychic keening – a wave of doom and agony had emanated in tandem with the blast of heat and rockcrete. And, as the debris settled in the wake of the detonation, so too there was a lull in the chattering and shrieking that had filled his mind since the moment they had made planet-fall. 'The tyrant is dead.'

'They did it,' murmured Octavius, his mind flashing back to the instant that Broec had turned away from him and plunged back into the tyrant's lair to support Shaidan.

Korpheus had struggled to his feet and was looking out across the incredible scene of devastation. 'The effect will not last forever. The swarm will be disoriented for a while, but its communal synapses will eventually reroute. It will find another creature to act as its coordination node. The hive tyrant is key, but it is not irreplaceable – this is the strength of the tryanid's organic organisation.'

'Yes,' agreed Octavius, 'our window is brief. We must get word to Commander Kastor so that he may press the advantage.'

As he spoke, there was a whining roar in the sky, and they all looked up. A torrent of warm air blew down at them, whipping up eddies from the dust and sand all around them. Shielding his eyes with his hand, Octavius saw a Mantis Warrior Thunderhawk drop down through the cloud layer, its guns tracking in all directions, but firing nothing. The front hatch was open long before the gunship crunched to the ground, its huge hydraulic landing legs crushing the corpses of dozens of gaunts. Shimmering in his emerald power armour in the mouth of the Thunderhawk, Captain Audin of the Second Company nodded a greeting to Octavius and jumped down off the ramp before it cracked against the uneven ground.

'Time to leave, captain?' asked the Mantis Warrior, as he took in the desolation around him. 'The Deathwatch offer no quarter, I see.'

'Time to leave, captain,' replied Octavius, bowing slightly. 'Thank you.'

Audin was caught by something new glimmering in the depths of Octavius's complicated blue eyes. Unless he was much mistaken, it looked like respect. From the Thunderhawk he had already seen that the Mantis Warriors' detachment was not amongst the Marines waiting for extraction, and, swallowing his grief, he wondered what they had done to transform the opinion of the eminent captain.

THE LITTLE CELL-LIKE room overlooked the principal landing bay of the *Veiled Salvation* and it was cloaked in darkness. The ceiling-high windows were armoured and reinforced with an invisible energy field, but they provided an unbroken view of everything that happened in the space below. The occupant was clearly allowed to look out, but, because of the darkness within, nobody down on the brightly lit bay-floor could see anything inside.

Inquisitor Lord Parthon stood right up to the glass. His cloak hung loosely around his shoulders and his wide eyes glinted like deep water, casting the events outside into miniature reflections, as though the landing bay actually existed within his head, and everyone else was just seeing some form of projection.

He was quite alone in the little room and, contrary to the concerns of his conspiracy-crazed subordinates, he had very little paranoia about it. The fact of the matter was that no living being would have been able to enter that chamber without him noticing. It may have been pitch dark next to the entrance and Parthon may have been pressed up against the glass without even the hope of catching a glance behind him through his peripheral vision, but he would have seen anything that moved.

In fact, his eyes had failed decades before. It had taken him months to notice, since he had hardly ever used them. Human eyes are such fragile things, and he did not care for such weaknesses. He was better off without them; his psychic powers more than compensated for such physical iniquities and they had no need for light. Just for the sake of form, he toyed with having his eyes repaired. However, even though the kinds of ocular implants available to inquisitors were far superior to

those that might be seen on other servants of the
Emperor, he did not care to have lumps of metal and
flashing lights bolted to his face. Unlike that fool
Agustius, he had no desire for people to be aware of his
disabilities, such as they were. It was not that he had a
fear of technology – far from it. He was simply uncon-
vinced that he needed the implants and utterly
convinced that a better solution would present itself
when the right time came. In the mean time, he would
live in darkness and nobody else would be able to see his
eyeless sockets.

It had not taken him long to find a solution. Just after
he had started the Herodian project he had made contact
with the eldar of the Iyanden craftworld. They had been
even more devastated by the tyranids of Hive Fleet
Kraken than had the Imperium on Ichar IV. The swarm
had overrun the gigantic space-borne city and destroyed
thousands upon thousands of its warriors. The Iyanden
eldar had been on the point of utter annihilation when
Pirate Prince Yriel and his infamous Eldritch Raiders had
swept in from the outer reaches of the galaxy and exter-
minated the forces of the Great Devourer.

Despite his heroism, Yriel's timely intervention was
not enough to save the Iyanden eldar, and it was unlikely
that the craftworld would ever recover its losses – the
eldar life cycle is long and complicated, and not given
over to rapid population increases. The eldar are not
mon-keigh, whom they say breed like rats. An additional
problem for the eldar was the fact that the Great
Devourer clearly enjoyed the taste of eldar flesh, and a
splinter of the Kraken Hive detached itself from the main
swarm and set off in pursuit of the fleeing craftworld,
pestering it all the way out into the lost regions of
uncharted space.

Much later, Parthon had been monitoring the occur-
rences of attacks by tyranid splinter fleets in the outer

reaches of Ultima Segmentum when he noticed an odd psychic signature in the warp, hidden in the darkness of the hive's own warp shadow. The signature turned out to be that of the Iyanden craftworld, which had sustained a peripatetic existence since 993.M41, keeping one step ahead of the ravening horde but simultaneously managing to hide its own immense form in the warp shadow cast by the hive mind.

Parthon discovered that the Iyanden eldar had still not managed to recover their lost numbers and that, in fact, they had resorted to constructing Wraith-guardians to protect themselves from the tyranid swarm that pestered them continuously. These Wraiths were artificially constructed warriors, fashioned by the unparalleled artists and artisans of Iyanden.

It was then that Parthon realised that the Iyanden eldar and the Ordo Xenos had a common purpose on the fringes of Ultima Segmentum: the eradication of the tyranid menace. And he offered them a 'deal'. In return for some eldar technology, which Parthon would use to fashion a weapon that would rid both the Imperium and the Iyanden eldar of the tyranid threat, Parthon would agree not to tell the Imperial Navy where the weakened Iyanden craftworld was hiding. The auspices of the Ordo Xenos were wide and flexible for those with the appropriate predilections.

In addition to various pieces of a psychic amplification array, which Parthon gave to Grendal on Herodian IV, the artisans of the Iyanden craftworld had also gifted Parthon with a new pair of eyes. The artisans had honed their craft on the production of Wraiths, and the eyes were vastly superior to anything natural or artificial produced by humanity. They were also beautiful beyond human comprehension, and Parthon had never let anyone look into them in the full light of day, lest they spontaneously realise that his gaze contained a glint of eldar. In the half-light that always enshrouded him, they looked merely like unusually reflective eyes.

'Suffer not the alien to live... past its usefulness,' whispered Parthon, misting the glass window slightly with his breath. He looked down through the haze and saw his old friend Agustius talking with Inquisitor Dvorn, the head of the retinue that had been awaiting the return of the Inquisitor Lord. Dvorn was a good man, reflected Parthon, watching the expression on Agustius's face turn to rage.

'THEY DIED WELL,' said Octavius as Audin joined the team in the main compartment of the Thunderhawk, where Korpheus was inspecting the Grendal-machine. Neleus was administering to his armour, muttering the necessary litanies of purification to cleanse its spirit after its contact with the foul aliens. Motionless in the corner, Ashok was already out of his armour, relieved to be free of its constraints and sitting silently in meditation, his hood drawn deeply down over his face. And laying out on one of the benches that were bolted into the walls was Kalypsia, still unconscious but breathing evenly.

'Thank you, captain,' said Audin. 'I had no doubt that they would.'

The two Marines watched Korpheus working for a few moments.

'What is that?' asked Audin, indicating the machine.

'I'm not sure,' replied Octavius honestly.

Korpheus looked up from the machine. 'We have to deactivate it, captain.'

'The inquisitor may not approve, Korpheus,' cautioned Octavius, throwing a glance towards the sleeping Kalypsia. 'Why do you think so?'

'If she is right and this machine is some kind of conduit to the hive mind, it may still be functioning. In which case–'

'–in which case this is an operational decision and I can make it. Fine, disable the device,' said Octavius with some satisfaction.

Korpheus paused. 'Inquisitor Grendal will die,' he said. 'He is organically fused to the machine.'

'Have you ever seen anything like this before?' asked Audin.

'No,' confessed Korpheus. 'The technology is alien to me.'

'The technology is alien,' said Kalypsia, sitting up on the bench and sliding her legs down onto the floor. She reached up and touched the wound on her head. The blood had dried, but there was a strange pus seeping out around the edges. 'If Grendal dies, will that compromise the machine itself? It must not be damaged.'

'I can't tell, inquisitor,' replied Korpheus, surprised to see her upright so soon. 'But the two appear to have formed some kind of symbiotic unity, so I would guess that killing Grendal will have an adverse effect on the machine.'

'The machine must not be damaged,' repeated Kalypsia, almost robotically.

'Inquisitor,' intoned Octavius. 'When you said that the technology is alien, what exactly did you mean?'

Kalypsia regarded Octavius for a moment and then turned back to the machine, her eyes slightly glazed and her face placid. 'The device contains a mixture of tyranid genetic material and eldar technology, captain.' She said it as though it was the most natural thing in the world.

In the corner of the room, Ashok raised his head from his prayers and stared at the inquisitor. He had known that she had been hiding something from the start, but he would not have guessed this. As he watched her circle the machine in the centre of the compartment, he saw something different in her eyes. They seemed dull and lifeless in the middle of starbursts of bloodstains where her ruptured capillaries had spilt blood all around during the psychic explosion. But the red sclera had already faded back to white.

Even Neleus stopped tending to the machine spirits of his ancient armour and turned to look at the inquisitor. He had been able to understand that the Ordo Xenos might be interested in new technologies that could combat the Great Devourer and he had even managed to stomach the idea that the xenos creatures had somehow exploited that experimental technology to combat the forces of the Imperium, but even for him this latest revelation seemed like a step too far.

'The tyranid material forms an organic bond with the occupant, assimilating him into the structure of the machine and affecting a symbiotic union. Meanwhile, the amplifier array that was borrowed from the Iyanden eldar forms a concomitant union with the user's mind, boosting his psychic potency to incredible levels.'

Kalypsia stopped in front of the machine and stared at the broken figure of Grendal, his shoulders pierced through with spikes and his skin meshed into the substance of the chair around him. 'Incredible, isn't it.'

'You certainly seem to know a great deal about this machine, inquisitor... What does it do?' asked Octavius, still conscious of Korpheus's warning.

'It sends out a disruptive signal into the depths of the hive mind, confusing the swarm and attacking the synaptic nodes using their own relay system. It assaults the hive from within, captain.' As she spoke, Kalypsia climbed up onto the machine, tracing her fingers along the arms and shoulders of the ruined figure of Grendal. 'This is the future of the war against the tyranids.'

'We must deactivate the machine,' said Octavius levelly. He was not yet sure what to make of Kalypsia's revelations and she was hardly behaving like herself at the moment. Perhaps that blow to her head had done some internal damage. Either way, his responsibility was for the integrity of the mission itself, which, as far as he was concerned, had been completed when Shaidan and Broec took out the hive tyrant down on the planet's surface. Anything that jeopardised the team's safety at this stage constituted an unacceptable risk and he could not permit it. The ethics of transporting alien artefacts were not his concern.

Korpheus nodded to his captain and stepped back up to the machine, where Kalypsia was still kneeling in Grendal's lap, running her hands around the tips of the vicious spikes that pierced his shoulders. As the Techmarine approached, her head snapped round and she hissed at him. 'I will deal with this, Marine. Perhaps I can disconnect these things without damaging anything... or anyone.'

Over in the corner of the compartment, Ashok had risen to his feet and he was striding forward towards the machine and the inquisitor. His black eyes glinted distantly and his cloak billowed out behind him as though blown by an invisible wind. 'Stop her,' he hissed, drawing the sound from somewhere deep in his chest and projecting it across the chamber.

But it was too late. The elaborate machine started to tremble underneath Kalypsia, shuddering and rattling as though in spasms of pain. Then it bucked violently and jets of steam hissed out of vents and exhaust tubes, sending plumes of mist and smoke around the compartment in the Thunderhawk. A terrible scream jabbed into the air, but the Marines couldn't tell whether it came from Kalypsia or from the Grendal-machine itself. Screeches and shrieks echoed through the mist, staggering the Marines under the sonic onslaught. A piercing psychic cry punched into Ashok, lifting him off his feet and sending him skidding back away from the machine, crunching him into the far wall.

Bunching the muscles in his face, Octavius yelled into the haze, pushing himself forward against the typhoon that had whipped up around the machine in the centre of the chamber. Through the swirling maelstrom he could see Kalypsia's writhing form, still riding the bucking Grendal-machine. He charged forward, fighting against the eddies and currents of air, bursting through into a pocket of sudden calm in the centre.

The machine fell abruptly silent, and the smoke started to waft peacefully around the room. Octavius took another step towards the machine.

Kneeling on the broken body of Grendal, exhausted and slightly manic, Kalypsia worked her hands around behind his head, searching for some kind of release mechanism that would eject the old inquisitor without ruining the machine itself. She leaned against him, peering over his shoulder and into the intricate workings of the device in which he was enthroned.

Like a chill breeze, Kalypsia suddenly felt breath against her neck. She pushed herself back and stared into Grendal's face, looking for any sign of life. There was nothing. She sighed slightly and then leant forward again. As she did so, Grendal's eyes suddenly flicked open and his arm flashed free of its restraints, grasping her by the neck and holding her face less than a centimetre from his own. She gazed into his eyes for an instant and her own widened in ineffable horror.

Breaking into a run, Octavius launched himself forward, diving at Kalypsia and knocking her clear of the skeletal arms. The two crashed to the floor, rolling away from the machine. Kalypsia fell into an unconscious heap, but the captain turned just in time to see Grendal lurch up out of the machine and then fall flat on his face against the floor, lifeless as a corpse.

* * *

As THE DUTIFUL Dvorn led the fuming Agustius away, Inquisitor Lord Parthon shook his head in disappointment. He had expected more of his old rival. Long ago, he had given up expecting more *vision* from the old Thorian, but he had at least expected more competence.

Had the old fool seriously believed that he would be permitted to thwart Parthon's plans in his own battle cruiser, out in the forgotten reaches of the Segmentum Obscurus where Parthon's word carried life and death?

It was certainly true that the research programme on Herodian IV skated close to the line, but it was all officially sanctioned, albeit by Parthon himself; Parthon was the source of his own sanction in these scarcely trodden parts of the galaxy. Even he would have to admit that the cost of his experiment was rather high, but he thought that even Agustius would have been able to see the gains: the loss of one, thinly populated system should be insignificant next to the advantage that his weapon might bring in the future.

But the old Thorian had always been a puritanical and sentimental fool.

Even when he had stolen Parthon's files and run off to hide with the Navy, Parthon had not entirely given up on his old friend. He had sent a few of his guardsmen to board the Inquisitor Lord's gunship, to let Agustius know that his actions had not gone unnoticed. But the idiot had not even understood the warning. Had Parthon really wanted to kill his friend, he would not have sent such bumbling guardsmen to do an assassin's job. If he'd wanted Agustius dead, he would be dead.

But the old Thorian wouldn't let it go. He had to return to the *Veiled Salvation* to throw his allegations at Parthon – to accuse him of pushing his radicalism to the point of heresy. The poor, naïve fool. Did he really think that he could take over the glorious *Veiled Salvation* as easily as Parthon had coopted his little Deathwatch kill-team? He

would find precious few Thorian sympathisers on
Parthon's own battle cruiser.

Parthon never ceased to be amazed by the remarkable
combination of naivety and arrogance displayed by his
old sparring partner. Agustius really seemed to believe
that right and wrong were starkly demarcated, that one
ended exactly where the other began and that this line
was self-evident to all those of right-mind who cared to
look. He was genuinely convinced that Parthon knew
where that line was and had deliberately overstepped it
and he was stupidly confident that the rest of the authorities would see this too, once he had explained it to
them. The idea that Parthon may draw the line somewhere else, or simply not draw a line at all, never even
occurred to Agustius.

In any case, breaking into a secure vault in the bowels
of an Inquisition battle cruiser, stealing several sensitive
files, fleeing into the middle of a battlezone and killing a
number of another inquisitor lord's retainers – these
things were definitely crimes, no matter who you asked.
And Agustius would have to answer for them, just like
anyone else.

HE HAD ALWAYS known that the recovery of alien artefacts
for analysis by the Ordo Xenos was one of the roles of the
Deathwatch, but Octavius had never liked it. It was a grey
area in the ethical composition of the elite force and it
was not something of which many Chapters of Space
Marines would approve. It certainly caused tensions
between the more radical branches of the Inquisition
and the Ecclesiarchy, not to mention the puritans in its
own ranks. Inquisitor Lord Agustius would never have
sanctioned this mission.

He was not certain that his own Imperial Fists would
tolerate such practices and he was certain that successor
Chapters such as Broec's Black Templars would rebuke

them bitterly. Perhaps it was for reasons such as this that the exploits of the Deathwatch were sealed into the hidden annals of the Inquisition. After all, it seemed that Broec had given his life for the recovery of this bastardised, alien technology. For a moment, Octavius wondered whether he would have done so as willingly had he been told the true purpose of his mission from the outset. Where does duty end and conscience begin?

Pulling his thoughts together, he admonished himself: duty comes before everything. He was a Space Marine and a Deathwatch captain. It was not his place to judge the ethics of his missions, rather it was his duty to ensure their success. He was a perfectly-honed tool of the Ordo Xenos, and he could not wish for masters more bathed in the glory of the Emperor's light.

Looking out of the view-screen in the small observation tower of the Thunderhawk, Octavius could see the fury of the ongoing space battle that raged around the atmosphere of Herodian IV. It didn't look good, and it seemed as though the beleaguered Imperial fleet was in the process of withdrawing from the conflict. In the opposite direction, ahead of the speeding gunship, still held in reserve outside the main theatre of combat, loomed the massive shape of the *Vanishing Star*.

It would only be ten minutes or so before they would reach the Gothic-class cruiser and Octavius was still unsure exactly what to report. He was confused by Kalypsia. She had clearly lied to him and had certainly not given him the kind of respect due to a captain of the Deathwatch. However, he was concerned that the true extent of the lie had still not been revealed. From her conduct it seemed that she knew a great deal about the design and function of the strange Grendal-weapon and Octavius wondered what her connection with the emaciated corpse might be. He suspected that the two must be connected through Brutius Parthon himself and if the inquisitor lord was involved, then it looked like the lie was a deliberate attempt to cover something up.

If the Grendal-weapon was really a conduit into the hive mind and if it was partially constructed out of tyranid organic parts, wasn't it possible that the device was like a glaring psychic beacon, calling the swarm to the Herodian system, just as the vanguard genestealer organisms called the hive to suitable worlds? After all, this was its first appearance in this sector and it had gone straight for Herodian IV. That, at least, was a working hypothesis, and it would explain why Parthon was so keen to remove the evidence.

But there was more. Shaidan had described how the activation of the weapon had changed the behaviour of the swarm and Octavius himself had seen how the swarm had subsequently seemed able to pre-empt the protocols and strategies of the Deathwatch. Octavius formulated a secondary hypothesis, wondering what Agustius would think of events. It seemed that the machine's psychic facilities had been swamped by the presence of the hive mind, inverting its functions and draining the psychic signatures out of Grendal along with his physical tissues.

He leant his forehead against the view-screen, hoping that the answers would just settle naturally into his mind, as though they could infuse through the glass from the infested space outside. He had not been able to contact Agustius since boarding the Thunderhawk, and he really needed the council of the old man now. A Deathwatch captain may be one of the most powerful figures that the Imperium could deploy on the battlefield, but he could not go up against an inquisitor lord like Parthon without perfect certainty. And, at the end of the day, as Kalypsia was so fond of pointing out, he was merely a soldier in the service of the Emperor and his Inquisition.

Reaching a decision, Octavius turned and exited the observation tower, striding down the corridor towards the main compartment in which they had left the machine, Grendal's corpse and the unconscious Kalypsia. None of the Marines had felt the need or the compulsion to move the inquisitor into more comfortable surroundings. The riveted metal floor of the drop-compartment in the prow of the gunship was more than she deserved. Octavius punched the release on the door and strode into the chamber, ready to confront Kalypsia and demand to know the truth.

As THE DOORS hissed open, a blast of hot, humid air gusted into Octavius's face. In the centre of the compartment, the mysterious machine was humming with life and floating slightly off the metal deck. Strapped into it, with two barbed spikes jabbed through her shoulders, was Kalypsia. Her hair was billowing out around her head and her eyes were blazing with a deep green fire. As he stared into the burning emeralds, he could see no trace of the pale, shallow grey that had been there before.

'Kalypsia,' he whispered, knowing that she could hear him as he stalked towards her. 'Kalypsia, you must get out of the machine.' He couldn't believe that she would try to use the weapon after all that had happened, but his voice remained level and calm. 'You must get out,' he repeated softly.

Very slowly, Kalypsia opened her mouth, keeping her narrowing eyes fixed on Octavius. Then she threw her head back and screamed. It was an inhuman wail – the kind of braying shriek that they had heard so many times over the last couple of days.

Octavius drew his sword and took another step towards her as she closed her mouth and levelled her eyes on his once again. They seemed to flare and throb with an alien fire and then a blast of warp energy burst out of them, punching into Octavius's chest and knocking him off his feet.

As the captain sprawled back onto the floor, his chest-armour smoking and smouldering, Ashok and Audin came charging into the room, summoned by the strangled cries of Kalypsia.

The Mantis Warrrior drew his bolt pistol instantly, and Ashok stormed forward with his staff jousting out in front of him, pointing directly at the ungodly figure of Kalypsia. Without a moment's hesitation, Ashok loosed a stream of flickering energy into the punctured body of Kalypsia, watching her writhe and twitch as the psychic onslaught pummelled her chest. She glowered at him with those emerald eyes and Ashok recoiled slightly, realising that there was almost nothing of Kalypsia left in that body.

Squinting her eyes, she sent another ball of warp fire sleeting across the compartment, but Ashok was ready for it, driving his staff into the crackling sphere and dispersing it harmlessly. He studied her again, wondering whether there had been anything of Kalypsia in the woman who had decided to strap herself into that alien machine – he had seen her soul before, and it had not looked this evil. She had been ambitious, manipulative and even wreckless, but she was no fool and her purpose had been clean.

Parrying another flaming blast of warp energy, Ashok recalled the moment at which Grendal had suddenly regained consciousness and stared into Kalypsia's soul. He could still see the look of horror on her face and he shuddered at the thought of what could have been transferred into her mind in that instant. What terrible things had laid dormant in Grendal's tortured mind while his body was sucked dry and his soul siphoned away? And what power! Kalypsia had been a weak psyker, capable merely of defending her mind from the encroachments of others – although not from Grendal, it seemed – and now she was a blaze of hate and flame.

As Ashok fenced with the lashes of power that emanated from the Kalypsia-machine, Neleus thundered into the compartment and opened up with his storm bolter, blasting a hail of hellfire shells into the floating monstrosity, riddling Kalypsia's body with lethal flecks of metal.

'Brace yourselves!' cried Audin as he strapped the unconscious Octavius into one of the Marine-harnesses against the wall. Then he flicked a grenade into Kalypsia's lap and punched the release for the main prow doors.

With a creak and the whirring of gears, the far wall started to unfold out into space, falling flat like an exit ramp. The compartment decompressed instantly, and the controlled atmosphere of the Thunderhawk was spat out into the vacuum. Ashok drove his staff down into the deck and gripped it with both hands, standing firm against the torrent of escaping air, while Neleus reached out a casual hand to brace himself against the doorframe.

Kalypsia screamed and convulsed in the chair, struggling to free her hands in order to deal with the grenade in her lap, but they were fused to the chair beneath her. The machine bucked and whined, as though it were willing itself to remain in the Thunderhawk. A tremendous shriek pulsed out of the device, rippling through the gunship and out into space, deafeningly loud but also resonating with silent, psychic terror.

Then Kalypsia's head slumped forward and the burning green faded from her eyes, leaving shallow pools of grey. She looked up for a moment, confused and dazed, and as she did so the machine finally gave up its resistance and blasted out into the vacuum of space, tumbling and spinning helplessly. After a second, Audin thumbed the remote detonator and the Kalypsia-device erupted into a blue plasma star, pristine and radiant like the light of the Astronomicon itself.

EPILOGUE:
CONVICTIONS

THE DOORS INTO the conference room on the *Vanishing Star* slid open with a mechanical whir. It seemed like an age since Octavius had last been there, standing like a sentry behind the confident, young inquisitor as she toyed with Commander Kastor. That was when he had first met the immaculately gleaming Captain Audin; if he could take back the discourtesies that he had done to the Mantis Warrior at that time, then he would. But this was not the time for regrets, this was still the time for action. This time, he was proud to stand side by side with Audin as the doors opened.

Commander Kastor was waiting for them, standing at the back of the room with his hands clasped behind his back. The projection screen had been dropped down over the wall and Kastor was inspecting the progress of the ongoing battle. When he heard the door open, he turned immediately.

'Captain Octavius, it warms my heart to see you again,' he said, walking hastily towards the Deathwatch Marine.

'I understand that the inquisitor is no longer with you.' He made a display of mock concern. 'And Captain Audin, it is good of you to join us.'

Bowing his affirmation and his greeting at the same time, Octavius couldn't help but smile at the direct manner of the commander. With all of the intrigues that had been plaguing his mind, he had missed the blunt honesty of military men and it reassured him to know that Kastor was now in charge of the theatre of war.

'Please, captain, sit,' said Kastor, ushering the wounded Marine to a chair.

'Thank you, commander,' said Octavius. Standing in the conference room of a Gothic-class cruiser, addressing a commander of the Imperial Navy, he felt underdressed without his armour. But his chest plates had been shattered by the warp blast from Kalypsia, and medicated bandages had been strapped around his abdomen to treat the blistering burns. Although his enhanced metabolism was working overtime to heal the wounds, they were still painful and awkward. He was grateful for the seat.

'How goes the battle, commander?' asked Octavius, as Kastor and Audin joined him at the table.

'I will not lie to you, captain,' began Kastor. 'It has not been pretty. While you have been planetside, enacting the sacred will of the Ordo Xenos,' he continued, almost sarcastically, 'the Imperial Navy has been suffering significant losses in the face of these vile organisms. We have lost a frigate already and, if it were not for the timely intervention of the Mantis Warriors' *Sword of Contrition*, we would also have lost a venerable Dictator-class cruiser. I hope that your time on the planet was well spent, captain, and that these losses have not been for nothing.'

Kastor regarded the Deathwatch captain carefully, watching for signs of confession. But there was nothing.

Octavius nodded firmly but wearily, unwilling to reveal the details of events on the planet to this commander – despite his admiration for the man and despite his rank, he was not part of the Ordo Xenos, and Octavius could tell him nothing.

'The hive tyrant has been destroyed,' confirmed Octavius. This was the salient information for the purposes of the current battle. 'Was this not evident from the behaviour of the hive fleet?'

Kastor eyed him with a mixture of satisfaction and disappointment. 'Yes, there was a shift in the coherence of the swarm about an hour ago and the tide of the battle turned a little in our favour. However, the tyranids quickly regrouped. As I suspected from the start, that was not enough to win this war, captain.' A look of sadness crossed his face.

'There was a second moment, not long ago, when a plasma explosion detonated near to your Thunderhawk... that seemed to coincide with some greater problems for the hive–'

Suddenly the lights in the room dimmed. A second later and the hiss of the doors sliding open again made them turn. Kastor immediately jumped to his feet and swept into a bow, while Audin rose smoothly from his seat. Octavius took a breath and then stood, turning to face the imposing, shrouded figure.

The silhouette shimmered in the half-light and points of light sparkled in its eyes. Fluttering out around him was a retinue of lethally silent, scarcely visible bodyguards, who slipped into the deep shadows of the dimly lit room.

Octavius bowed. 'Inquisitor Lord Parthon.'

'Ah yes, the valiant Captain Octavius,' purred Parthon. 'How nice to see you again. I should apologise for the tardiness of my appearance here. I was... delayed by matters of some importance on the *Veiled Salvation*.'

Nobody replied, but Parthon was quite used to filling rooms with restrained, palpable hostility. He often felt that it compensated for the lack of light.

'Lord Parthon, I am happy to report that the hive tyrant on Herodian IV has been destroyed,' said Octavius formally.

'Yes, very good captain,' replied Parthon without moving. The sparks in his eyes seemed to dance in the darkness. 'Is there anything else that you should report?'

Octavius considered the question. There was so much that he felt like he should say. There were accusations to be levelled and indignities to be recompensed. But he clenched his jaw and bit back his distaste for the radical inquisitor lord. 'No, Lord Parthon, there is nothing else to report.'

Even in the half-light, Octavius could see the faint, sickly glimmer of a smile dance over Parthon's shrouded features.

'Very well, captain,' responded Parthon smoothly, nodding almost imperceptibly. A smug satisfaction sank into the inquisitor's mind as he realised that the honourable captain's sense of duty could be relied on by him just as much as by the late Lord Agustius. Whilst it was clear that the boy scouts had recovered his experimental weapon and then destroyed it, presumably after discovering what it was – something that Agustius would have been proud of – it was equally clear that the valiant Imperial Fist took his responsibilities to the Ordo Xenos seriously. His discretion could be relied on.

'What of the young Kalypsia, captain?' he asked, unwilling to let go completely.

'She… she fell, my lord,' said Octavius carefully. 'It was a difficult extraction.'

'I see.' Parthon's voice was rich with sibilance.

'My lord,' began Octavius, 'might I inquire after Lord Agustius? I am keen to report to him and to continue on our way to the Obscurus Frontier. We have been delayed enough. I understood that he was enjoying your hospitality on the *Veiled Salvation*.'

Had they been able to see his face, Octavius, Audin and Kastor would have seen Parthon raise an amused eyebrow. Perhaps this captain could cause some trouble after all, he mused.

'I'm sorry to say that Agustius also… fell, captain. You will be now be escorting *me* to the frontier aboard the *Veiled Salvation* herself. I will be taking his place in the main theatre of conflict once this little skirmish is finished.

'Talking of which – Captain Audin, I assume that your battle barge, the *Endless Redemption*, is equipped with planetary bombardment cannons and an Exterminatus array?'

'Yes, my lord,' answered Audin simply.

'Then you will use it on Herodian IV – it is time to kill the planet. The Mantis Warriors will have the honour of the strike.'

'Yes, my lord. Thank you,' said Audin, his voice tinged with unease. He did not think that this was the kind of honour that the Mantis Warriors needed. His finest Marines had given their lives to prevent this and he was loathe to obliterate their deeds with such an indiscriminate device.

Kastor could not contain himself any longer. 'But the hive fleet is routed, my lord. Together with the Mantis Warriors, we have turned the tide. Your drop-mission was a success, Parthon. To have used the Exterminatus two days ago would have made sense: then it would have saved so many lives and ships, but to use it now looks like–'

'Careful, commander. Do not forget to whom you are speaking,' purred Parthon, amused by the yapping of this Naval officer. For a moment, a streak of ambient light sparkled against the medallion that hung around Parthon's neck, bursting like a tiny star against the dark silhouette.

Kastor stared at the little icon for a second, fighting back the words that bubbled into his mouth. Octavius watched the commander with sympathy – this was exactly what Kalypsia had done when she had first met Kastor in this conference room and it had been a trump card then as well. Instinctively, he pressed his hand against the pouch in his belt and remembered that he still had Grendal's medallion in there.

'Very well, Lord Parthon,' hissed Kastor, turning away and slumping down into one of the chairs.

'Come, Octavius, we have much to discuss,' said Parthon as he turned and swept out of the room, his bodyguards folding into step behind him.

Octavius paused for a lingering moment, contemplating the events of the last few days. Then he turned to Audin and bowed crisply. 'I will make sure that the names of your Marines are spoken with honour in the hallowed halls of the Deathwatch fortresses across the galaxy. Shaidan, Ruinus and Soron will be posthumously inducted into our ranks with full honours.' He paused for a moment before continuing. 'I would gladly serve with you again, captain.'

Taking a deep breath and pushing out his blistered chest, Octavius strode out of the gradually lightening room and followed after the Inquisitor Lord, following his duty above all else.

THE HUGE WARHEADS spilt fire out of their thrusters as they powered towards Herodian IV, where the roiling black clouds of the tyranid swarm still coursed and swirled over the surface. In the outer atmosphere, the gigantic mass of the Hive Ship was consumed in flames, as an intense and continuous stream of lance fire pressed into its chitinous shell, feeding the blazes with a colossal energy flow. The ugly monstrosity was falling into the atmosphere, and sheets of fire flooded the skies over half the planet.

After only a few seconds, the warheads pierced the stratosphere and screamed down towards the planet's surface. Some of them detonated in the air, exploding into vast sprays of viral rain that bloomed and blossomed into lethal weather systems, hailing biochemical death into the seas of xenos organisms on the surface below. Others blasted down into the ground, punching out great craters and exploding into superheated thermal shock waves that radiated out around the planet, incinerating vast swathes of organic matter.

From the viewing station of the *Endless Redemption*, Herodian IV looked completely transformed. When the Mantis Warriors had arrived, they had seen a planet overrun by the tyranid swarm, and they had watched its oily black shadow swim and writhe across the orange deserts. Now the black oceans where being rapidly consumed and vaporised by spreading plumes of burning orange, and obscured under coagulating layers of dirty clouds.

Standing before the ceiling-high viewing screens, Captain Audin of the Mantis Warriors' Second Company whispered a prayer to the Emperor of Mankind, asking him if this was really what the redemption of the Mantis Warriors should mean.

ABOUT THE AUTHOR

C S Goto has published short fiction in *Inferno!* and elsewhere. His previous novels for the Black Library include the Necromunda novel *Salvation* and the Warhammer 40,000 epic *Dawn of War*.

READ TILL YOU BLEED
DO YOU HAVE THEM ALL?

1 Trollslayer – William King
2 First & Only – Dan Abnett
3 Skavenslayer – William King
4 Into the Maelstrom – Ed. Marc Gascoigne & Andy Jones
5 Daemonslayer – William King
6 Eye of Terror – Barrington J Bayley

7 Space Wolf – William King
8 Realm of Chaos – Ed. Marc Gas-coigne & Andy Jones
9 Ghostmaker – Dan Abnett
10 Hammers of Ulric – Dan Abnett, Nik Vincent & James Wallis
11 Ragnar's Claw – William King
12 Status: Deadzone – Ed. Marc Gascoigne & Andy Jones
13 Dragonslayer – William King
14 The Wine of Dreams – Brian Craig
15 Necropolis – Dan Abnett
16 13th Legion – Gav Thorpe
17 Dark Imperium – Ed. Marc Gascoigne & Andy Jones
18 Beastslayer – William King
19 Gilead's Blood – Abnett & Vincent
20 Pawns of Chaos – Brian Craig
21 Xenos – Dan Abnett
22 Lords of Valour – Ed. Marc Gascoigne & Christian Dunn
23 Execution Hour – Gordon Rennie

24 Honour Guard – Dan Abnett
25 Vampireslayer – William King
26 Kill Team – Gav Thorpe
27 Drachenfels – Jack Yeovil
28 Deathwing – Ed. David Pringle & Neil Jones
29 Zavant – Gordon Rennie
30 Malleus – Dan Abnett
31 Konrad – David Ferring
32 Nightbringer – Graham McNeill
33 Genevieve Undead – Jack Yeovil
34 Grey Hunter – William King
35 Shadowbreed – David Ferring
36 Words of Blood – Ed. Marc Gascoigne & Christian Dunn
37 Zaragoz – Brian Craig
38 The Guns of Tanith – Dan Abnett
39 Warblade – David Ferring
40 Farseer – William King
41 Beasts in Velvet – Jack Yeovil
42 Hereticus – Dan Abnett
43 The Laughter of Dark Gods – Ed. David Pringle
44 Plague Daemon – Brian Craig
45 Storm of Iron – Graham McNeill
46 The Claws of Chaos – Gav Thorpe
47 Draco – Ian Watson
48 Silver Nails – Jack Yeovil
49 Soul Drinker – Ben Counter
50 Harlequin – Ian Watson
51 Storm Warriors – Brian Craig
52 Straight Silver – Dan Abnett
53 Star of Erengrad – Neil McIntosh
54 Chaos Child – Ian Watson
55 The Dead & the Damned – Jonathan Green
56 Shadow Point – Gordon Rennie
57 Blood Money – C L Werner
58 Angels of Darkness – Gav Thorpe
59 Mark of Damnation – James Wallis
60 Warriors of Ultramar – Graham McNeill
61 Riders of the Dead – Dan Abnett
62 Daemon World – Ben Counter
63 Giantslayer – William King

WWW.BLACKLIBRARY.COM

64 Crucible of War – Ed. Marc Gascoigne & Christian Dunn
65 Honour of the Grave – Robin D Laws
66 Crossfire – Matthew Farrer
67 Blood & Steel – C L Werner
68 Crusade for Armageddon – Jonathan Green
69 Way of the Dead – Ed. Marc Gascoigne & Christian Dunn
70 Sabbat Martyr – Dan Abnett
71 Taint of Evil – Neil McIntosh
72 Fire Warrior – Simon Spurrier
73 The Blades of Chaos – Gav Thorpe
74 Gotrek and Felix Omnibus 1 – William King
75 Gaunt's Ghosts: The Founding – Dan Abnett
76 Wolfblade – William King
77 Mark of Heresy – James Wallis
78 For the Emperor – Sandy Mitchell
79 The Ambassador – Graham McNeill
80 The Bleeding Chalice – Ben Counter
81 Caves of Ice – Sandy Mitchell
82 Witch Hunter – C L Werner
83 Ravenor – Dan Abnett
84 Magestorm – Jonathan Green
85 Annihilation Squad – Gav Thorpe
86 Ursun's Teeth – Graham McNeill
87 What Price Victory – Ed. Marc Gascoigne & Christian Dunn
88 The Burning Shore – Robert Earl
89 Grey Knights – Ben Counter
90 Swords of the Empire – Ed. Marc Gascoigne & Christian Dunn
91 Double Eagle – Dan Abnett
92 Sacred Flesh – Robin D Laws
93 Legacy – Matthew Farrer
94 Iron Hands – Jonathan Green
95 The Inquisition War – Ian Watson
96 Blood of the Dragon – C L Werner
97 Traitor General – Dan Abnett
98 The Heart of Chaos – Gav Thorpe
99 Dead Sky, Black Sun – Graham McNeill
100 Wild Kingdoms – Robert Earl
101 Gotrek & Felix Omnibus 2 – William King

102 Gaunt's Ghosts: The Saint – Dan Abnett
103 Dawn of War – CS Goto
104 Forged in Battle – Justin Hunter
105 Blood Angels: Deus Encarmine – James Swallow
106 Eisenhorn – Dan Abnett
107 Valnir's Bane – Nathan Long
108 Lord of the Night – Simon Spurrier
109 Necromancer – Jonathan Green
110 Crimson Tears – Ben Counter
111 Witch Finder – C L Werner
112 Ravenor Returned – Dan Abnett
113 Death's Messenger – Sandy Mitchell
114 Blood Angels: Deus Sanguinus – James Swallow
115 Keepers of the Flame – Neil McIntosh
116 The Konrad Saga – David Ferring
117 The Traitor's Hand – Sandy Mitchell

118 Darkblade: The Daemon's Curse – Dan Abnett & Mike Lee
119 Survival Instinct – Andy Chambers
120 Salvation – CS Goto
121 Fifteen Hours – Mitchel Scanlon
122 Grudge Bearer – Gav Thorpe
123 Savage City – Robert Earl
124 The Ambassador Chronicles – Graham McNeill
125 Kal Jerico: Blood Royal – Will McDermott and Gordon Rennie
126 Bringers of Death – Ed. Marc Gascoigne & Christian Dunn
127 Liar's Peak – Robin D Laws
128 Blood Bowl – Matt Forbeck
129 Guardians of the Forest – Graham McNeill
Coming Soon
130 His Last Command – Dan Abnett
131 Death's City – Sandy Mitchell
132 Junktion – Matthew Farrer

DATE DUE

10/21			